Prais

Murder on Skis Mysteries

Finalist for Best Mystery Series
— Chanticleer International Book Awards

The Man Who Had 9 Lives

"Bayly's engrossing latest in the Murder on Skis Mystery series."
— The Prairies Book Review

"The beauty of the setting in the mountains of Colorado will dazzle the reader."
— Authorsreading.com

Witch Window

"A gripping mystery set in a stunning Vermont landscape."
"Best Books We Read" list for 2022
-— Independent Book Review

Back Dirt

"Skiers, mystery lovers and history buffs will enjoy Phil Bayly's newest novel."
— Adirondack Daily Enterprise

"Phil Bayly spins a captivating yarn."
— Reader's Favorite

American Fiction Awards Finalist

Loving Lucy

"A chilling mystery."
— Vail Daily

Murder on Skis

"More twists and turns than a slalom course."
— Saratogian

The Man Who Had 9 Lives

A *Murder on Skis* Mystery

Other ***Murder on Skis*** **Mysteries**
by Phil Bayly:

Murder on Skis

Loving Lucy

Back Dirt

Witch Window

The Man Who Had 9 Lives

A *Murder on Skis* Mystery

Phil Bayly

The Man Who Had 9 Lives

A *Murder on Skis* Mystery

WWW.MURDERONSKIS.COM

ISBN: 978-1-60571-643-5

Cover Design: Carolyn Bayly, Debbi Wraga &
Daseugen / istockphoto.com
Laifalight / istockphoto.com
Kosmos111 / Dreamstime.com
Cover Photo: Carolyn Bayly
Cover Model: Dr. Alan Justin
Author Photo: Carolyn Bayly

Printed in the United States of America

The Man Who Had 9 Lives is a work of fiction. The people, places and groups in this novel are a work of fiction. This work is an act of the author's imagination.

The Minnie's Gap Ski Resort does not exist, nor does the town of Dog Mountain or the county of Lonesome.

The many landmarks and the colorful history of Browns Park do exist. I paid my first visit there in the 1980s, as a reporter for KJCT Television The spirit and perseverance of generations of people in Browns Park is a rich history of how the West was truly won, by people of all colors.

To Carolyn. Her belief fools me into overlooking evidence that I have overestimated my abilities.

"Not heaven itself upon the past has power; But what has been has been, and I have had my hour."

—John Dryden, English Poet, 1685

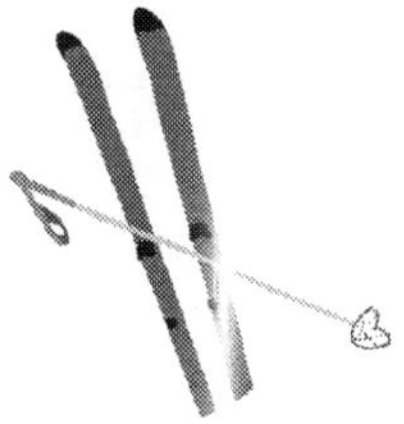

1

"This place comes with a strange story," the deputy said.

"Which one?" another deputy asked.

"Which place?"

"No, which strange story?"

"True," agreed the first deputy. "There are a lot of them."

The two law officers were standing guard over scattered human remains discovered on Diamond Peak. And they weren't wrong about the unusual tales.

It had not been a normal month, even for Lonesome County. It began with an avalanche several weeks before.

"Do you believe you've ever died?"

It was an odd question coming from the man who only minutes before had been pulled from beneath the snow. But the ski patrol member tending to him suspected the avalanche survivor was in shock.

"Like a cat," the rescued man slurred. His voice was weak. His jaws ached from clenching them. He was exhausted after struggling to live.

"I believe that humans have nine lives," he said. "I can't prove it. I'm a man of science, but I believe it."

The man then seemed to doze off. His body temperature was warming under a blanket. His feet, still buckled into his ski boots, dangled in the same hole that nearly became his crypt.

"Stay with us," the ski patroller urged. "We don't want you to sleep on us just yet. Do you hear me, Dr. Anderson?"

Who could blame the man, thought the ski patroller at Minnie's Gap Ski Resort. Dr. Anderson had survived a terrifying experience. He was helpless until rescuers reached him. His brain must have been a chamber of horrors down there under the snow.

"Is this yours?" a second ski patroller asked as he approached. He was wearing the same red jacket as his colleague, the one with the white cross on it. The patroller held out a somewhat flattened cowboy hat.

"Yes, it is!" Dr. Anderson said with a slight laugh, followed by a hoarse cough. He reached out with his left arm and accepted the hat, happy to be reunited.

"Maybe you should wear a helmet," the first ski patroller said.

Anderson shrugged and used his one good hand to push out some dents in his tan George S. Bailey 1922 cowboy hat.

"Holy shit!"

The first skier to reach the spot where the avalanche buried Dr. Anderson had stammered obscenities about the enormity of the task before him.

The rescuer, a man who said he was from Norway, clawed at the snow like an animal. His fingers started to burn. When he pulled off his gloves, there was blood seeping from under his fingernails.

"Hang on," the man had shouted at the snow. "Just hang on. Hang on!"

Twelve inches of freshies had fallen. The entire ski resort was excited about the day ahead. The snow had been fluffy champagne powder.

Now, in the area where the slide had covered its victim, the snow was hard like packed dirt.

The Norwegian rescuer was on his knees. He could feel the sweat on his back. A layer of PolyPro fastened to his flesh. He pulled down the zipper on his jacket and continued to dig.

"I got a sick feeling in my stomach," the rescuer would later say with a Scandinavian accent. "As soon as I heard the crack behind me, and then the roar, I knew what it had to be. I turned around. I feel selfish for saying this, but I was glad that it wasn't me in its path."

The Scandinavian man who dug furiously through the snow was later identified by the ski patrol as Ullr Skadi, a professor at the nearby community college. He told the ski patrol that he was Norwegian.

"I saw the skier below the slide. I saw it roll over him. Then, he came up. He was trying to swim to stay on top. Then, he disappeared."

Another man watching the victim was Ethan Johnson. He was an avalanche educator at a backcountry ski store in Steamboat Springs. He made the two-hour drive to Minnie's Gap that morning.

Johnson rode a chairlift up behind Dr. Anderson and planned to ski to the edge of the ski resort's boundary. Then he thought he would climb a ridge and ski the chutes that presented themselves out-of-bounds.

"I watched him as the snow carried him downhill," Johnson would later say. "I kept checking landmarks so that I would have a general idea of where he was when the avalanche ended.

"When everything stopped moving, I skied over to the last place I saw him. One guy was already looking for him and then a snowboarder joined us. I kicked my skis off and tried to get to the spot in the runoff where I thought I'd last seen him. I was calling for him. I was looking for a ski tip or a pole or something."

"He didn't have an avalanche beacon on," someone from the Colorado Avalanche Information Center, in Boulder, would later say. "He wasn't required to have a transceiver on him. He was in-bounds. We don't have many avalanches *inside* a ski resort's boundary. This was unusual."

"There were three of us looking for him," the snowboarder said. Her name was Margaret Lynch. "Periodically, one guy would call out to us to be quiet and listen. Then he'd yell at the snow, 'Hey, can you hear me? Yell, if you can hear me!' We had to be quiet, hoping we'd hear his response from under the snow."

"I think the avalanche came down from a couloir above us, long and narrow," Johnson said. "I've jumped into that couloir before. That made this kind of spooky."

"In cold clinical terms," the spokesperson for the Colorado Avalanche Information Center would say, "the older bed surface of snow, below the fresh snow, was a rain crust. It had rained and that layer of snow froze and became slippery.

"Then, we got twelve inches of snow. The fresh snow didn't bond with the rain crust. As the layer on top grew heavier, it slid downhill."

"Thank God he was wearing a blaze-orange jacket," the Norwegian said. "Maybe six centimeters of one sleeve was sticking out of the snow. His hand was above the snow too. But I don't think I would have seen it. His glove was gone. It was that six centimeters of orange."

"We couldn't get him out," the snowboarder said. "He wasn't moving, not an inch. When the Scandinavian guy yelled that he'd found him, me and the other guy ran over and just started digging like mad. Now, three of us were digging. I remember one of them kept saying to the snow, 'Hang on, hang on, hang on.' I think he was hoping that the guy under the snow could hear him."

"When we started to uncover the victim, his arm was twisted behind him at a grotesque angle," Skadi said. "It looked like it had been pulled loose from the socket. The arm was straight up in the air. The rest of the fellow was like sixty centimeters under the snow. It was pretty sickening. I was sure he was dead.

"When we dug down to the victim, he was face down. There was a lot of blood. He must have really scratched up his face. We reached down and scraped away the snow from his mouth and nose, trying to give him a pocket of air. That's when he moved his head to the side. I couldn't believe it."

"I thought I was dead," the victim later disclosed. "I once had a ski racing coach who gave us a little lesson on surviving avalanches. He said that we had an average of twenty minutes to live, if we got buried. That terrified me. I didn't know if anyone had seen what happened. I was afraid I was alone. I tried to stay calm, but I was terrified."

The victim's full name was Hunter Anderson. He was a doctor from the nearby town of Dog Mountain. He was the *only* doctor, which made him a valuable member of the little community.

"The avalanche was almost sixty-five feet wide. Not a particularly large one, but deadly," the spokesperson for the Colorado Avalanche Information Center would later explain.

"It came down a gully or a couloir," he said. "It was six-feet deep. Life expectancy can depend on how far down the victim is pulled. If it is totally dark to the victim, it can resemble being underwater. There won't be much air to breathe, or even room to expand his diaphragm."

"I couldn't move, not even my fingers," Dr. Anderson said. "I had a small pocket of air around my face. I spit so I could see which way gravity pulled the spit. Then I'd know which way I had to dig to go up. That's what I had been taught, but I was kidding myself. I couldn't dig. I couldn't move.

"And the spit didn't drip in any direction. Now I knew that I was flat on my stomach. But I was completely disoriented down there. And when I was trying to use every crumb of what I'd ever been taught about avalanches to save myself, I was terrified. I realized there was nothing I could do."

"About fifteen to twenty people a year are killed in avalanches in the United States," the speaker for the Colorado Avalanche Information Center would say. "This is the third bad winter we've had for avalanches in Colorado. And we have more avalanche-related deaths than any other state.

"Dr. Anderson was lucky. Witnesses got to him within minutes. In less than an hour, a helicopter reached the scene and the survivor was airlifted to UCHealth Yampa Valley Medical Center in Steamboat Springs. But those two skiers and the snowboarder probably saved his life."

The ski patrol had asked Dr. Anderson if he was skiing alone. He said that he was. Then they asked him if he saw anyone else skiing near him. He said that he had not. The ski patrol was trying to ascertain if there was anyone else buried beneath the avalanche.

"I was pretty sure that I was the first skier down the slope that morning," Anderson told them. "I was excited to get first tracks in the powpow."

The ski patroller smiled. He knew the feeling.

Anderson examined his orange ski jacket. It was ripped open along the arms and torso. Goose down was being carried away in the wind. It looked like someone had slashed his jacket with scissors.

"It's funny," Dr. Anderson later said. "When the ski patrol got me out of the snow and sat me down and wrapped a blanket around me, I looked at the view. My feet were dangling in the same hole that was almost my tomb. But I was seized by how beautiful it was up there. I could see Browns Park, off in the distance. I was thinking about what a great day it was to go skiing."

"Thank you," his rescuers had heard him whisper to them.

"Then he said something odd," the Norwegian skier added. "It was almost like he was talking to himself. He said, 'That's eight.'"

2

Weeks prior to the avalanche, a car pulled into a campground in Irish Canyon. The six campsites were secluded from the road by the dense pinyon pine and sagebrush.

The driver parked at campsite number four toward the back. Half of the sandy soil and cheatgrass was covered with old compact snow.

His was the only car there. The nearby cliffs offered accessible petroglyphs carved by prehistoric man. But campers and hikers did not use the Irish Canyon Campground in the winter.

The driver of the car pulled himself out from behind the steering wheel. He looked in both directions and saw no one.

The canyon was narrow there. Yellow-white walls towered overhead, carved by nature into the likenesses of castles, carousels, and layer cakes.

The man sipped from an energy drink while he waited, leaning against the car's fender. He fidgeted a bit, looking at his watch and looking toward the entry to the campground. No one, except the man he was awaiting, was likely to come.

He remembered how Irish Canyon got its name. Three Irishmen robbed a saloon in Rock Springs, Wyoming. It was well over a century ago. They stole money and liquor. They got as far as the canyon before they celebrated, enjoying the liquid proceeds from their robbery.

After waiting for the engine to cool, the man pulled open the hood of his car.

With a pair of needle-nose pliers, he loosened two clamps and worked off a rubber hose near the radiator.

Having succeeded, he placed the good hose in a brown paper bag and pulled out a hose with a crack in it.

Reversing the process, he coaxed the bad hose into place and fixed it to that spot with the needle nose and clamps.

He placed the paper bag on the floor of the backseat. Opening the trunk, he lifted a two-gallon container of water and walked to the exposed engine compartment. He poured the water on and around the cracked hose. He thought it would give the appearance of a cracked hose some authenticity.

"I've got a problem," the man had said when he placed a phone call. "My car broke down. I'm not far from where we are supposed to meet, but could you come here? You know cars better than I do. We can talk and I'll bet you can get my car running. You're better at this stuff than I am."

The man on the other end of the phone call, Nat Sanchez, agreed.

"Thanks, Nat," the caller said. "You're a lifesaver. I made it as far as the Irish Canyon Campground. I'm by the bathroom. I was hoping to use it, but it's locked."

Arrangements having been made, the caller pocketed his phone and walked around the campsite. He was looking for a rock. He wanted something heavy, something he could lift over his head with two hands.

He spotted a yellow rock about the size of a throw pillow. It was near the firepit and a green picnic table. The rock was dense in the middle and had lots of edges.

He considered where to hide it. He chose a place behind the front tire on the passenger side of his car.

"Can I talk to you?" Nat Sanchez had asked when he phoned the man two days earlier. "Unless my eyes are deceiving me, I think you have done something that is not your nature. I'm not looking to get you into trouble. I know times are hard. But I think you've taken a lot more money than we agreed to. Let's talk about it, face to face. I haven't told anybody yet, not even my wife."

"You have to be mistaken," the man calmly told Sanchez. "You may not understand what you're looking at, my friend. It can be a little tricky when you look at that data. If you don't think it's fair, though, we'll work it out. I'm sure everything will be fine."

"Well, that makes me feel a little better," Sanchez said.

They had agreed to meet in the town of Dog Mountain. The man said he'd be returning from a job in Dinosaur,

Colorado. Sanchez said he'd be coming from Casper, Wyoming.

"Bring a sandwich," the man told Sanchez. "We'll eat lunch in the park and enjoy the great outdoors. I won't even object if you bring a couple of cold beers."

It was only an hour before they were scheduled to meet that the man had placed his phone call to Sanchez.

When Sanchez arrived at the campground, the man heard the car's tires crushing the gravel on the dirt and stone road. The vehicle rounded into view. They exchanged a wave. Sanchez pulled into the parking spot next to the disabled vehicle.

"What happened to your car?" Sanchez asked.

"It was driving just fine, and then steam started to rise from the hood," the man said.

"Sounds like a hose," Sanchez said.

"See what I mean?" the man praised him. "You haven't even lifted the hood and you already know what the problem is."

"Well, let's take a look and see if I'm right," Sanchez told him.

The man opened the driver-side door to reach for the hood release.

Sanchez was wearing a tie. So he tucked it into his shirt and zipped up his jacket. He had heard of guys wearing ties getting them wrapped around the fan and pulled into the engine. It was a horrible way to die, he thought.

"That's what it is," Sanchez said after lifting the hood. "Look at that, a cracked hose."

"You know your cars," the man said as he stood next to Sanchez to see for himself.

"Funny, I don't smell any coolant," Sanchez remarked as he looked over the rest of the engine.

"What's that?" the man asked.

"Nothing really. It's just odd," Sanchez said with his head buried in the engine compartment. "You don't have another radiator hose with you, do you?"

"I don't."

A crushing blow to the back of Nat Sanchez' head drove the bridge of his nose straight into the radiator cap. He grunted. A broken nose wouldn't kill him. It was the blow to the back of his skull, at the base, that killed him.

Sanchez slid down the grill of the car. His head bounced off the bumper and he dropped to the ground. Another blow with the rock assured the outcome.

Nat Sanchez, the man called a lifesaver only moments ago, was lying lifeless in front of the other man's car.

The killer wiped any telltale blood splatter off the yellow rock, walked up the dirt road to another campsite and tossed the rock back amongst others.

He had already found a spot to dispose of Nat's car. It was nearby. The vehicle probably would not be found until spring or summer.

The body would be taken to a pasture far from the campground where he died. Undressed, the corpse of Nat Sanchez would provide nutrients for a hungry wildlife population all winter. By spring, there would be little left of the human remains, and no evidence of how they got there.

The man gave a fleeting thought to how he arrived at this point. Where had his life stepped onto a path he never intended to follow?

But the past was the past, he told himself. Now, he had a chance to follow a new path, live a new life, at Dog Mountain and Minnie's Gap Ski Resort.

3

"There's nothing small about the new ski resort called Minnie's Gap," JC Snow told his television audience in Denver. He was standing in the center of the ski resort's shiny new village, far from Denver and almost in Utah.

"But it must leap the same large obstacles that have prevented virtually any new ski resort from opening in Colorado for decades," JC continued.

"Why is it so hard to open a new ski area?" the anchor back in Denver asked him, as viewers listened in.

"There's a long list of challenges that other attempts have failed to overcome," JC told her. "First, the cost.

Investors had to come up with $100 million. The infrastructure alone has required building a small city, providing roads, electricity, a wastewater treatment plant, buildings, the chairlifts and lodges."

"And we watched, with interest," the anchor added. "Minnie's Gap worked its way through some difficult environmental reviews and local opposition."

"That's right. But here we are now," JC said. "We're standing in a ski-resort village at the base of slopes offering two thousand vertical feet of skiing and snowboarding and an average of three hundred inches of snow a year."

"I can't get past that $100 million price tag," the anchor told him. "That's going to be paid for by selling lift tickets?"

"Not even close," JC told her and the viewing audience. "The modern method of making money from a ski resort is selling the real estate that surrounds the slopes. And not only the one- and two-million-dollar vacation homes and rentals. Remember, this was a blank canvas. They have built and own every single building. Minnie's Gap LLC owns it all."

Local residents knew that the mammoth ski resort wasn't even located at the place they had called Minnie's Gap all their lives. *That* location was over the border in Wyoming, about an hour's drive north.

But Minnie Crouse was a legend in Browns Park. And how could you ignore the legend of this land when looking to name the ski area?

Skeletons of dinosaurs had been found there. Famous mountain men like Kit Carson had walked the ground there. The park was used as a hideout by famous outlaws like Butch Cassidy. And people like Minnie Crouse had carved out a living that most people could only dream of.

The wind caught JC's hair and tossed it. There was a sharp slap of cold air accompanying the breeze. The sun was down. The temperature had dropped into the teens.

The television reporter zipped his jacket higher up his chest. He had turned thirty-seven years old over the summer.

He was still fit. He worked at it. His hair and mustache were still dark. Only faint gray hairs were making their initial arrival on his head.

JC was on assignment at the ski village for one week. The entire state was intrigued by the first season of the new ski resort. It meant new jobs, new money and a new place to seek pleasure.

The Minnie's Gap Ski Resort wasn't far from the bones of the last attempt to build a new ski area. It failed and was now a ghost town. There were unfinished subdivisions, a partially constructed ski lodge, half-built ski lifts and half-cut ski runs.

JC was pleasantly surprised when his news director had agreed to this idea for a story on Minnie's Gap. Everyone in the newsroom was aware of JC's obsession with skiing. And so were his television viewers. Colorado had its own obsession with skiing, and it made JC only more popular with his audience.

The story, JC explained as he pitched it to his superior, was not a fluff piece about a new location for skiers and snowboarders to link turns. The story, JC insisted, was possibly the biggest economic investment on the Western Slope since oil shale in the 1980s.

"Oil shale went bust," JC told the news director, Pat Perilla. "This might go bust too. If it does, the flames will be worth watching."

"You're clear. Nice job," a producer's voice announced in JC's earpiece. It was Monday night and JC had just finished his first live shot at Minnie's Gap. He was assigned to be there the entire week.

He turned to view the new resort village that had been framed as his background for the broadcast. The architecture was designed to resemble an old horse ranch. The buildings looked like old bunkhouses, old barns, horse stalls and old ranch homes. The pedestrian walks, where they weren't lined by stores and restaurants, were lined with fencing that looked like old corrals.

Above the reach of children, lassos decorated the walls of the buildings, along with horseshoes, spurs and branding irons.

It was all lit in a warm glow. The lighting was intended to look like it came from a giant campfire. It was slightly orange and cast long shadows. And there were plenty of actual fires burning in outdoor pits.

"You hungry?" he asked his photographer. The man carrying the camera was Bip Peters. He had happily fallen into the role as JC's photographer on "road trips."

"Yeah, I'm hungry," Bip responded.

JC's road trips had become one of the brands of his television station. He was known to viewers for traveling across the country to pursue a story they would find interesting. Over the past few years, he'd reported from Vermont, Upstate New York and Montana, as well as distant corners of Colorado. His stories tended to involve tales of murder and political scandal.

"It moves the needle," the news director liked to say about JC's road trips. The idea of an imaginary gauge measuring popularity suggested that their TV station lured more news viewers because of JC's compelling coverage.

Their first live shot from Minnie's Gap marked the end of a long day. The drive from Denver that morning had been draining. It took nearly eight hours to arrive at the middle of nowhere.

They left Denver, heading west on I-70, and turned north at Silverthorn. They followed Route 9 until turning onto Highway 40 and passing through Steamboat Springs. They stopped for lunch at a Mexican restaurant with a large mural of Frida Kahlo on the wall.

After passing through Craig, the presence of human dwellings on Highway 40 dissipated. The land beyond that point was largely left to grazing cattle.

The occasional farm, with its dense-green irrigated fields in the summer, stood in stark contrast with the rest of the horizon. In the winter, everything was brown, except for the snow.

Bip turned their news car off Highway 40 and headed north on Colorado Route 318. Until recently, 318 was the only paved road in Lonesome County.

A herd of wild horses kicked up dust as they ran away when the SUV approached. The occasional mule deer dashed across the road. Much of the land, in every direction, was unspoiled by human hands. They were on the edge of Browns Park.

They turned right onto Route 10N. It was unpaved dirt.

They rode through Irish Canyon as it was getting dark. The canyon walls were steep and sometimes hugged the road on both sides. As the walls of the canyon tapered off, Bip turned the car right, onto the access road to Minnie's Gap Ski Resort.

This was where you would find the county's other paved roads. The asphalt still looked fresh, a dark black. The painted lines on the road were still bright yellow and white.

The cluster of lights coming from human dwellings and business establishments required a moment to adjust their eyes. They had been staring at open plains for hours.

And the buildings they now passed were new. Only a few years ago, this landscape was just more windswept snow piling against more snow fences placed on more brown pasture.

It had been a long drive. In the ski village, they found themselves among human beings, aside from each other, for the first time in hours.

"Hey, they speak English here," Bip quipped the first time they spoke with a local resident. "Just like back in the United States."

Remarks like that were not unusual upon someone's initial arrival in the area of Browns Park. It was beautiful, but remote.

Visitors would climb out of their car and say things like, "Where the hell are we?"

The land was officially categorized as "semi-desert." In the summer, newcomers would quip, "Anyone ever think of buying a sprinkler?"

But the beauty here was sculpted by God. It wasn't fertilized or fed chemicals. It looked like it looked hundreds of years ago. It hadn't changed much and probably couldn't be improved upon.

Winters on the valley floor were mild. Only a few inches of snow covered the ground, and sometimes it was swept away by the wind or melted by the sun. From the valley floor, the ski mountain rose quickly. That's where the deep snow was.

"How about we pull on the feedbag for a spell," Bip said in his best Western cowpoke impression. He looked toward a cowboy-themed restaurant in the ski resort village.

The restaurant was called Peg Leg. It was named after a one-legged horse thief who lived in the area long ago.

The restaurant's interior was the reproduction of a tack room in a horse stable. There were saddles and bridles and barrels and carefully placed hay against the faded barnwood walls. There was a stuffed horse in the corner and walls full of lariats, branding irons and old cowboy boots.

A plump waitress wearing a smile, blue jeans and a shirt with pearl snap buttons arrived to take their order.

The journalists both ordered a dark beer called *Big Bad Baptista.* It was made by a craft brewer in Salt Lake City, Utah. The ski resort wasn't any further from the border with Utah than it was from Wyoming. They were near the spot where the borders of those two states met the border of Colorado.

"Hey, you recognize that guy?" JC asked Bip as they sipped their beer. "Picture him with shorter hair."

Bip gazed over his shoulder at a man with shoulder-length dark hair. The smile on his face looked like it was a permanent fixture. He was greeting diners as he passed by each table. Everyone seemed to have something to say to him, and he answered with a pat on the shoulder, a handshake for the men or a kiss on the cheek for the women.

"I don't recognize him," Bip said. "But I may be the only one who doesn't."

"He was in some movies a while ago," JC said. He struggled to remember the actor's name or the movies he was in. "Women loved him. His name is on the tip of my tongue."

The man moved with care not to let anyone feel left out. He finally reached his table, already occupied by a beautiful woman with skin the color of milk chocolate.

"Benjamin Maple!" JC blurted. "That's who it is. He was a young star, like twenty years ago. Then he kind of disappeared." JC remembered a few of the actor's movies and jogged Bip's memory.

"What's he doing here?" Bip asked.

"I don't know," JC said. "But it looks like he's welcome to come here anytime."

The waitress arrived at the table with their food, ribs for Bip and barbeque chicken for JC. Chicken had been his favorite food for as long as he could remember.

"Is that the actor, Benjamin Maple?" JC asked the waitress.

"Benny?" she replied with her smile, stealing a glance in his direction. "He's quite a character."

"What's he doing here?" JC inquired.

"He lives here," she said. "Everyone knows Benny. He's like the local celebrity. Oh, Roman is too. That's the woman with him. She was in movies too."

"Are they part of the investment group who built the ski area?" JC asked.

"I don't think so," the waitress answered pensively. Then her smile returned. "They're just a bonus!"

4

The woman at the table with Benny Maple at the Peg Leg restaurant wore a worried look on her face. She was speaking quietly to the movie star. At times, she'd drape her hand over his arm. JC thought she was on the verge of tears.

JC and Bip finished their dinner and the waitress brought a second round of the craft beer they were drinking, *Big Bad Baptista.*

Bip was twenty-nine years old. He had dark hair that he spiked. He grew up in Telluride. JC admired his skill on a snowboard. The reporter also liked working with him as a news photographer. They had gotten to know each other, and what one another expected when covering a news story.

JC thought Bip was handsome almost to the point of perversion. The reporter had gotten used to the subtle head turns from women when Bip walked by. His good looks didn't prevent him from seeming approachable. He always looked like he was thinking about something funny. Women seemed to like that.

"What's Robin doing while you're gone?" Bip asked JC.

"She'll be in Denver. I just spoke with her while you were wrapping up your gear after the live shot. Robin drew the short straw and was sent to a four-hour planning commission meeting in the suburbs."

"Wow, feel the goosebumps on my arm?" Bip smirked. "There is nothing more boring to a news photographer than a planning commission meeting. I know they're important, but after taking a shot of the board members and members of the audience, and then a shot of a board member chewing on his pen followed by a shot of another board member twirling a paperclip on her finger, I wrap it up with a picture of a member of the audience sleeping."

"Oh, it got even better," JC smiled. "She waited three hours for the item on the agenda that the producers were interested in, and it was tabled. She waited for three hours, and her story was tabled in thirty seconds."

Bip started laughing. It was a knowing laugh. It was sometimes the nature of the business they were in.

"But," JC proceeded, "that Robin is a sharp pencil. As the audience was filing out of the room because they weren't interested in anything else on the agenda, she saw a new proposal quietly advancing. Someone wants to build a shopping center on top of some wetlands outside Denver."

"Seriously?" Bip reacted. "Was someone trying to slip it in unnoticed?"

"That's what Robin thinks," JC agreed. "She'll probably break the story tomorrow. Environmentalists are going to go nuts."

"She's a good reporter," Bip told him. "Management made a good decision moving her from producer to reporter."

"I know," JC agreed. "We were lucky to have her as our producer for as long as we did."

"Well, you had a lot to do with her becoming a reporter," Bip said.

"She wanted to move to reporting and she had everything it takes," JC stated. "But she never would have pushed management to give her a chance. That's not her style."

"And now she's the most popular television reporter in Denver, as far as the male demographic," Bip reminded him. "You'd better watch out. Now, everyone knows she's beautiful *and* smart."

"I'm not concerned," JC confided. "I've still got the female demographic, and they decide what's on the television set."

"You'd better not blow it," Bip told him. "I mean Robin as your girlfriend. Don't blow it."

"Why does everyone say that to me?" JC said defensively.

"Uh, because they know you," Bip declared. "You've gone through a few. I only met Shara once, but that romance was legend in the newsroom. And yet, you blew it."

"I suppose so," JC agreed, with humility. "I thought Shara was a goddess. But we never seemed to work it out when we had a problem. It always became a bigger problem. It's not like that with Robin. She brings me peace."

They drank their beer and the waitress brought the check.

"Poor thing," the waitress said as she placed the check in front of JC. "Someone just ran over Roman's Boston Terrier."

"They ran over her dog?" Bip inquired. "Did they kill it?"

"Yes," the waitress said sadly. "He was the cutest little thing."

"That sucks," Bip muttered.

"It's awful. That's probably why she looks so upset," JC agreed. "Anyone who has owned dogs for awhile has probably lost one to a car. Yeah, it sucks."

Out the window of the restaurant, JC could see the warm light illuminating a tall statue of Minnie Crouse, the namesake of the ski resort whose homestead was over the border in Wyoming.

The site of Minnie Crouse's old cabin was now underwater. The land was taken by the federal government and flooded for a new reservoir in the 1960s.

It was still a point of contention among the ranch families. Minnie lived in her home until the last day. With the water approaching her front door, she set her cabin ablaze.

Now, her name was reborn as the moniker of a destination ski resort. Her likeness stood where she could watch it all.

Skiers and snowboarders who spent a day on the slopes were walking past the window of the Peg Leg restaurant. Many were in a state of exhaustion. They were heading for the parking lot. The dining room at the Peg Leg was filling up.

It looked like the new ski resort was off to a promising start. And JC wondered where the people were coming from.

The closest "big city" was Rock Springs, Wyoming. It was seventy-five miles away and only Wyoming would consider it big. It had a population of just under forty thousand.

The airport there had two flights, daily, to and from Denver. To drive from Denver would take four hours. And it took five hours to drive from Salt Lake City.

JC hoped to set up an interview with the ski resort's management and get some answers.

"Hey, do you recognize him?" JC asked Bip, nodding his head to a new customer walking in the door.

"That's the congressman from Durango, isn't it?" Bip said. "Jonathan Oaks?"

"It is," JC said. "Though, he's a former congressman. Remember, he decided not to run for re-election."

"What's he doing here?" Bip asked.

"He's an investor in the ski resort," JC informed him. "He probably doesn't have the deepest pockets of the investors, but he's the one who is best known to the public. And, at least for the time being, he's the managing partner here. His title is president, I think. He's got someone else doing the day-to-day stuff, like fixing broken water fountains. But *he* decides what goes on here, and *his* is the last word on matters."

Like the movie star who had already arrived, Congressman Jonathan Oaks had a few tables to stop at on the way to his own. He shook hands and exchanged quips with faces familiar to him. There were smiles all around.

Oaks was a handsome sixty-two-year-old. His dark hair was quickly surrendering to gray. He was tan. He looked like he was spending time on the slopes. For dinner, he was dressed in a thick ski sweater and jeans.

"There are rumors that he's thinking about running for governor," JC told Bip. "Or maybe he's looking at the U.S. Senate seat that's opening up in a couple of years."

"Would this be a stepping-stone?" Bip asked.

"It would enhance his resume with voters," JC assessed. "He was in Congress for eight years. Being here would give him some chops as a businessman. If Minnie's Gap is a success, he could tell the private sector that he knows what it takes to prosper. And if it fails, he could blame red tape and tell those same business owners that they would have a sympathetic ear in the Capitol."

JC stood up from his table as the congressman passed by.

"Congressman Oaks," JC said as he extended his hand. "I'm JC Snow and this is Bip Peters. We're with the news out of Denver with channel—"

"Of course, JC," the former congressman said as he shook the reporter's hand. "I remember you. I always thought you were fair when you were reporting."

"Thank you, Congressman," JC said. "We're here doing some stories about the opening of your new ski resort. It's an interesting venture."

"Yes, it is," Oaks said. He smiled but it resembled a grimace. "It's a big bite to take, but we're off to a great start. Someone told me you were here. And I know *your* background as a skier. So, while you can't admit it, I know you're secretly pulling for us."

"Could we bother you for an interview?" JC asked. "Perhaps we could stop by your office tomorrow?"

"That would be fine," the former congressman said. "We want everyone to know what we're doing here. We want them all to come pay us a visit. Call my office and set up the interview. I'll look forward to seeing you."

"And when can we expect to see you re-enter politics?" JC asked him. He knew that politicians never closed the book on a political career. As a breed, they seemed to be intoxicated by the whole business.

"I don't know if that day will come," Oaks responded. "The style of politics today seems to be so negative. If a politician just provides voters with a checklist of things they hate, they can win a lot of support. Candidates behave like it's too risky to come out in *support* of anything in particular. Just list all the things they hate and people they're *against*. A lot of voters fall for that."

"But I'm not hearing you say that you'll never run for office again," JC asked.

"A politician never says never," Oaks laughed.

Hands were shaken again, JC said that he'd schedule an appointment for the next day, and the president of Minnie's Gap, LLC, moved on.

"I'd vote for him," Bip said when the former congressman was out of earshot.

"You can't blame him for becoming frustrated with Washington," JC stated. "Television journalism took a big step in the wrong direction when we put the little 'D' or 'R' under the names of politicians. It gave viewers an excuse not to think. They don't actually have to listen to a politician's idea and decide if it is a good one. Now, they just look at the little 'D' or 'R' and let their bias do the thinking."

"By the way, are you?" Bip asked.

"Am I what?" JC responded.

"Are you secretly pulling for this place to be a success?"

"He's right," JC said. "I can't publicly endorse a new ski resort. But could you imagine if I was hoping a $100 million investment on the Western Slope would fail? By the way, do you want to take a few runs tomorrow before we start our workday?"

"Sweet," was the only response Bip needed to make.

Before reaching his own table, Congressman Oaks stopped and exchanged words with the actor, Benjamin Maple. But his attention was really focused on the woman, Roman Holiday. They grasped hands. Then she embraced him. Her face was hidden behind her dark hair as the tears returned.

5

The animal pulled mightily with her hind quarters, trying to unearth the treasure. She alternated between tugging backwards and digging at the ground with her paws.

She was pregnant. Her appetite was insatiable. This would provide good nourishment to await her pups.

It didn't take long to expose the carrion. Human carrion. The wolf sank her teeth with satisfaction into the putrefying flesh.

The animal's gray muzzle was covered in dried blood. She ripped savagely at the neck and jawbone. She exposed and devoured the tongue. The wolf's bushy tail with a black tip was horizontal. She was in prey mode, feasting on the discovery.

She was led to it, across the sagebrush slopes and sandy soil, by following her exceptional sense of smell.

The brisk wind caressed the carnivore's thick winter coat. The sky was dark. The stars hanging from a black ceiling over Diamond Peak were as bright as anywhere in the world. But a far-off sodium vapor lamp illuminated a corral at a Browns Park ranch.

The wolf was part of a growing pack that began with the first pups born in Colorado since the 1940s. They were expanding in number, and they were spreading out.

She had passed a large red rock nearby. One side was sloped and could provide shelter for the night. It was next to a solitary, dead pine tree with bare branches bleached almost white by the sun.

She would bring some of her supper to the rock and lie down. She could slumber for a few hours and return to her discovery at dawn, for breakfast.

With a jawbone to gnaw on, she settled under the cover of the boulder. It was red sandstone. The side that was angled toward the earth had some letters scratched into it, with the numerals 1838.

Of no consequence to the wolf, what remained of the human corpse would probably be found next May or June. That was when cattle would be brought back up for summer grazing.

The livestock had already been taken down to their winter pasture. There would be no cause for humans to set foot on this soil until the cowboys returned with their cattle.

By the time someone found what was left of Nat Sanchez, his bones would be scattered by this wolf and other wildlife that would follow. Every living carnivore on Diamond Peak would be searching for nourishment over the cold months ahead.

Minnie's Gap Ski Resort was built on Dog Mountain.

In 1839, an exploration party was being led by Thomas Jefferson Farnham. They were hoping to reach Oregon but encountered hardships in the mountains of Colorado. They were starving. So much so, they cooked and ate their beloved dog.

Dog Mountain was the next summit southeast of Diamond Peak. West of Diamond Peak's dark brown rocks and gnarled ponderosa pine was Browns Park.

It used to be called Browns Hole. Some say the name came from those brown rocks. Others say it was named after a French-Canadian trapper named Baptiste Brown. No one really was certain where the name came from. And events taking place in that valley were as mysterious as any in North America.

Underfoot in Browns Park, there were lost graves of honest men, honest women, bad men, bad women, and their victims.

There were hardworking ranchers and cattle rustlers. Sometimes, they were one and the same.

There were bank robbers and cowboys who cheated at poker. There were stories of buried loot that had never been recovered.

Browns Park was forty miles of meadow. It was accessed from a few narrow notches in the mountain walls that surrounded it, like Irish Canyon.

The Ute and Shoshone used to seek out mild winters there, before being driven away.

Archaeologists found signs of prehistoric man dating back ten thousand years. The petroglyphs in Irish Canyon were left by the Fremont people. There were repeated carvings of a man with antlers protruding from his helmet. In some carvings, he carried a weapon in one hand and a shield in the other.

It was mountain men like Kit Carson and Jim Bridger who originally called it Browns Hole. They wintered there too, holding a legendary rendezvous at Fort Davy Crockett each year.

Then, Browns Park became a safe harbor for notorious outlaws. The most famous was Butch Cassidy. He and others on the "Outlaw Trail" would come to Browns Park to hide out.

There was cunning behind their selection. Half of Browns Park was in Colorado. Almost half of it was in Utah. The rest was in Wyoming.

Outlaws could escape a posse by crossing over the border into another state. In Browns Park, the border of another state was always a short ride away.

Many notorious thieves and gunmen made Browns Park their home. They lived peacefully with the ranchers and farmers there.

Butch Cassidy once worked for the father of Minnie Crouse as a ranch hand. The outlaw was known to be good with horses.

Butch's sister, who lived in southern Utah, said that he got the name "Butch" when he worked for a butcher in Rock Springs.

The Green River cut a path through Browns Park, though the river was rarely green any longer. The Flaming Gorge Dam, built in the 1960s, had submerged the glacial till that gave the river its natural color.

The dam permanently raised the water level and maintained a constant current. The Green River no longer froze in the winter.

Modern residents of Browns Park were hardy people. Cattle had brought prosperity to the valley. Children still grew up to be riders and ropers, just as their parents had. Only their parents probably used an outhouse when they were young and were lucky if they had electricity.

There were still ruins in Browns Park of small log cabins or dugouts that someone once called home.

And Browns Park was still sparsely populated. It was remote and rugged.

It was a cowboy life. Bonds between brothers and sisters were strong, growing up on a vast ranch and working alongside each other at an early age.

There were also a few outfitters living in the park. They took care of visiting hunters and fishers in the national wildlife refuge. There were river guides who took tourists whitewater rafting in the Flaming Gorge National Recreation Area. Or they could raft through the towering Gates of Lodore, another narrow entrance to Browns Park.

That's where swallows built mud houses on the sides of the cliffs. They stuck their heads out and chirped at the world as it went by.

East of Browns Park was a sliver of land called Lonesome County. It included a piece of Diamond Peak, all of Dog Mountain and the valley in between. The town of Dog Mountain, named after the peak, was the only incorporated municipality in the county. That made it the county seat.

Dr. Hunter Anderson, the man who almost died in the avalanche, was a welcome addition to the small town of Dog Mountain. His office was closer for Browns Park residents than the seventy-five-mile drive to Rock Springs.

Dr. Anderson wore his right arm in a sling since the avalanche. But he quickly resumed office visits. He could do most of the daily routine with one hand.

He was handsome, with a thick mane of white hair on his head and blue eyes. He was single and had just acknowledged his sixty-fifth birthday. He had grown up in Denver, attended medical school there and joined a prominent office of general practitioners. He was intelligent and had a good bedside manner. He enjoyed the success and the financial rewards associated with his achievements.

But he suffered a tragedy. It became painful to remain in surroundings that reminded him of the life he had lost. At the time his colleagues were planning their retirement, Dr. Anderson packed up his belongings and moved to remote Lonesome County.

Throughout his prosperous career, Anderson had dreamed of living the cowboy life. He was also looking for a generous helping of ski bumming. Leaving Denver, he reached into a box and grabbed a cowboy hat, a gift from long ago, and headed west.

He opened an office in the small central business district of his new hometown. On the receptionist's desk, for all to see, he displayed a brass antique microscope made in Austria over a century ago. His family had given it to him as a gift when he completed medical school.

"It's a Reichert," he'd proudly tell patients who asked. "It's a beauty, isn't it?"

He wore his cowboy hat and added a pair of cowboy boots to his costume. He felt like a cowboy. His new start in a new town brought him happiness that he hadn't felt in years.

Dr. Anderson lived in what fashionably had become known as a "Tiny House." It had everything a single man desired. It was clean, there was heat and a roof overhead. It had a bed, a kitchen, a shower, a living room, a porch and a magnificent view. It was 250 square feet.

He purchased five acres just inside the town limits and set up house. The tiny home was the talk of the townspeople for a while. It always gave him something to discuss during appointments with patients. Though lately, all they wanted to talk about was the avalanche that nearly killed him.

At the end of each day, Dr. Anderson would place his cowboy hat on his head and pull on a long black coat made of wool. He locked the door to his office in town and drove home past fence posts strung with barbed wire and tin cans. The cans were hung by ranchers, intended to ward off predators hungry for livestock and chickens.

Dr. Anderson would arrive home at his small plot of land and enter his small house, loving the new life he had chosen.

The structure he lived in was about the same size as the cabins the settlers of Browns Park first built for shelter, the ones now lying in ruin across the landscape.

He wasn't unlike the pioneers who set out from Iowa, Illinois or Missouri. Many of them walked to Browns Park to find a life that would fulfill their dreams.

Dr. Anderson loved nature and loved the same undisturbed horizon his predecessors had admired. He too was willing to work hard to achieve his dream.

"What are we up to today?" Bip asked as they worked on breakfast.

"We've got a little time before we have to be anywhere," JC told him. He leaned toward his news photographer as if to conspire. "Let's kill the hill."

"I thought you'd never ask," Bip said with a grin, tossing aside his napkin and pushing his chair away from the table.

After pulling on boots and layers of clothing in their rooms, they made the short walk to the base lift. They were pleased to see that they got there before most of the crowd. The only ones who stood alongside them were a group of skiers who showed up first every morning. They called themselves "The Corduroy Crew."

Most of them were retirees who lived on or near the mountain. Most of them skied every day, usually only two or three hours on the best snow. Then they went home for lunch, planning to return in the morning to ski the best snow again.

As JC and Bip rode up the side of the mountain, they listened to the metal clatter of the chairlift as it approached the upper terminal.

At the top, they pushed toward a wooden sign on a post indicating that they had arrived at a steep run called Ute Chute. It was a double black diamond. They would have to drop in, a plunge of about ten feet. JC was on his skis and Bip was on his snowboard.

As Bip strapped into his board, they admired the magnificent view. Browns Park opened up in the distant valley below them.

They could see the southern end of the park and the Gates of Lodore. And they could see the land that was part of Dinosaur National Monument, a spot where an abundance of fossils had been found of the great creatures.

"You know that chickens are related to the tyrannosaurus rex?" Bip stated. "They share similar molecular proteins."

"And I eat them every chance I get," JC responded. "That's how tough I am."

Ignoring the metallic noise of the chairlift behind them and the skiers unloading, they continued to marvel at the untamed landscape that unfolded before them.

"In a million years," Bip said, "families of cockroaches will vacation at a park named 'Human National Monument.' They'll gaze at fossils of human beings and ponder their extinction. A cockroach child will ask her parents where all the human beings disappeared to."

"'They killed each other,' the parents will say," JC added. "The little cockroach child will ask why the humans all killed each other. And the parents will tell her, 'Because they could.'"

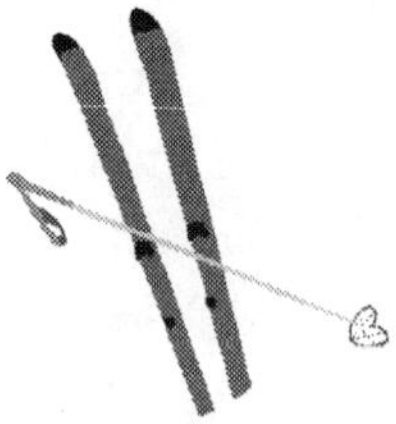

6

"He called again," the voice said quietly, choking back sobs on the other end of the phone.

"Oh my," former Congressman Jon Oaks replied. "What did he say?"

"He said that he had a riddle." Roman Holiday had to stop to compose herself before continuing. "He asked, 'What is black and white and red all over?'"

"My God," Oaks gasped. "Your dog. Oh, Roman."

"Then, he asked how Olive's day was at school. He named the school and Olive's teacher." Roman Holiday's voice was hoarse.

"What's wrong with your voice?" Oaks asked.

"I think it's from crying so much," she said. "Maybe it's just the tension. Should I go to the police?"

"I thought he told you not to contact the police," Oaks reminded her. "Roman, right now, he's little more than a stalker. He's probably no worse than some of the fanatic followers that you had in Hollywood. We don't even know who he is. And if you get police to find him and arrest him for killing your dog, they'll write him a ticket and he'll be free until the case goes to trial months from now. In the meantime, he might really become outraged. He might go after Olive next."

"Oh Jon, what am I going to do?" she squeaked. She felt she was near a complete breakdown, and she wouldn't resist.

"I'm going to think of something, Roman." Oaks spoke in a measured tone. He was the voice of reason. "Let's buy time until I figure out how we're going to catch him. Keep talking with him. Don't call the police. I'm not going to let anything happen to Olive, or to you."

Roman Holiday was the second-ranking Hollywood star residing in Lonesome County behind Benny Maple. As a younger woman, Roman had a couple of supporting roles in a couple of TV shows. She also had a few lines in a few successful movies.

Ultimately, she was pretty enough for Hollywood, but not talented enough.

But in Lonesome County, she was a hometown girl. She was born and bred there. She grew up a cowboy on a cowboy ranch. She could ride and she could rope.

She was fourth generation in the Browns Park area. Her skin was dark and flawless. Her parents said that she was black. Some people saw it, others didn't. Her great-grandfather had been the outlaw Isom Dart.

Isom Dart had been a slave in Arkansas until the end of the Civil War. Then he became a talented rider and bronco buster. Like a number of young men in Browns Park, he became a cattle rustler.

He was popular in the valley, until he was gunned down at his ranch. Legend says that he was murdered by the famous bounty hunter, Tom Horn, at the hire of the cattle barons.

Roman's father was named Arliss Holiday. Roman repeatedly had to disappoint those who asked if she was related to the gunslinger, Doc Holliday. "His name has two L's" she'd tell them. But it never stopped Hollywood publicists from claiming that she *was* related to the gunman.

Roman's parents named her after a popular 1953 film starring Audrey Hepburn and Gregory Peck. It was called *Roman Holiday*, and it got her seeing stars.

Until then, she wanted to be a cowboy. She thought playing cowboy was fun. But Hollywood was her destiny.

She was beautiful, with shoulder-length black hair, a great figure, a lovely smile and eyes that beamed.

But she was also fragile. She lacked confidence and sometimes had difficulty coping. When Los Angeles became too much, she came back home.

Lonesome County loved having her back. She was their movie star. They were proud of her. Her parents had both passed away, but she would always have a home there.

She had a secret affair with Congressman Jonathan Oaks, who was married but not very attentive to his wife or three grown children.

They were twenty years apart in age. She gave him the energy that was lacking in his marriage. He found Roman exciting and he was in a constant state of arousal. He was infatuated.

Eventually, Roman ended the tryst. She lacked confidence in herself, but her return to Lonesome County slowly peeled away the reckless habits of Hollywood. She returned to the principled code of behavior taught during her upbringing on the edge of Browns Park.

The congressman and the actress remained friends after their breakup. She realized he was more of a father figure than a flame.

Roman had a daughter, Olive. Her full name was Palmolive. Roman liked the ring of the name, even when others thought it was ridiculous. Again, the name made more sense in Los Angeles than it did in Dog Mountain.

Olive was eleven years old, meaning that Roman either conceived during her waning days in California or the early days of her return to Lonesome County. Most thought she got pregnant before she came home.

Roman never named the father. She was raising Olive as a single parent. Those in town offered various opinions about who and why she was protecting the father. There were rumors that Olive's father was a very famous actor, and the reason Roman quit acting.

But her life in Lonesome County had been pleasant. No one made a big fuss about her. A lot of people had known her parents and everyone behaved like old friends.

The anonymous phone calls to Roman were a recent source of torment. They joined the letters that had already been harassing her. It was like something out of a movie she once had a role in.

It began when Roman started receiving letters with no return address. Inside the envelope would be one page with words cut from various magazines.

The content of the letters was lewd. They suggested that the sender knew something about her sex life, that he or she had peered into her window when Roman was naked or making love to a man. And the letters warned her not to contact police or "There will be a price to pay."

Roman was terrified. She reached out to her father figure, Congressman Jonathan Oaks. He offered her advice and tried to help her weather the storm.

Now, the phone calls had begun. The stakes had grown. The stalker began talking about Olive.

Roman had not told Olive about the threats. When the phone calls came, Olive was never home. Roman took that as further proof that the caller was watching or knew her routine.

Not wanting to terrify her daughter, Roman would try to seem casual when she insisted on driving Olive to the end of their road and wait for the school bus with her.

Roman tried to sound matter-of-fact when telling Olive not to talk with strangers and not to accept a ride in a truck or car offered by a stranger.

"Mom, you don't live in Los Angeles anymore," would be a standard impatient response from the eleven-year-old. Olive had grown up in Lonesome County, a community largely without crime.

Olive was tall for her age. Her figure hadn't begun to develop. But she had pretty eyes. And the texture of her brown hair was the envy of grown-up women. The adults in Lonesome County said that Olive was going to be a beauty, like her mother.

Jim Bridger gazed over JC's shoulder. Below the portrait, JC was reading a book while lying on the bed in his hotel room. The book was about Browns Park, where Bridger and other famous mountain men had gathered each winter for an annual rendezvous. On another wall of the room, there was a print of one of those mountain-man meetings at Browns Park.

The book told JC that the annual rendezvous allowed the mountain men to sell the skins of animals they had trapped or shot since the last gathering. Their earnings went toward the purchase of gunpowder, flour, fishhooks, sugar, coffee, knives and whisky. It was everything the frontiersmen would need to survive in seclusion until next year's rendezvous.

The variable between how much money the men would earn for their pelts, and how much money they would spend on supplies, was determined by how much money they squandered on gambling at that gathering.

Browns Park, or Browns Hole as it was known then, also offered shelter from the harsh winter weather up in the mountains. First Natives would erect their teepees in the park, during the winter season, for the same reason.

The hotel where JC and Bip were staying at Minnie's Gap Ski Resort was called "The Fort." It was a nod to Fort Davy Crockett, the name of the trading post where the old mountain-man rendezvous used to take place. The painting of the fort, on the wall of JC's room, illustrated a square of log cabins and warehouses. Teepees were erected outside the perimeter.

"Hi Clint," JC said as he put his book down when he answered a ring on his phone.

He listened to what Clint had to say.

"Wow," JC responded. "That's an unexpected development. I'm flattered. I'm going to have to think about it though. You know that."

The two men shared assurances that they'd talk again.

He ended their call and heard a knock on the door to his room.

"It's open. Come on in," JC said.

Bip Peters entered. JC hopped off the bed. They were heading for breakfast.

"You made your bed," Bip said. "Impressive. Were you a Marine?"

"I was a Duck Hawk," JC told him.

"A what?" Bip laughed.

"A Duck Hawk," JC told him, smiling. "It was an organization I belonged to when I was in grade school. We went camping and learned about the outdoors. But we also learned about being disciplined, like making our bed. A Duck Hawk is another name for peregrine falcon."

"They could have named you after the peregrine falcon, one of the scariest predators on earth?" Bip quipped. "But they named you the Lame Ducks?"

"The Duck Hawks," JC sneered.

JC and Bip ate breakfast in the hotel's dining hall. It was included in the cost of the room.

The dining room was called "The Rendezvous." It was big and cavernous, with lots of shellacked wood posts and tables to match.

They talked over their plan for the week. They were scheduled to interview former Congressman Jon Oaks, the managing partner of Minnie's Gap, in about an hour. He would discuss all the new housing and construction jobs provided by the resort, in an area sorely in need of jobs.

There were so many jobs, though, many of them went to people from outside the area. The town of Dog Mountain began as housing for all the construction workers.

Until the ski area was constructed, there was not a single hotel, bar or store in Browns Park. Not one. There were no neighborhoods, no cul-de-sacs. If you lived in this corner of Colorado, you lived in a ranch house or a bunkhouse.

And most of the locals were too busy running their ranches to also apply for the new full-time construction jobs. Though, quite a few ranchers did end up moonlighting at the construction site. The money was too good to leave on the table.

There were eight hours until their next newscast. JC and Bip planned to gather local reaction to the project. Some, they would find, loved it and some loathed it.

Each day of coverage would include some footage of skiing and snowboarding, interviews with guests, and a warranted dose of input from those who said the environment and the culture was being harmed beyond repair.

"It's a nice change to be on a road trip with you that doesn't have anything to do with someone's gruesome death," Bip said as they sipped their coffee.

"Consider it my present to you," JC smirked. "I'm giving you a vacation from murder."

A woman arrived at the table and introduced herself as their server. She said that she was Ute and grew up just over the border in Utah.

"What would you be doing this winter if you didn't have this job?" JC asked.

"Probably working at the discount store in my hometown," she said. "This job is better."

She agreed to do an interview after they ate. They would do it outside, to sidestep layers of permission they would need from the hotel's ownership.

She was an attractive young woman. She glanced in Bip's direction more often than she was taught during her training in hotel hospitality.

"Do you snowboard?" Bip asked the server.

"I'm always impressed by your attention to detail," JC murmured to his companion.

"I do!" she said as her dark eyes brightened. "I love snowboarding."

"Maybe we can take some turns together," Bip said with a smile. "You can show me around."

"That would be fun," she said sincerely. "My name is Sunny."

Sunny left and turned her attention to other tables. She walked with grace, like she knew Bip was still watching her.

"What, I'm not good enough company on the ski slopes?" JC jabbed.

"You don't snowboard," Bip responded, laughing.

When it came time to sign the bill for breakfast, JC noted there was a heart next to Sunny's name. JC pushed the receipt with the heart toward Bip.

"Here, this must be for you."

7

The only soul who Roman Holiday told about the threatening letters and calls, besides Jonathan Oaks, was Benny. She swore him to secrecy.

The famous actor, Benjamin Maple, had moved to Lonesome County about a year prior to Roman's return.

He had never heard of the place. He had never been there. That was part of the attraction to him. No one in Hollywood had heard of it either.

Benny just wanted to disappear. He knew that his career in movies had flamed out. His fame and famous friends had been intoxicating for a while, but then turned toxic.

Barely twenty years old when he became a hit, he learned the ropes of film stardom. Then, he learned how tempting it was to take that rope and hang himself with it.

The business of being famous demanded being on display every waking moment. Hollywood stars—and he was one of them—were a target for paparazzi and critics. And stars had an orbit of phony friends.

However, he loved the women who accompanied celebrity. He would never forget the women. He began to ask himself why they sought him out. And when a few of his films flopped, he wondered where they had disappeared.

Benny left Hollywood and moved to Lonesome County when he was in his late thirties. He didn't leave a forwarding address. A financial advisor had told him that he had enough money coming in royalties that he didn't need to work anymore.

He bought a small ranch at the base of Diamond Peak. It cost him a fraction of what property like that would cost in Los Angeles. It was cheap to live in Lonesome County, though sometimes he wondered why he didn't have more money.

Benny and Roman were naturally drawn to each other by their respective celebrity. They had mutual friends on the West Coast, though they had not known each other there.

They had a brief romance in Lonesome County. It was the talk among the local populace during gatherings at the historic Browns Park School or Lodore Hall.

Roman called him Benny Ray. But Benny eventually found the romance exhausting. It reminded him of the life he escaped. That Hollywood dream had become his nightmare. He was still trying to wake up.

Roman and Benny Ray remained close friends after their breakup. In fact, he never stopped relying on her. He often called her on the phone. Sometimes they'd just talk about what was on television. Sometimes he asked her to help him choose something to wear when he was going out on a date. He asked for her help when he had errands to run or paperwork that he didn't understand.

She was always there for him. She was his true friend. She didn't complain. And she didn't voice an objection when he slept with other women. Roman and Benny Ray were best friends.

Roman and Olive lived on the ranch where Roman grew up. It was just south of Irish Canyon. There were horses and 250 acres of cedars, piñons and sagebrush. In the spring, red flowers grew from the claret cup cactus.

A pond was fed by snow that melted and ran down the mountains. The pond was lined by cattails and reeds. Currently, the cattails, reeds and saplings were bent by the weight of snow.

Her ranch was much bigger when Roman's grandparents owned it. That was a source of bitterness.

The small four-room house that Roman grew up in was gracefully rotting a short distance from the new home Roman had constructed on the property.

The modern home had big bedrooms, a contemporary kitchen and a three-car garage. The living room windows were aimed at the canyon and Dog Mountain. The sunset often turned the canyon's red stone into a blaze of color.

But there was a window in the laundry room that framed the old house she grew up in. Every time she looked out that window, she saw her childhood and her parents and a perfect life. Then, the phone would ring.

Jonathan Oaks' office was on the third floor of a building in the resort village. His desk sat in front of a large window looking out on the ski mountain and the shopping area of the village.

"Sometimes," he told JC and Bip as they were shown into the office, "I just swivel my desk chair and watch everything going on. I can do it for hours. I watch the skiers and the snowboarders and the uphill skiers hugging the tree line. I watch how long the lift lines are or if there is something blocking pedestrians from getting into stores and restaurants. I can get on the phone and resolve an issue within minutes."

Oaks spotted Bip searching for an electrical outlet to plug in a camera light. Oaks motioned the news photographer toward a socket next to a couch.

The managing partner of Minnie's Gap Ski Resort was not new to television interviews. He served four terms in Congress. He was on television a lot.

"First we saw that movie star at the restaurant, Benjamin Maple," Bip said to Oaks while setting up his tripod. "Then we saw another movie star, a woman. And then we saw you. It's like Hollywood here."

"Hollywood for ugly people," Oaks laughed. "That's what they call politics, you know. And her name is Roman Holiday. That's the actress you saw, I believe."

"Right," Bip said, remembering.

JC recalled Oaks from past interviews when he was a Colorado congressman. He was accessible and friendly. He radiated a persona that said he was the same guy he was while growing up in a middle-class home in Durango.

But he was not like everyone else, JC thought. He was determined to achieve whatever he set out to achieve. He rolled up his sleeves and worked his way through law school. He had made a lot of money since then. He was smart and powerful.

"We should have had one of these in Congress," Oaks said to JC as he gestured toward the big overseeing window. "It would have been helpful to look out on the country and see if the laws we were passing were doing any good."

Oaks, JC thought to himself, didn't display that conceit so often found in Congress. He was popular with voters. His popularity grew when he walked away from it all, even though re-election to another term was a certainty.

"It's time I got a real job," Oaks joked at the news conference announcing he would not run again. He said that he would not become a professional politician.

During the interview in Oaks' office at Minnie's Gap, JC was reminded of how smart Oaks was. How confident he seemed.

"Vacation homes are quickly selling," Oaks said, after being asked where the money would come from to support such a big resort. "I can honestly tell you that we are selling houses and slope-side condos at a pace beyond our wildest dreams.

"Maybe we got lucky," the former congressman told him. "People wanted to move out of the city during the Covid crisis, and that is just when we started to build. People put money down on condos and houses that didn't even exist."

"Is that where the real money is coming from?" JC asked. "Selling houses rather than selling lift tickets?"

"Right now, I'd have to say yes," Oaks informed him. "What troubles me is that we also want to be a profitable ski mountain."

"What's troubling about that?" JC asked.

"The *cost* of skiing is a growing problem," Oaks responded. "As a kid, I used to ski every chance I got. Too many young people today can't afford it—not if they're paying for college and a car and an apartment.

"When I'm in Durango, I ask young people if they ski. Too many of them say, 'I can't. It's too expensive.' And that makes me ask myself, where are our future skiers and snowboarders going to come from?

"Colorado set a record for skier visits last year, so a lot of people don't share my concerns. But the skiers who ski the most are sixty-five years old and older. Think fifteen years down the line. Who is going to be skiing then, if younger people don't start skiing?"

"The new emphasis to bring people of color to ski areas is a great turn of events," JC said. "And that will help pay the bills."

"Yes," Oaks agreed. "We're working hard to become diverse, reaching out to people of color who will enjoy this sport. That should help. But those young people face the same problem. The ski industry has to figure out a solution or we're going to price ourselves out of business."

"I could talk about skiing all day. But let me move to another subject," JC said. "You grew up in Durango. After you left Congress, you moved back to Durango. That doesn't always happen. Members of Congress often come to consider Washington their home, rather than the district they came from."

"I never left Durango," Oaks told him. "I kept my home there, my three kids went all the way through school there, and my wife and I still live there. Brenda did a great job raising those kids while I was in Washington. I'm sorry that

I was away so much, but I had a job to do. That's one reason I left Congress, to return home to my family."

"And yet, you're here," JC noted, "working five hours away from home."

"Closer to a seven-hour drive," Oaks winced. "What can I say? This project is providing thousands of jobs on the Western Slope. It will change lives. I won't have to do this forever."

"You were born in Durango?" JC asked.

"I was. Do you know why my father moved to Colorado?" Oaks asked rhetorically. "He read the book *Atlas Shrugged*. Have you read that?"

"Ayn Rand," JC responded. "All about hard work being rewarded. Earning success versus success being given away like a constitutional right. Colorado was like an uncharted Utopia, in that book."

"Exactly," Oaks agreed. "And people here *want* to work hard and *will* work hard, but they need somewhere to work. That's what we're providing here, a chance to work hard."

That ended the interview. Bip began to wrap up his light, cords, tripod and camera. The intercom on Oaks' desk buzzed.

"Frank Green is here," the receptionist reported. "He's come to fix your computer."

She was told to send him in. JC heard a click on the door, meaning it had an automatic lock. Probably, the journalist thought, a mind-set from security measures Oaks enjoyed in Congress.

"Hi Jon," the tall man said. JC noticed the air of familiarity coming from the man.

"JC, Bip, this is Frank Green," Oaks announced. "Frank, these gentlemen are television journalists from Denver. They're doing a story about the ski resort."

"News guys, huh?" Frank said. "Are you going to interview Doc Anderson? He was nearly killed in an avalanche a few weeks ago. He's a lucky man."

JC and Bip looked at each other. They were aware of the avalanche. It was in the news.

"Frank grew up here in Browns Park," Oaks revealed.

"That was a long time ago," Frank responded seriously. He looked at JC and Bip to explain. "I moved away when I was still a kid. I moved back here recently."

"Frank walks on water around here," Oaks said. "He owns the only computer store. That saves us from having to drive two hours to a big-box store. And I don't know who would fix them if Frank wasn't around."

"Jon, you could probably find a *YouTube* video in five minutes that would tell you how to fix this. And it's free, instead of what you pay me for a 'house call,'" Frank laughed.

"Frank, you can't teach an old dog new tricks," Oaks said, smiling. Frank gently shooed the managing partner from behind his own desk and the serviceman seated himself in front of the computer.

"Don't let Frank make you think I'm the only Neanderthal in Dog Mountain," Oaks happily told JC and Bip. "House calls keep him very busy."

"You're all going to pay for my purchase of a private island in the Caribbean," Frank jested, never taking his eyes off the computer. He was hitting the keys and responding to the software when prompted. "I'm going to move there and never come back. So, all of you had better figure out how to find *YouTube* so you can fix your own computer."

Frank Green had blond hair that was thin and straight. It always moved in the direction of gravity. He had a growing paunch but engaging smile and eyes that seemed to notice a lot.

Green liked to tell people that the nearby Green River was named after him. He was joking.

He'd tell people that just about anything with the name green was named after him. Green apples, green crayons, golf greens.

"My ancestors discovered the bean," he'd joke. "That's why they're called green beans."

His mastery of computers and all things related to computers was unquestioned.

"People love their computers in Lonesome County," Frank told JC and Bip. "This county was not named by mistake." Frank never looked away from the data provided on the screen, trying to solve the riddle.

"It can be lonesome out here. But folks don't feel so alone, having their computer," Frank continued telling his audience. "They have their social media and they can have a live video chat with family members who live on the East Coast—or in France, for that matter."

"So, you're a popular guy," JC said. "You give them all that." Frank looked up for a moment.

"You make me sound like Jesus," he said as he looked back at the screen. "Funny, since *your* initials are JC."

Bip gave JC a look saying that their camera gear was packed up. JC rose and informed the men they would be leaving.

"Thank you, gentlemen," Oaks said as he walked them to the door. "You know, there's a cocktail party tonight that you might enjoy. You might meet someone you'd like to interview. Please come. My receptionist will give you directions."

"Are you going to have any time to go sightseeing?" Frank asked, looking up but not rising from behind the computer. "This is beautiful country. Nothing quite like it. Right, Jon?"

"That's true," said Oaks. He turned to JC and Bip. "If you grew up watching Westerns, you can't do any better. There's a boulder on Diamond Peak. Some people call it Signature Rock. The year 1838 is etched in it, and some fading initials or letters.

"Imagine, you can put your hand on the same spot where Butch Cassidy might have put his hand. Have you been there, Frank?"

"I probably rode my horse by it when I was a kid," Frank said. "But I don't remember it."

"That's really cool," Bip said.

"A lot of locals know about it," Oaks told them. "It's easy to find. From the road out of town, you can see the upper half of a tall dead pine protruding over a hill. Not a needle on it, just dead branches. It's been bleached white by the sun. The rock is right there."

That night, in a darkened room, Roman's tormentor slouched over a table with a single lamp. Gloves covered his hands. On an envelope, he applied a self-adhesive sticker with the typed address of her Dog Mountain ranch. He looked over a single page that would be folded and stuffed in the envelope.

"I have some friends who would like to meet Olive," it said. "And they have friends, and they have friends."

He slipped the message into the envelope and before sealing it, dropped in five condoms.

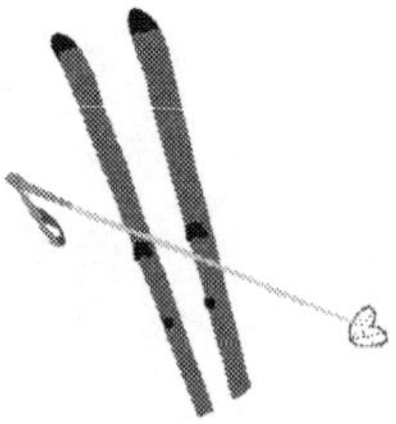

8

"The mud, the blood and the beer," JC responded.

He had just been asked why he preferred being a reporter on television rather than being an anchor.

"This is where the action is," he told three people he had just been introduced to. "It's like being a football *player* instead of being the head coach. Both are fun, and I remember an interview with a very successful football coach who used to be a player. But he was a much better coach.

"He said he dreamed about football every night. I asked him, 'In your dreams, are you a coach or a player?' He smiled and said, 'Definitely, a player.'"

At the conclusion of their second day of reporting from Minnie's Gap, Bip and JC had cleaned up and proceeded to the party that Oaks invited them to.

JC phoned Robin, with Bip adding comic asides to the conversation while he drove the 4x4 to their destination.

Their four-wheel-drive vehicle was a news car owned by their TV station. It was unmarked. The days of using news cars as billboards, with their TV channel and other graphics splashed on the side, were fading.

It was because news cars had become targets of smash-and-grab robberies. The thieves knew that expensive cameras and electronics could be found inside news cars. The bright graphics advertising a TV station had become a bullseye on the vehicles.

JC and Bip arrived at a large home with enormous two-story windows overlooking the ski runs of Minnie's Gap.

Walking in the front door, they heard the sounds of a party. Dozens of people were talking at once. There was laughter and the chime of cocktail glasses striking one another when someone called for a toast.

The cocktail party was attended by well-dressed people wearing lots of jewelry. Some wore ski sweaters that were much too expensive to actually ski in. Some wore expensive Western wear, like boots made from a skin they would never expose to snow. One man wore a battered cowboy hat and his arm in a sling.

The crowd was clustered in the living room below the big windows. The guests held drinks and conducted conversations with each other in groups of three or four.

All of them seemed to belong to a set of people that JC imagined were in Jon Oaks' circle of acquaintances.

The men and women were all well cared for. If they needed cosmetic surgery, they'd seen to it.

If the women had a figure they labored to get or paid dearly for, they showed it off with plunging necklines or low-cut backs.

"Have you been skiing yet?" a woman asked JC. He guessed her age to be in her fifties. She wore a satin sleeveless turtleneck blouse, exposing arms toned at the gym.

"Not enough," he answered. "Too much work and not enough play."

"I understand that you race," the woman's husband said to JC.

"When time allows," he responded with a smile. "And you?"

"I do," the man said. "Not very well, but I enjoy it. You should do some gate training with us. If you see us set up on the race hill, come over and hop in line."

"I'd enjoy that," JC told him. "Goodness knows I could use some training. My schedule doesn't allow me to do anything on a regular basis."

"We've all gotten so busy," the woman agreed. "I'd love to go skiing tomorrow, but my group scheduled a pickleball court at eleven."

"Yes," the man added, smiling at his wife. "Everything has now taken a backseat to pickleball."

It was dark out. But through the wall of windows, JC saw the headlights of grooming machines prowling the slopes, preparing for the next day of skiing.

"They're PistenBullys," said Frank Green as he approached JC and the couple. "They're German. They're one of the best snow groomers you can buy. But prepare to pay a half-million dollars if you want a good one."

"I've always been kind of fascinated by the grooming machines," JC admitted.

"They promise eighty-mile-per-hour corduroy," Green told him. "You know, they have video games that put you behind the wheel of one of those things."

"I'm sorry," the woman interrupted with an apologetic expression on her face. She was looking at JC but put her hand on Green's arm. "May we steal Frank? We're having trouble with our computer at home."

The woman and her husband steered Green away and JC found himself alone again.

The expansive, and no doubt expensive, home was on the edge of the ski resort village, located high up Dog Mountain. A ski run passed within feet of the patio downstairs. In the morning, the homeowners could take a last sip of coffee in their own kitchen and be on their skis before they swallowed.

"What may I get you, sir?" a roving waiter asked. He was dressed in a white vest and black pants. His presentation was formal.

"What do you have?" JC asked with a smile.

"You have no idea," the waiter smiled back. "If you've ever heard of it, it is probably here in the liquor pantry."

"Glenfarclas?" JC asked. "The Scottish whisky?"

"Ten or twenty-one?" the waiter asked, referring to the age of the whisky he had to choose from.

"You weren't kidding," JC said with a small laugh.

"No sir," the waiter smiled. "May I get you the twenty-one?"

"You'll be my friend forever, if you do," JC told him.

And as if this waiter was put on earth only to serve JC, he was back with a twenty-one-year-old Glenfarclas within a couple of minutes.

"Anything else, sir?" the waiter asked.

"Just one question," JC asked.

"Certainly, sir."

"May I live here for all of time?"

"You'll have to take that up with the hosts, sir," the waiter told him with a grin. "I'll be rooting for you."

With the waiter's departure, JC turned to admire the view out the windows. He watched the groomer work high on the mountain.

JC thought groomers painted a romantic picture, like a fishing boat on the bay at sunrise. Those groomers represented the potential each morning brought with it. Anything wonderful was possible with a new morning.

As he turned, he found himself facing a small group of people he had never met. They said hello. One of them was a housing developer named Gerhard Snyder. He said that most of his business was in Denver, but he built the employee housing for the ski resort.

Snyder introduced JC to a woman in the group who looked familiar. She was the lesser movie star of Lonesome County, Roman Holiday.

She wore a low-cut blouse. Her black hair rested on her bare shoulders. Her browned skin was perfect. As they conversed, her eyes were trained on him as though he mattered, even though they had barely met.

The developer and the rest of the cluster dispersed. It was just JC and Roman Holiday facing each other. But JC noticed that the eyes of men and women alike followed Roman around the large living room.

"Do you realize that everyone watches you?" he asked.

"Oh, that. I stopped noticing that when I lived in La-La Land," Roman said, rolling her eyes. "They're all very nice to me."

"I was hoping you two would meet," interrupted a gregarious voice. It was Jon Oaks. "JC, I'm glad you could make it. You've met Roman?"

"We were just getting acquainted," JC told him.

"Roman is doing good work, rescuing horses who would otherwise be on their way to extermination," the former congressman said.

"Slaughter, Jon," Roman said to Oaks with a ribbing smile. "That's the term we use." Then, she turned her eyes back to JC. "I'm starting a horse-rescue nonprofit."

"JC, you ought to visit her horse ranch," Oaks suggested. "It might be a good story."

"It might," JC agreed. He turned to Roman. "We're not here for very long. I imagine you're in a constant state of fundraising. Are you near here?"

"Just down the road," Roman said with a smile. "On the other end of Irish Canyon. Why don't you come out tomorrow?"

"Great," JC said. "I'll bring my photographer." It caused JC to wonder where his photographer had gotten off to.

"We'll see you tomorrow," JC said to the actress. "Excuse me."

JC scanned the faces of the crowd. He did not see Bip. He toured the large room and climbed a staircase to look at the party from a balcony. He did not see Bip, but the balcony provided a view of the fantastic room.

When the doors to the kitchen opened, and a server carried a tray out of the room, it disclosed a stainless-steel castle of culinary undertakings. It looked enormous and restaurant-quality.

He also saw a figure who did not fit in with the rest. JC climbed down the stairs and gently pushed the door into the kitchen. He saw Bip talking with the same young woman who had served them breakfast.

"Hey JC!" Bip greeted him. "Look who I found!"

"Hi, Sunny," JC said. Bip explained that Sunny was working for the party's caterer. She was dressed in the same white vest and black pants as the waiter who brought JC's whisky.

"We might go out and do something tonight, when her shift is done," Bip told him. "After we go back to the hotel, can I borrow the car and come get Sunny?"

"Yes," JC said. "I'm used to it," he told Sunny. "My boy is growing up. Soon, I may have to get him his own car," JC joked and left the kitchen.

"Having a good time?" a man asked JC. He turned out to be the party's host. He was a retired banker from Connecticut.

"Let me introduce you to another one of our colorful characters in Lonesome County. He's a professor at our community college here. Biochemistry. We're lucky to have him. And he's from Norway!"

The two men eyed each other suspiciously. JC noted the professor's long hair, neatly combed. The party host continued to provide some sort of commentary, but JC wasn't listening anymore.

"May I present Dr. Ullr Skadi?" the party host said. "Dr. Skadi, this is JC Snow. He's a television reporter from Denver."

"Mr. Skadi, is it?" JC asked with skepticism.

"Professor Skadi," the man said, emphasizing the *Professor*. "And it's Ullr, like cooler," emphasizing the *cooler*.

"Is that Portuguese, you said?" JC asked.

"No, Norwegian," the professor responded tersely. "I'm from Henningsvær."

"That city has a lot of Portuguese influence, then?" JC pursued.

"None that I'm aware of," Professor Skadi said to his inquisitor. "Perhaps you're thinking of Lisbon."

The party host seemed confused by the conversation. He excused himself, leaving the professor and journalist alone.

"Spook?" JC asked in a low voice.

"I never liked that nickname," the professor whispered as he looked to see if anyone was listening to their conversation. "Why did you give me that nickname?"

"Because you were one of the spookiest men I'd ever met," JC told him. "Of course, that was before you began combing your hair."

"Yes, well, people grow," Professor Ullr Skadi responded. "Nothing stays the same."

"Am I to guess that things that don't stay the same include your social security number and your fingerprints?" JC asked. "And why aren't you using your real name? What's wrong with Steven Hemingway? It makes you sound smart, like a novelist."

"What makes you think Hemingway is my real name?" Skadi inquired. "And you may have heard there are a few undesirables around the country inquiring about Hemingway's whereabouts."

"Yep, I did notice that," JC said with a smirk.

JC met Steven Hemingway four years ago in Montana. Spook was a member of a militia group living in the woods. Aside from Hemingway, the membership was mostly dim-witted. But Spook enjoyed playing with their toys, specifically guns and explosives.

The leader of the militia gave Hemingway a free pass to detonate the explosives within the compound. No one got hurt. In return, Hemingway gave the group credibility when deep-pocketed donors came by with their extremist views and their checkbooks.

JC found Hemingway to be brilliant. A curious kaleidoscope of temperament, but brilliant.

Then, in one capstone evening in Montana, Hemingway detonated the militia's entire stockpile of munitions and disappeared into the night. Most of the compound burned. Again, no one was hurt.

Another guest at the cocktail party joined the discussion, greeting Professor Skadi. JC surmised that he was a fellow faculty member at the community college in Dog Mountain. The secret and sensible discussion between JC and Hemingway would have to pause, so JC was happy to return to a non-sensible one.

"You're from Norway, huh?" JC asked Skadi.

"That is correct," Skadi/Hemingway winced, as his fellow faculty member listened in.

"You must drive a Fjord," JC said, laughing a little. He was proud of that one.

"Funny," Skadi replied without smiling. For the second time, the extra member of their conversation departed, confused.

"My, you're a crankypants," JC said. "It must be all those winter days in Norway without sunlight."

"I'm not oblivious to your mocking tone," Skadi said. Again, he was scanning the room to see if anyone was taking note of their conversation.

"Why did you change your name?" JC repeated. "There's no warrant for you in Montana. I don't think they even know you existed. You're pretty good at that, by the way."

"That was in Montana," Skadi/Hemingway said. "Elsewhere, there is a shortage of Steven Hemingway fan clubs."

"So, you teach college kids how to blow stuff up?" JC asked with a grin.

"There's not as much demand at community colleges for that curriculum, as you would imagine," Skadi told him.

"Hmm," JC murmured. "No class called Arson 301?"

"Not on the syllabus," Skadi responded.

JC looked at Hemingway. He was clearly trying to improve his appearance. He still looked fit. But his unruly blond hair was now neatly brushed and had grown long. He wore a button-down shirt, a tie and a sport coat. JC had only seen him wearing camouflage before this.

Another stranger attending the party joined their conversation.

"You're better-looking than I remember," JC said to the professor. "Have you had work done?"

"You're an idiot," Skadi said.

"Nose job?" JC prodded.

For the third time, the additional member of their circle departed, uncomfortable with the topic of conversation. JC started laughing.

"You're still an idiot," Skadi repeated. "You're starting to annoy me."

"Has it really taken this long?" JC chuckled.

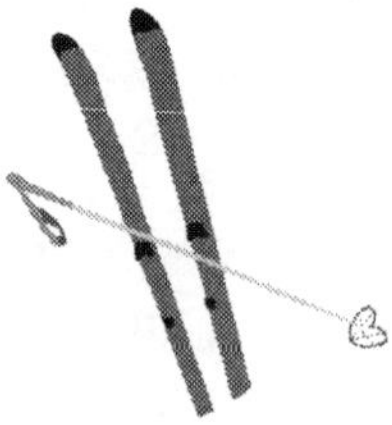

9

"This one is named Sneak, because he can sneak anything by you. He'll sneak an extra apple out of the basket. He'll even sneak a carrot out of my sweater, and I won't feel him picking my pocket!"

Roman Holiday, the beautiful forty-two-year-old former actress laughed when she spoke about her horses. Her voice was like a warm blanket. It was something you wanted to wrap yourself in. JC thought he heard, almost but not quite, a Southern accent.

He vaguely remembered her from a small role she had on television, in a show starring someone else. But she was stunning to look at. Her red-and-black-checked work shirt and blue jeans showed off her figure. She may have quit Hollywood, but she brought home what she learned.

She lived at the end of a long driveway of packed dirt and gravel, east of route 10N. She could hear it when a vehicle approached her house, because it would rumble over the cattle guard.

"This is Buggy," she said. "I call him that because he attracts so many flies. It's alright now because it's a winter morning. But you should see him in the summer!"

Steam poured from the nostrils of the horses as their warmth hit the cold air. There was a bit of frost on their manes. Bip was capturing all of this on his camera.

"There used to be more wild horses in the park. There are still some, but there used to be more," she said as she looked at her four-legged friends. "They love the snow," she giggled as a horse trotted over to her, seeking attention.

"They miss Missy, though," she said. "That was Olive's dog. Olive is my eleven-year-old. Missy was hit by a car recently. We're all terribly sad, even the horses. Missy was friends with the horses. If Olive was sleeping over at a friend's house, Missy would sleep in the stables with the horses. She wanted to."

JC and Roman exited one of three corrals attached to a new barn behind Roman's house. There was more land sectioned off by fences, for more horses. There were a few other outbuildings in the distance.

They walked along the dirt yard. There were patches of snow and tracks dug by pickup trucks and other farm vehicles. Roman bent over and picked up a rock. It was about the size of an orange.

"I don't know where they keep coming from." She smiled and looked at the stone as she tossed it in her hand.

"My father told me they rolled down from those cliffs." She pointed at some cliffs a mile or two away. "He said it probably took a thousand years for them to get from there to here."

There was a bucket at the foot of a post by another corral. There were other rocks already in the bucket. She tossed her new rock in with the rest.

"My grandfather picked up enough rocks and built that well," she said, pointing at a well with walls made of stones.

Roman was quite photogenic. And she instinctively demonstrated all the tricks as she caressed her horses. She knew to drop her arm when it might block her face from the camera. She knew not to show the back of her head to the lens.

"Here's Mort!" She laughed as the former carriage horse inside the next corral approached her. "I stole that name from my grandfather. He named a horse Mort because the animal reminded him of an ugly neighbor."

JC laughed and stroked the horse on the neck.

"And here comes Maude! I stole that name from my grandfather too. He told me that Maude was Mort's ugly wife!"

"These are rescued horses?" JC asked.

"Yes," Roman said, turning her attention to the reporter while still stroking Mort's neck. "I have ten rescued horses right now. But I have room for about one hundred, so I'll be adding more."

"You told me that Mort was a carriage horse," JC said. "What about the others?"

"Yes, Mort was a carriage horse in Philadelphia," she said. "He developed problems with his feet, so he couldn't work anymore. He was sent to slaughter, but we intercepted him. We have some former racehorses, too.

"Maude was an attraction for a traveling amusement company when she was a pony. But full-grown horses cost more to feed, and they wanted another pony. Maude was sold and on her way to the slaughterhouse when we got her. Canada and Europe eat horse meat, you know."

"So, will you adopt these horses out to good homes?" JC asked.

"Oh no, they'll live out their lives here," Roman replied. "Many of them have injuries that make them no use to anyone. And their medicine can get expensive."

She bent over and picked up another rock. Then she walked JC into the barn, with Bip and his camera trailing. There were two more horses in barn stalls.

She deposited the rock into a bucket by the tack room.

"Is this your cash crop?" JC asked.

"Rocks?" Roman laughed. "I wish I could find someone to sell them to."

Maude walked through a door from her outside corral and into her stall in the barn. Roman approached and stroked the horse's forehead.

"Whether they've been injured or they're perfectly healthy horses like Maude, they feel the same sense of betrayal. They were all loved and useful, and then they were abandoned. They feel that emotionally, like humans do.

"When they arrive here, they don't trust me. Many have been beaten or starved. Their hearts have been broken. I have to win their trust back, and that takes a long time. No, this is their home now, forever."

"That must get expensive," JC remarked. Roman gave a little laugh and rolled her eyes.

"It does," she agreed. "And as I add horses, because I have the room, it will get more expensive. I've established a nonprofit to raise money to feed them and pay for their medicine. My horse rescue group is called Hollywood for Horses."

"Your pole gate at the end of the drive has an 'H' lying on its side and an upright 'W,'" JC observed. "That stands for Hollywood?"

"Pretty much," she told him. "The ranch actually began as the Lazy HW. The H is lying on its side because in the language of cattle brands, that means it's lazy. The name goes back to my grandfather. The H stood for Holiday and the W stood for Wait. That was my grandmother's maiden name. But it stands for 'Hollywood' now!"

"Did you say this ranch has been in your family?" JC asked.

"I grew up here!" she said with enthusiasm. "The ranch was two thousand acres at its peak. That Lazy HW was their brand. Of course, we don't brand any of our horses anymore."

"So, who owns the rest of the land now?" the reporter inquired.

"That is a sore spot in our family," Roman told him, though her parents and a brother were all dead. "That's a sore spot for every multi-generational family around here."

Roman walked out of the barn with JC to show him more of her property.

"The federal government took a lot of my parents' land. They took the land of a lot of ranchers. The ranchers were paid, but they didn't have much choice. The government wanted the land for a wildlife sanctuary, a public recreation area and Lord knows what else. They flooded a bunch of land to make a huge reservoir west of here. All the ranchers could do is watch."

"You love this land, don't you?" JC prompted her. Bip had been rolling his camera the whole time. He had fitted Roman with a wireless lapel microphone. She was careful not to brush it with her arm or hand. She knew the tricks.

"This land is a part of me," she said with sincerity. "And having this horse rescue, this is what this land was made for. We're on the edge of Browns Park. We're standing on a footprint of history. My great grandfather was an outlaw and great horseman, Isom Dart. He was a former slave.

"But he didn't behave like an outlaw when he was in Browns Park," she said. "He worked hard just like everyone else."

"What was your life like, growing up as a child here?" JC asked.

"Well, you have to understand. There are three people per each square mile in Lonesome County. So, life revolves around family and ranch," she said.

"I grew up having chores to do every day. I grew up respecting hard work. But it also allowed me to grow up in the greatest playground in America. We'd play every day. My brother was still alive then and we had friends. We'd ride our horses and explore old cabins and Indian campgrounds.

"And everyone seemed to have a story to tell about their grandparents or great grandparents. Some delivered the mail on horseback. Some were sheriffs and some were outlaws. We'd play outlaws and sheriffs all day. It was a wonderful childhood."

"Was there prejudice?" JC asked.

"Because I'm Black?" Roman asked, almost laughing. "No. I don't think they even noticed. We've all been here forever. We're way past that. If an outsider came in, I don't know what would happen. But I'm just Roman to everyone around here."

JC looked out beyond the corrals. There was room for plenty more horses on Roman's land. There was sagebrush, three and four feet high, pushing through the snow. There were poplar and apricot trees, greasewood and juniper pines.

"I'm sorry that you didn't meet Olive," Roman said, smiling. "She's in school right now."

"You seem so at home here," JC told her. "How did you get into acting?"

"Oh, sometimes you take for granted the things that you hold dearest," she said as she scanned the landscape. "I was doomed the moment my parents named me after a motion picture. Los Angeles seemed so glamorous to a girl living in a semi-desert."

"You started with school plays?" he asked. She laughed.

"My brother and I used to put on performances for our mother and father and aunts and uncles in our living room. Then I did some television commercials in Rock Springs," she said. Her mind was wandering back to days when she seemed destined for fame. "Then I was offered a job doing infomercials for a cosmetics outfit. They loved my skin.

"That led to moving to Los Angeles and that led to a TV show and that led to a couple of movies and that led to a broken heart," she said. And suddenly she looked like she was reliving the pain. Her eyes lowered and her smiling face looked to be on the verge of tears.

"Sorry," she said quietly. She looked up and glanced at Bip. "I have a girl you should meet."

"I'm sort of seeing someone," Bip said. JC figured that Bip was thinking of Sunny, since there was no regular female companion back in Denver.

"Well then," Roman said, looking at JC, "how about you? She's pretty."

"I'm taken," JC said with a smile. "And she is much too good for me."

"That's a nice thing to say," Roman said with a smile. "She's a lucky woman. Do you cook for her? Women like men who cook."

JC heard Bip snort.

"I'm afraid that I don't cook," JC informed her. "Mankind is better off, believe me."

Bip was wrapping up his gear. The interview was over. JC told Roman that they'd include her story in that night's newscast. He asked for specifics about her Hollywood career and she supplied him with names of shows and movies she was in.

"You should interview Benny Ray," she said. "He's much more famous than I am."

"Benny Ray?"

"Sorry, you probably know him as Benjamin Maple. I call him Benny Ray," she said. "His middle name is Raymond."

"I'd like to interview him," JC told her. "Do you have his phone number?" He handed her his reporter's notebook and a pen. She scribbled it on a clean page.

"I'll tell him that you're going to call," she said. "I've got to take him his laundry this afternoon."

"You have his laundry?" JC asked.

"I do his laundry sometimes. If I didn't, he'd wear the same pair of underwear for three days in a row." She rolled her eyes but smiled at the same time. "Boys will be boys."

"Are you and Benny a couple?"

"It's a long story," she said and looked at the ground. "I guess we're in what you would call 'a situationship.'"

She walked JC and Bip to their car. "Give me a ride to the mailbox?" The mailbox was at the end of the long driveway. She said that she would walk back to her house.

In the car, JC asked her about the ruins of a log cabin that he had noticed on her property, closer to the road than the home she grew up in.

"That was the home of my other great grandparents, on my mom's side," Roman told them.

The log cabin had no roof and none of the walls were the same height. The top logs all had a crust of old snow on them.

Over the years, the missing logs had been repurposed, Roman told them. There was no glass in the remaining windows, but an apple tree and an apricot tree remained in the front.

"Oh, my grandmother loved to plant apricot trees," Roman said. "There are a lot of them on the property.

Bip drove over the cattle guard and stopped at the mailbox by the post gate to let Roman out of their car. JC thanked her again for allowing them to visit. She thanked them for getting the word out about her horse rescue.

He watched Roman in his side-view mirror as Bip drove away. She slipped a letter out of the mailbox and opened it. And just before disappearing over a hill, JC watched as Roman dropped her head into her hand and let the envelope and its contents fall to the ground.

10

"People mistake being negative with being smart," JC said.

"I know," his assignment editor responded. "And they usually prove just the opposite."

The voice on the phone belonged to the assignment editor at JC's television newsroom. His name was Rocky Bauman.

"So, you received an email complaining?" JC asked.

"Yeah. The sender insisted that we bring you back to Denver. I'm not really sure why, though. They usually complain about how much violence there is on the news," Rocky said. "This time, they seem to be complaining that there isn't *enough* violence."

"It's kind of nice to report on a story that doesn't have to bleed to lead," JC said.

"The complaint was sent from a community computer at the public library in Dog Mountain," Rocky said. "Anyone can use it. You must be rattling somebody's cage. Any idea who?"

"We've been playing nice," JC asked. "I can't think of anyone I've offended."

"Then I'm already sorry I mentioned it," Bauman said, changing the topic. "But that brings me to another topic. Could you be more careful when you type the scripts that you send us?"

"Rocky," JC replied. "They make these phones too small. The keyboard is designed for the fingers of a ten-year-old."

JC was not a technophobe. But his adult-sized fingers on a child-sized keyboard was the stuff of autocorrect legend. "Crops" was substituted for "corpse" and "mango" for "mangled."

His thumb was all but incapable of making a clean strike on the caps key. So words like "Investigation" became "Zunvestigation." "Police" became "Zpoluce." He also couldn't seem to make a clean strike of the "i."

"I need a producer, Rocky," JC said. "She used to do a splendid job of sending my perfect scripts."

"There are needs and there are wants, JC. I know what you *want*," Rocky said. "And you can't have her. Robin is a reporter now, and a damn good one."

"You'll get no argument from me about that," JC surrendered.

The call from Rocky had come immediately after their live shot. Bip had framed JC in front of a large ice rink at the Minnie's Gap Ski Resort. A number of families were enjoying an evening of figure skating.

Bip informed JC that he had plans for the evening, if their work was done. The plans involved Sunny, their breakfast waitress.

So, JC had the evening to himself. He pulled out his phone and slowly walked down a cobblestone path lined with stores and restaurants. He called Robin. They related events of their respective day. Robin said that she remembered the actress, Roman Holiday, on a sitcom she used to watch.

"Hey, have you happened across a guy named Gerhard Snyder?" she asked.

"That name sounds familiar," JC told her. "Can you tell me anything more?"

"He built the housing for the employees at the ski resort," she informed him.

"That's right. I met him last night," JC remembered. "Only briefly. But I met him. Why?"

"That's the guy who is trying to build that shopping center on the wetlands outside Denver," she said. "He won't return my calls, so I'm going to come there and corner him. Our fearless leader gave me his blessings. I'll need to borrow Bip for a few hours, okay?"

"Of course," JC said. He was quietly smiling at the news that she'd be joining him.

"I'll get there Friday," she said. "In time for you to buy me dinner."

"That's a long drive," JC said.

"I know. So, I'll fly to Rock Springs and get a ride to the ski resort. Don't give up your hotel room. You'll be done with your assignment, I'll get my work done and we can enjoy the weekend there. We'll drive back to Denver together on Sunday. Okay?"

Rocky was half right, JC thought. It wasn't really a producer that JC wanted there. He wanted Robin.

Hanging up the phone, JC wandered the cobblestone paths of the resort village where cars weren't allowed. The paths were heated from beneath the stones so the snow wouldn't pile up.

JC listened to the nylon legs of ski pants rub together as skiers walked on the path beside him. Vacationers looked both exhausted and energized. They were enjoying their adventure.

He stopped to look at a poster stapled to a thick upright log. The log was covered in posters. This one advertised a winter carnival being held in the town of Dog Mountain that weekend.

It was called *IcEscape.* It was said to celebrate a mountain man's escape from pursuing Arapaho warriors, over a century ago. He did so by climbing over slabs of broken ice in the river. The carnival included a race over an obstacle course of ice sculptures and a playground sprayed with water until it froze.

Almost back to his hotel, JC entered a bar next door. It was called *Snapping Annie's.* It was named for the first non-Indigenous woman in Browns Park. She arrived there in the 1850s.

The bar's interior had walls of simple wooden planks painted a light green, though it was hard to tell with the low lights. There were old photographs on the wall. They were of Browns Park and its inhabitants.

He climbed onto a stool. The bar was also made of simple wooden planks painted brown. Behind it, above the bottles of alcohol, there were televisions showing taped ski races or death-defying stunts being performed on skis and snowboards.

There were also tee shirts for sale, boasting the bar's logo. It included an image of a rough-looking woman with a menacing grin. A pair of crossed skis was behind her.

"How did you enjoy hobnobbing with the upper crust of Minnie's Gap?" a voice asked from JC's right. He looked in that direction and saw Frank Green, the computer store owner.

"Hi Frank," JC said, extending a hand to shake. Frank took it with a smile.

"Have you met Benny?" Frank asked, nodding to his companion on the other side of him. It was Benjamin Maple, the former movie star and most famous man in Lonesome County.

"We have not had the pleasure," JC said as he leaned over to shake the man's hand. "My photographer and I saw you the other night at dinner. At the Peg Leg?"

"Oh yeah," the man said with a friendly look. "I love their barbeque. It's one of my many addictions."

Benny Maple had shoulder-length dark hair. He had the face of a child, with happy blue eyes. He was slightly exotic-looking.

"My mom was from Thailand," he explained. "Dad was a white boy from Los Angeles. They were both beautiful to look at. I don't know what happened to *me*. Maybe good looks skip a generation." He laughed at this. His man-child's face lit up.

"Do you have any craft beer from Dog Mountain?" JC asked the bartender who stood before him.

"Not yet," the bartender replied. "One of my friends is going to open a brewery here soon. The tanks are up. They're fooling around with their recipes. We're hoping one will be named after Snapping Annie."

"Do you like whiskey?" Benny asked. "Try what we're drinking. It's called 10th Mountain Whiskey."

"It's distilled in Vail," Frank added. "The name is a tribute to the Army's 10th Mountain Division. As you know, they trained around the site of what became Vail, during World War Two."

"I'll have what they're having," JC told the bartender.

"I was just out at Benny's house fixing his computer," Frank said. "He gets so many emails from women with no clothes on. And he opens every attachment, expecting to find more! His computer is a vacation resort for malware."

"I'm sure every one of those young ladies goes to church on Sunday and does volunteer work on Wednesdays," Benny laughed as he slapped Frank on the shoulder. "And none of them look like they're suffering from any virus."

"What brought you to Lonesome County, Benny?" JC asked.

"It's not what brought me to Lonesome County," he said with a grin. "It's what chased me out of Hollywood."

"Well, what chased you out of Hollywood?" JC persisted.

"I forgot what was real, there," Benny said. He was still smiling. "Real people arrive there at the train station, but if you meet them five years later, something's happened. It happened to me too."

"Really?" Frank said. "You always seemed like you were just being yourself in your movies."

"I don't know if I ever changed," Benny explained. "But it required more and more drugs to be myself." He started laughing and looked at JC. "I was a junkie. I have no one to blame but myself for what happened to my career."

"Not as glamorous as it looks?" JC asked.

"No, the problem is that it's *more* glamorous than it looks!" Benny shook his head, as if he was still trying to make sense of it. "I could name ten of the most beautiful women in motion pictures. I slept with every one of them. I thought, one by one, that I was in love with them all. But it didn't make sense. We weren't in love. We didn't even know each other. We were just ready and able!"

"That's a problem I'd like to have," Frank laughed. "Where do I sign up?"

"The problem," Benny tried to explain. "The problem is that it isn't real. And once you sign up, it's like you can't bring yourself to resign. It's addictive behavior. I started taking drugs because I didn't think I was worthy of these women, or even of friendships with really impressive men.

"Then it started affecting my work. I was showing up late to the set or not showing up at all. They gave me a lot of chances because I always apologized. I don't think I yelled or cursed at anyone during the entire time I was making movies. I was just a nice guy having a good time who was insecure and wasn't reliable and wasn't talented enough to get away with it."

"Wow," JC said. "I don't think I've ever heard that complete a mea culpa."

"Well," Benny said, "I let a lot of people down, not just myself."

"So, now you're sober?" JC asked.

"Oh, hell no," Benny laughed and slapped the bar.

"Benny, you're the most functional drug addict that I know," Frank said as he pulled himself up from the barstool.

"That you know of," Benny responded.

"I've got to go to the store," Frank said. "I want to see if my employees left me any cash."

That left JC alone with Benny Maple, the ex-movie star.

"Do you think of making a comeback?" JC asked.

"Nah," Benny said. "Well, Roman makes me look at scripts sometimes. And I know she reaches out to movie producers to try and get me a part. But those producers know I haven't changed. Hell, if they asked me if I changed, I'd say 'no.' My momma didn't raise a liar." He laughed at that.

"Are you and Roman a thing?" JC asked.

"Why," Benny said. "Are you interested? She's a great woman, man. You should go for it. Don't hurt her, though, or you'll have me to answer to." He was pointing at JC, but he was still wearing a grin.

"No, no," JC responded. "I kind of thought that you two were together. I saw you at the restaurant together. And I was at her house today. She was doing your laundry?" Benny smiled at that.

"Yeah, she does that. She's my best friend. She's like my sister," he said. "Okay, once in a while there are fringe benefits, you know? But we're not in love or anything. We're just tight. We're close."

JC bought another round of whiskeys. Benny spoke about how comfortable he was in Lonesome County. They were interrupted from time to time when people who liked Benny would stop to say hello or just slap him on the back while passing by.

"Is there something going on with Roman?" JC asked. "Something bothering her?" Benny gave him a blank look.

"What do you mean?" the actor asked.

"I'm not sure," JC told him. "When we were leaving her ranch today, I saw her reach in the mailbox and open a letter. I thought she might collapse. Something in that letter seemed very troubling to her."

"She is a hero in this place," Benny stated. "They love her here. And with looks like that, what could possibly trouble her."

But JC noticed that Benny wasn't smiling anymore.

11

"Do you think that you've ever died?"

JC could see Dr. Anderson's face, so he knew he wasn't joking.

"Like, did I die on the operating table?" JC asked. "Only to be resuscitated?"

"Yes, but not just that," the doctor said, pushing back his cowboy hat. "Let me ask you–have you ever experienced a close call? Maybe so close a call that you think to yourself, 'Why aren't I dead?' or 'How did I live through that?' Think about it for a minute before answering."

Dr. Hunter Anderson's right arm still hung in a sling, healing after arthroscopic surgery to repair damage suffered in the avalanche. The abrasions on his face had mostly healed.

He maneuvered his fork through some mashed potatoes with his left hand. JC saw that it was awkward. Anderson must have been right-handed.

"I can only eat softer foods right now," the doctor told JC. "I can't use my right hand yet to cut with a knife. It's more of a disadvantage than you think. I can't cut cheese or bread to make a grilled cheese sandwich. I can't spread peanut butter. It's good for me to see what my patients go through."

JC was working on some fried chicken. As usual, he'd ordered dark meat only. He looked through a window onto the main street in town, waiting for his lunch companion to continue his story.

"That avalanche could have killed me," Anderson finally said to JC. "Maybe it did. But perhaps my spirit lived on and now I'm living in my next universe."

"So, you think that perhaps you died in that avalanche?" JC inquired.

"Yes, exactly," the doctor said. "So, I'm dead in that universe. But since my personal universe is solely based on my being alive, my life continues in *this* universe. In *that* universe, my friends and family have already gone to my funeral and my body has been donated to a medical school. But in *this* universe, my life continues, and I am now having a conversation with you."

"So, the world doesn't really exist without you," JC theorized. "Only your world exists?"

"Essentially, yes," Anderson said. "It's quite narcissistic, I know. It's all about me. But what if my existence really *is* all about me? What if *you* only exist because *my* brain needs you to exist. And, in turn, what if *I* only exist to you because *your* brain needs me to exist?"

JC had agreed to have lunch with Dr. Anderson after they encountered each other on a sidewalk in downtown Dog Mountain. They had nearly collided. JC was on foot, inspecting the fledgling new town, and the doctor was locking his office door to take an hour for lunch.

"You're the television reporter from Denver, aren't you?" Anderson had asked. "I moved from there. I used to watch you each night. That was quite an adventure you had in Montana," he had said.

"That seems like a long time ago," JC told him.

"Tell me," the doctor now asked. They sat at the table in a restaurant called *The Hole*. "Are you sure that you didn't die in Montana during that confrontation with the serial killer?"

"You're suggesting that I did?" JC replied.

"I'm suggesting that you might have," Anderson stated. "But you still exist in your next universe, perhaps this one. My theory is that humans have nine lives."

"Like cats?" he asked.

"Exactly," Anderson said. "The legend that cats have nine lives may be as old as man itself," Anderson said.

"Someone has really studied whether cats have nine lives?" JC inquired.

"Oh yes. Including me," the doctor said, nodding. "No one really knows who started this notion, but you can find it in ancient Egypt. It was also believed by the Celtics in Scotland and Ireland. How did those civilizations in ancient Scotland and Egypt, who never met one another, come up with the same belief? Perhaps because it is true. And perhaps the cat is a metaphor for mankind."

"How many times do you believe you've died?" JC asked.

"Eight," Anderson said without hesitation.

"You think that you're almost at the end of your rope?"

"No, no, no," Dr. Anderson laughed. "I just had a rough start. I can live on this last life until I'm one hundred. I won't bore you with the details. But I was in the Army Reserve and served in Desert Storm. I think I died there a couple of times. I was also very sick as a child. I think I died. And the avalanche, I believe, was the eighth time I died."

"Are there any other doctors who share your philosophy?" JC asked.

"There are a few of us," Anderson said matter-of-factly, as he lifted another forkful of mashed potatoes. "But they needn't be doctors. You said it yourself, it's a philosophy. But it's an educated philosophy. And being a doctor doesn't hurt the overall perspective. Now, how about yourself?"

"Myself?" JC asked.

"Yes, I asked you to think about any near misses in your life," Anderson reminded him. "I don't expect you to come up with all of them. I didn't give you much warning. Let's start with your close call in Montana. A man wanted to burn you to death. Who's to say he didn't?"

"In a past universe," JC added.

"Exactly," the doctor said. He seemed excited to have someone to share his theory with. "Now, how about another?"

JC shrugged but put his memory to work.

"I had a humdinger of a crash in a ski race a couple of years ago," JC said. "I was knocked-out cold for about five minutes."

"Alright," Anderson declared. "For the sake of argument, let's say that's two times that you've died. Do you have another?"

"I was in a horrible accident on my bicycle when I was a child," JC remembered. "I was bedridden for over a month. I had scars for ten years." He was suddenly experiencing a relative flood of dumb things he did that almost got him killed. Or maybe they did.

"A sniper was shooting at me a few years ago," JC added. "He didn't hit me, though."

"Lousy shot," the doctor assessed. "Or maybe he wasn't. Maybe you died."

"Wow, and there was a time when I was a little kid," JC suddenly remembered. "I nearly drowned. I remember floating to the bottom of a swimming pool. I was so young, I didn't even know how to swim. But I remember my dad diving into the pool. He was wearing his clothes. He pulled me back to the surface. He saved my life."

"That was quite heroic of him. He saved your life," the doctor repeated. "At least, in this universe he did."

"You've given me something to think about, Doc," JC said with a smile. He wasn't convinced, but it was an interesting exercise.

"I don't expect you to be convinced all at once," Dr. Anderson said. "And yet, you have a number of plausible death experiences. And you've barely given it any thought."

After lunch, Dr. Anderson pulled on his long black coat and departed to open his office for afternoon hours. JC took the opportunity to continue his inspection of downtown Dog Mountain.

He stood on the wooden steps of the hotel where he had just eaten lunch. It had the appearance of an old hotel, but was constructed only nine hundred days ago. It resembled a stagecoach stop. It was actually *called* the Stagecoach Stop. On the side of the building, there was a replica of a two-story outhouse. It was put there to add charm.

Dog Mountain was the newest town in the state. It was an urban experiment. It was three years old.

Not since Battlement Mesa, during the oil-shale boom days of the 1980s, had a town just risen overnight in Colorado. Such a thing used to be commonplace in the days of the gold and silver rush. Then, they were called boomtowns.

Dog Mountain's very first buildings were erected to house all the construction workers coming to the area. There were no hotels and no apartments to rent. Two thousand laborers were coming, and they had nowhere to sleep.

Minnie's Gap, LLC, chose the town's site, north of Irish Canyon, and construction began without pause. For the first year, a constant cloud of dust hung over the site.

New roads and curbs were built. Nearly a thousand modular and mobile homes were put in place. A permanent town hall was constructed from local stone.

Pronghorn antelope watched from nearby hills. They were curious about all the noise.

A school was built for the children of the workers. Children from the ranches in Browns Park also attended the school. It was much closer than prior alternatives.

A small downtown was built. The new general store was a replica of the local landmark, Lodore Hall. Plenty of new stores looked like old log cabins. Others were Victorian or just wood-plank facades. There was an Old West feel. Many of the new stores had false fronts.

JC walked the length of the downtown area. It was neither big nor busy. In the center of the central business district, the sidewalks were raised and made from wooden boards. And there were wooden awnings overhead, to protect shoppers from the weather.

Most of the storefronts were full, but not all of them. The stores sold things permanent residents needed. There was a hardware store, a diner, Frank's computer store, a phone store, a gas station, a bank and a small grocery store.

Dr. Anderson's office looked old on the outside. But inside, there was every modern requirement of a physician's office. Long-time residents of the area thought he was a Godsend, a nearby general practitioner.

Over time, many of the modular homes were replaced by sturdier permanent houses. In three years, the town of Dog Mountain had gone from being no place to someplace.

JC saw deer antler arches at the four entrances to the new city park. It reminded him of Jackson, Wyoming.

The mascot of Dog Mountain's new combination high school-middle school-elementary school, he noticed, was the pronghorn.

There was nothing phony about the new town or its people. Its elegance and flaws were genuine.

And there was a turnover occurring in the population of Dog Mountain. Fewer construction workers were needed and more employees were required at the ski area.

There were also employees of the small Lonesome County government workforce. That included judges and attorneys and clerks to operate the new courthouse. Before that, county court proceedings had taken place in neighboring Moffat County.

There was a new community college. It consisted of two buildings, so far. One for classrooms and one for offices. There was a feed store next door.

And at the end of Main Street, there were still a couple of trailer parks. The trailers were older models, the first ones to arrive on site. They were dented and dirty. JC saw more clusters of old mobile homes when he peered down side streets.

To give everyone something else to do, Dog Mountain staged a lot of festivals. JC saw posters advertising the upcoming IcEscape carnival, coming that weekend. And he saw a fire truck hosing down a playground behind the school, growing a thick layer of ice.

And there were two older posters. One advertised a Charles Dickens festival that had been held at Christmas. The other poster invited guests to the "First Snow Carnival" back in November. It marked the initial snowfall of the winter. The poster said it was the oldest celebration of its kind west of the Mississippi River. The event was in its second year. There wasn't much competition.

Until the town of Dog Mountain was built, every road in the county was dirt except State Highway 318. And the paving of more roads was causing some controversy. With big changes like that, planning board meetings sometimes became rancorous shouting matches. It was a source of bad blood among otherwise good-natured people. The meetings became a prime source of entertainment in Lonesome County, the closest thing they had to reality television. And it was available on livestream with closed captioning.

Population 1,842, Dog Mountain was still the kind of community where traffic had to stop to let bighorn sheep cross the road. But the Browns Park families who had been there for generations complained that paradise was being paved over.

JC thought about his lunch with Dr. Anderson. The conversation had turned to the avalanche that nearly took Anderson's life. Or perhaps it did, JC thought with a grin.

Anderson had told him the harrowing tale of being buried alive beneath the snow. And he spoke of his rescuers. They were the only reason he was alive, at least in this universe.

"One was a man from Norway," he told JC as he reset his hat on his head. "His accent would appear and then disappear. I suppose he's losing it. He's probably been in this country a long time."

Longer, JC thought to himself, than the doctor imagined.

12

“Have you checked your mailbox today?” the voice asked her.

“No,” she replied, meekly. She sat down at her kitchen table. The phone was pressed to her ear.

The voice, Roman thought, was disguised. It didn’t matter. The malice was real and unblemished. She was terrified.

“Why are you doing this?” she quietly squeaked.

“Go check your mailbox,” the voice told her. “And no police, for Olive’s sake.” Then the call was disconnected.

She looked out the window, through the laundry room, at the home she grew up in with her parents. They couldn’t help her now. No one could help her.

Roman's eyes wandered toward the front door. It was the portal to the path to her driveway and to the mailbox. She felt helpless to resist his command. Go check the mailbox.

She walked down the long driveway. Her legs felt weak. A couple of horses nickered to get her attention, but she ignored them.

The bright sun reflected off the snow lining the dirt road and made her squint her eyes. She didn't notice the landscape she loved so much. She didn't notice her great grandparents' log cabin that she adored. She simply put one foot in front of the other, holding closed a jacket that she hadn't even bothered to zip up.

Roman stood in front of the mailbox. She looked up and down the road. There wasn't a single vehicle. There usually wasn't. She usually loved that about her road.

Grasping the latch with her hand to open the door on the box, the wind was blowing strands of hair across her face. The only sound she heard was her own heartbeat.

She pulled the latch and opened the mailbox. She expected to see a box or an envelope, but there was none. She was relieved.

But she thought that she saw something move. She lowered her head to get a better look into the mailbox. Something was moving at the back. She moved her face closer to the opening and her eyes adjusted to the dark.

She suddenly recognized the delivery in her mailbox. It was staring back at her, twitching, looking for an avenue of escape. A live rat.

Roman screamed and lunged backward, at the same time falling to the ground. She sat on the mix of snow and dirt, her legs curled up at her side, and began screaming, then sobbing, then screaming again.

"Why me?" she screamed. "What do you want?" She began to cry uncontrollably.

Through her tears, she saw the rat edge toward the opening of her mailbox and leap to the ground. It landed within inches of her legs, but she didn't react. She had no will to protect herself. She was powerless. The rat scurried away, following a dirt path in the road.

Roman remained seated on the mix of dirt and snow, her shoulders heaving to the pattern of her wail.

"You saved the man buried in the avalanche?" JC asked.

"It was a terrible thing to watch," Steven Hemingway, now known as Ullr Skadi, said academically. "But my role in the rescue was just another undertaking to better the circumstances of my fellow man in my adopted country. I feel like I have to prove myself—as an immigrant to the country, you know."

"You're not an immigrant!" JC blurted. "You're not from Norway."

They were in Hemingway's small office at the community college. It was located close to the ski resort. At night, those at the college could see the lights at the ski mountain. Its proximity was a useful recruiting tool for the college. The school had an outstanding ski racing team.

"What's your angle?" JC asked. "Why are you suddenly from Norway?"

"We've already gone over this," Professor Skadi said. "Why do you think I need an angle? I'm just trying to bring my years of learning at the academy in Norway to share with this great land of opportunity. And if I did have an angle, it might be to hide my whereabouts from those who think Steven Hemingway deserves to be punished in some fashion."

JC shook his head in amazement. But he found that the whole thing also amused him. Hemingway was again proving his brilliance by pulling off this deception.

"By the way," JC needled. "Your Norwegian accent needs work. The guy who was buried by that avalanche told me he was rescued by a man whose Norwegian accent came and went like waves on a Florida beach."

"He was in shock," Professor Skadi responded. "At the time, he didn't know Norwegian from pig Latin."

"And let me pry into *your* life for a moment," Hemingway/Skadi said. "How is that beautiful woman you were living with in Montana? She was gorgeous. Shara?"

"Yes, Shara," JC said without emotion. "We've gone our separate ways."

"So, you blew it," Hemingway said. "I've heard that you tend to do that."

"You heard that all the way back in Norway?" JC sneered.

"Word of mouth is a powerful tool," Hemingway chuckled.

"By the way, Ullr," JC said.

"If you are going to address me," Hemingway interrupted. "I prefer you address me as Professor Skadi."

"Don't I recall a pagan god of skiing named Ullr?" JC asked him.

"Very good. If I taught a class in Scandinavian folklore," Hemingway said in a condescending manner, "I'd encourage you to enroll in my freshman-level course. Then you'd also learn that Skadi was the *goddess* of skiing."

"So, as Ullr Skadi," JC suggested, "you are both the god and goddess of skiing?"

Hemingway, or Skadi, beamed at JC.

JC was aware that Hemingway was closeted. It was another feat the reporter marveled at when they met in Montana. Hemingway would find lovers amidst men inside a violent homophobic militia camp.

"Ullr Skadi. I am the god and goddess of skiing. Deliciously appropriate," Hemingway said. "Don't you think?"

"That was a great interview with Oaks, JC." The voice on the other end of JC's phone belonged to his news director, Pat Perilla.

"You know," Perilla continued, "high-ranking people in his political party tell me that Oaks is the popular choice to be their candidate for governor. They're telling anyone else thinking of running that they won't be seriously considered in the event that Oaks runs."

"Wow," JC said. "So, he's already got the nomination locked up?"

"That's what I'm being told," Perilla said. "Two years from now, you may be calling him Governor Oaks. So keep your lines of communication with him open. It could come in handy down the road."

"My God, Jon, what am I going to do?" Roman asked into the phone. She sounded exhausted. She had told Jon

Oaks about her frightening encounter at the mailbox. She sounded like she was near her breaking point. Oaks could hear her sobbing.

"I'm going to end this, Roman," Oaks finally told her. "I should have done this before. I'm taking matters into my own hands."

"Oh God, Jon. I don't want you to get hurt. I couldn't take it if I lost you," she said.

"Don't worry about me. It's time that this creep pays for hurting you like this," Oaks stated. "He said 'no police?' He's going to regret that. They're the only ones who could save him."

"What are you going to do?" Roman asked.

"The less you know, the better," Oaks said with determination.

"Jon, be careful," is the last thing Roman said before Oaks hung up the phone.

Roman was emotionally spent as she sat on the couch in her living room. She was in a state of terror, but now she was also frightened for Jon.

She felt some relief, though. Oaks had promised he was going to end it. And Jon Oaks was a man of his word.

She jumped as her phone rang. She stared at the device without moving. As it continued to ring, she recognized some of the numbers she could see in the readout. It was Benny Ray.

"Could you come over?" she pleaded as she picked up the phone. "Please?"

"Sure," he said. "I'm on my way."

"No police makes no sense," Benny implored. He was sitting on the couch next to Roman. She had barely moved since he arrived. She only got up to get him some water to drink and some paté and crackers. She wasn't hungry, but he was.

"Roman," Benny said, "this is what police are good at. You know that I'm not often in favor of having cops around. They tend to frown on people who get high all the time. But this isn't kid stuff. This stalker keeps elevating his game. He's dangerous."

Roman stared at Benny Ray. She absorbed his every word. She knew that Benny Ray had her best interests in mind, as did Jon Oaks. She was lucky to have them both.

"Let's call the police," Benny said to her. She just looked at him. Finally, she raised her eyebrows. It was a signal of compliance. If Benny Ray thought they should call the police, then they would call the police.

"Would you talk to them?" she asked meekly.

"Yes, of course," he responded.

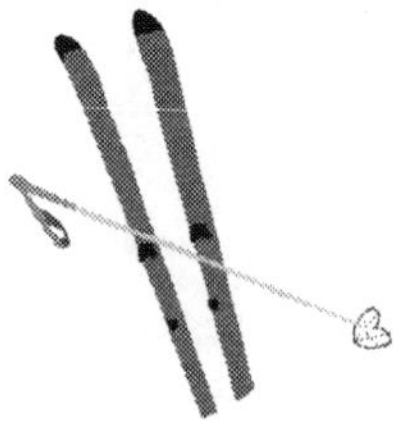

13

"To serve and protect," he said when he took the oath.

The police chief in the small town of Dog Mountain was a man named Bob Newell. He was in his fifties and had been the police chief for all three years that the police department had been in existence. Before that, he was a detective in Denver's police force.

His jurisdiction as chief included every square inch of the town, up to its borders. Beyond the town limits, Sheriff Henry Nidever was in charge of the rest of Lonesome County. The relationship between the two law officers could be described as an uneasy peace.

Chief Newell's hair was getting gray at the temples. He was overweight and embarrassed about it. He'd leave any foot chase to his younger officers.

But he was smart. His eyes radiated intelligence. Whatever first impression his appearance might allow, his sharp mind quickly demonstrated that he was someone to be taken seriously.

Newell accepted the police chief's job in Dog Mountain, at a significant pay cut, because he wanted his time on earth to calm down some. Being a police officer in a major metropolitan area put a lot of stress on his family life.

During his last year in Denver, his marriage was in trouble and so was one of his two teenage kids. Newell brought them all to Dog Mountain to save his family.

It seemed to work. He and his wife bonded again. Together, they helped their children adjust. The teenagers took up skiing and learned to ride horses.

The girl had always been good at making new friends. It didn't take long for her to adapt to Dog Mountain.

The boy resisted change at first. The urban tools he'd sharpened in Denver weren't of much use in Lonesome County. But eventually, he decided that his new life was sort of like going on vacation and never having to go back home.

The police department had added three new full-time officers since the ski resort opened. More hires would probably come.

Dog Mountain was still a small town, but it was growing. As of now, the biggest gatherings came on the weekends for what the chief thought was an endless list of festivals and carnivals.

And the central business district had to be patrolled. Dog Mountain's downtown was a tiny collection of stores on three blocks. But there were proposals before town planners to open stores on a fourth block.

The call to the police department from Benny Maple went to the desk of an investigator. Joe Walker was one of two investigators on the force. And the call caused Investigator Walker to come into the chief's office.

Walker suggested that the call he had on hold be put on speakerphone in Newell's office for both of them to hear.

That being agreed to, Benny Maple explained the ordeal that Roman Holiday had been enduring.

"Why didn't you call us sooner?" Chief Newell asked.

"I know," Benny responded. "But he told Roman not to contact the police." Roman was next to Benny on the couch, listening to everything.

The police chief devised a plan. It would require Benny to stay with Roman. If the stalker called again, Roman was to answer the phone and try to keep the caller on the line as long as possible. Benny was to call the chief.

Newell explained that they'd try to trace the stalker's call to a cell tower, try to figure out where the call was coming from. From there, the police would try to find the caller.

"You can do that?" Benny asked.

"We can try," the chief told him. "The way the caller knows Ms. Holiday's whereabouts means he is probably nearby. And he's probably alone. He's not making the call from a crowded room.

"In a little place like Dog Mountain, he might stick out. If the phone company can give us a quick location, and unless he's a pronghorn, Investigator Walker can probably chase him down."

Benny had been reading about pronghorn. He had learned they were among the fastest animals on earth, running over fifty miles an hour across open ground. He thought it was exciting to live in a place where pronghorn ran free.

But they weren't looking for a pronghorn.

The police chief made a call to the sheriff of Lonesome County. The sheriff did not have the volume of experience that the police chief had. But the sheriff might have the jurisdiction before this was through. The police chief thought that it was unlikely the caller was going to restrict himself to the town limits of Dog Mountain.

Roman had not told Benny much about Jon Oaks' vow to put an end to the stalking. She couldn't explain what Jon was planning to do. "The less you know, the better," Jon had said to her.

Not knowing what to say, Benny said nothing to the cops about Jon Oaks.

Benny dashed back to his home and returned to Roman's ranch with a bag full of clothing and things he would need to stay there for a prolonged period. They would wait for the next call, or letter, together.

If it was a letter, Benny thought, this could drag on. Investigator Walker had already come to Roman's ranch and collected the letters sent by the stalker. Benny figured the police would look for fingerprints.

Roman wondered if the stalker really was watching her, whether he'd call or come after her. He'd be angry that she'd involved the police. No call came that day.

The chief told her that they would be watching her house. He told her to call if anything out of the ordinary occurred. Anything.

A call came the next day. Roman hesitated. Benny urged her to answer the phone, reminding her that he was on his phone calling police.

"What did you find in the mailbox?" the voice asked Roman. She didn't answer.

"I didn't see Olive at school today," he said. Roman's heart raced. She had packed a bag for her daughter and told Olive to stay with a friend in town, and not to go to school or ever be left alone.

"She's sick. She stayed home," Roman choked. "She's here with me."

"Maybe I'll come check up on her," the voice said. "Maybe it's time to introduce her to my friends."

Roman's eyes grew. Tears began to form. She snapped her head toward Benny, who gave her a reassuring smile. He quickly wrote something on a piece of paper and pushed it her way. It said, "That means he doesn't know where she is." Roman gave him a relieved look.

"Tell me what I can do to make you feel better about all of this," Roman said. "Let's talk." The chief had told her to keep the menacing caller on the phone as long as possible. She was using the line of questioning the chief had told her to use.

"It might get him talking," the chief had said. "He might want to talk about himself."

After receiving Benny's call, Chief Newell got on a secure line to his investigator. The chief was at his desk at the station. Joe Walker was in his patrol car downtown.

"The phone company tells me the call is coming from here in town," the chief said. "Try the Stagecoach Stop," meaning the hotel. "It's a guess, but in a little town, it's where he might think he blends in."

"Got it," Investigator Walker said.

"I'm coming that way too," the chief said, jumping up from the seat behind his desk and out a side door to his patrol car.

Investigator Walker slowly drove by the Stagecoach Stop. The hotel and a big parking lot took up almost an entire block.

The patrol car, a white 4x4 with a black stripe stretching from the headlights to the tail lights, took a left turn to view the side of the building. Walker was looking for someone on the phone, probably in their car where they had privacy. There weren't many cars in the parking lot.

"He's still on the phone," the chief told Investigator Walker on the secure line. The chief was still on another phone line with Benny.

Walker turned left again and drove slowly past the back of the hotel. Left again, he turned onto the street where cars could angle-park next to the hotel.

The police officer spied a man on the sidewalk. Quickly, Walker identified the pedestrian as Dr. Hunter Anderson. Walker eyed the doctor's hands. He was not holding a phone.

But Anderson's eyes were fixed on a parked car. It looked like he was watching it.

Walker saw that a man was inside the car. He was wearing a cowboy hat and had long black hair. The rest of his facial features were hidden. But he was on the phone.

It was a black, late-model sedan. It looked like it had just been washed. The sedan backed out of the parking spot and headed east. Walker followed. At the intersection, he saw the police chief's patrol car. With a hand gesture, the chief said he would follow Walker.

After leaving town, the sedan drove east on Route 72 and turned south on Route 10N. It turned right onto the access road of Minnie's Gap Ski Resort. The two patrol cars followed.

"He has to have noticed us," the investigator said to his chief over the secure line.

"I'm sure he has," the chief replied.

"Have you called up the plate?" the investigator asked, meaning the license plate on the black sedan.

"Yes. I thought I recognized the car," the chief said. "Let's just see what happens."

The sedan passed new townhomes and large single-family homes as it proceeded up the access road toward the ski mountain.

There were empty lots that had been cleared for commercial development. The ground was covered with snow. Building would begin when the warm weather returned.

The black sedan turned into a parking lot in front of the administrative offices for the ski resort. The two town police cars were joined by a pair of patrol cars belonging to the sheriff's office.

The sedan parked in a spot in front of the entrance to the administrative offices. The four law enforcement vehicles positioned themselves to block the car in.

Police Chief Bob Newell and Investigator Joe Walker climbed out of their cars. Each law officer had a hand on their holstered revolver as they approached the sedan.

The car door opened and the man stood, facing them.

"You've got me, gentlemen," said Congressman Jon Oaks. He looked distraught. "I won't offer any resistance."

Chief Newell leaned to look inside the congressman's car. On the front seat on the passenger side, there was a cowboy hat and a wig with long black hair.

"May I see your phone, congressman?" the chief asked.

Oaks extended his arm and placed the phone in the chief's hand.

"May I?" the chief asked.

"Of course," said Oaks. He knew that an eventual court order would provide the same information.

The chief opened the flip phone and looked for the last call made from the device. The time of the last call ended only eight minutes ago. The call had been placed to a phone number belonging to Roman Holiday.

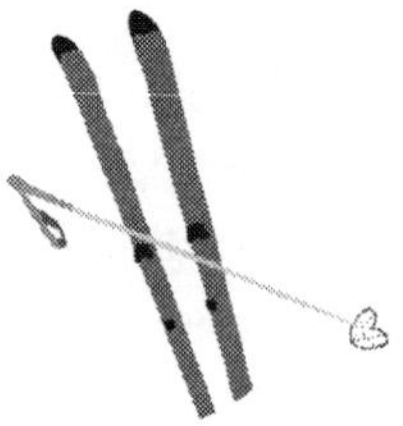

14

Her eyes were puffy and full of tears when Roman answered the knock at the door of her home.

"No doorbell," JC said.

"I don't need one out here," Roman told him, wiping her nose but wearing a slight smile. "If you hear a car cross the cattle guard, you know it's coming up your driveway."

"Are you okay?" he asked.

"I'm in shock," she told him. She was holding onto the door that remained between them. She stood in the doorway, but she still held the door, blocking him from entering.

"Should I have known?" she asked him.

"I don't know."

"How could I be so stupid?"

"You trusted him," JC told her. "He wasn't on your list of suspects."

A tall eleven-year-old girl appeared from behind the door and pressed herself against Roman's side. Roman put a protective arm around her.

"This is Olive, my daughter."

"Pleased to meet you, Olive. I'm so sorry about your dog."

"Thank you," Olive said sadly. The pitch of her voice was still that of a young girl.

"Your mom is a brave woman," JC told Olive.

"Not at all," Roman sighed. "And Jon knew that about me. He knew too much."

JC noted that Roman spoke of Jon Oaks in the past tense. That had to be good, JC thought, like she was done with him.

Roman glanced over JC's shoulder and saw Bip waiting, leaning against the 4x4 that the journalists had arrived in. Roman waved to Bip and Bip waved back.

"I'm on my way to his arraignment, JC said. "I'm not going to force you to do anything, but it's my job to ask if you want to make a comment on camera."

"No, I'm sorry." She said it as though she felt guilty for letting him down.

"That's alright," JC answered. "Maybe another time." He paused, trying to grasp the right words.

"Did I miss something?" he finally said. "Am I the only one who didn't know that you had a relationship with Jon Oaks?"

"No, and thank you for putting it so politely," Roman told him. "No one knew about it except Benny Ray and

Olive. And she didn't know that he was married." She looked at her daughter, rubbing her arm.

"I'm sorry," she said to her daughter.

"We were very discreet," Roman said when she turned her attention back to JC.

Dr. Anderson was asked to come to the police station and give a statement. He did so, telling Investigator Walker that he had walked away from his office to run an errand.

"My eye happened to spot a man inside a dark sedan. I swore it was Congressman Oaks' car," the doctor said. "Then, I saw that the man had long hair and was wearing a cowboy hat. I concluded that it was not Jon Oaks."

"So, you could not identify the man in the car as Jon Oaks?" the investigator asked.

"I stared at the man," Anderson told the investigator. "I wondered if the congressman had a brother who looked like him. Then, I became certain that it *was* the congressman, and that made the hat and long hair an odd addition to his ensemble."

Back in the car and heading for the Lonesome County Courthouse, JC remembered the automatic lock on Oaks' office door at the ski resort. It wasn't a habit formed in Washington, after all, he thought. It was a mechanism installed to ensure no one would barge in on Oaks and Roman Holiday when they were in a compromising position.

JC placed a call to Robin. She was on her way from Denver to Dog Mountain.

"Can you meet me at the courthouse? he asked.

"Well, this is sudden," she said over the phone. "You haven't even given me a ring."

"Be careful what you wish for," JC told her with a smile. "Seriously, you're not going to believe what happened today."

"I saw the news bulletin on my phone," Robin told him. "I can't believe it. I've got a driver bringing me down from Rock Springs. I'm not that far."

"Meet me at the courthouse," he said. "You're not going to want to miss this."

JC and Bip had already reported the arrest of former Congressman Jon Oaks to their audience in Denver. The breaking news interrupted regular programming with a message crawling across the bottom of the screen. It told viewers that JC would have a full report on the early evening news at five p.m.

"I'm taking the night off when we're done," Bip said as he drove them to the courthouse. "Maybe I'll go see Sunny, see what her hometown looks like. I'll need the car."

"What do you mean?" JC asked him. "Robin's arriving tonight."

"That's why I'm taking the night off," Bip told him. "I don't need to watch you two suck face and paw each other." Bip laughed.

"Wait a minute," JC protested. "We conduct ourselves with dignity and respect to those around us. I'll bet you haven't even seen us kiss."

"I have," Bip disclosed. "And it was disgusting. It was like watching my parents have sex."

"You're not even ten years younger than I am!"

"Well," said Bip, "maybe if I had a woman like Robin, I wouldn't be such a whore. Don't blow it." Bip was smiling. So was JC.

JC told Bip that if he did drive to Utah, he'd need to be back Saturday morning, ready to work.

"All weekend leaves are canceled," JC told him. "Robin is going to need you too. She has a story she's working on here. I have a feeling that we're not going home on Sunday."

The courthouse, like everything else in the town, was new. But it was built to look old. It was yellow sandstone with a false front, like a building Wyatt Earp would have walked out of.

The courtroom had a high ceiling and tall windows. The acoustics were awful. Words spoken at the front of the room seemed to drift up to the ceiling and get lost there.

Jon Oaks, the popular congressman and unannounced candidate for governor, was shuffled into the courtroom. He was still wearing the clothing he was wearing when he was arrested earlier in the day. He would be issued an orange jumpsuit at the jail when he was processed there.

Oaks was wearing chains shackled to his wrists and ankles. He looked disoriented. His normally perfect hair was unkempt. His tan face had lost its color. He looked scared. His eyes darted across the courtroom. He looked older.

Then, he lowered his chin and seemed to gather himself. When he raised his head, he was transformed. The intelligence had returned to his face. He even smiled at a deputy when the law officer instructed Oaks to sit down at the defense table.

Oaks spoke with respect when addressed by the judge. He answered, "Yes, Your Honor," and "No, Your Honor." This, despite being on a first-name basis with the judge for years leading up to this moment.

The lawyer standing next to the defendant was well-dressed. No doubt, he would be replaced by an experienced trial lawyer when this went to trial. *If* it went to trial, JC thought.

Once in a while, the defense attorney leaned over and whispered something to Oaks who would look back at him and shake his head, confirming his understanding.

JC was straining to hear the discussion between the judge, the attorney for the defense and the district attorney. They were speaking in low voices.

JC was sitting on a mahogany bench that looked like an old pew from a church. He was in the front row of the gallery where spectators were allowed.

The jury box was empty. In fact, the courtroom was mostly empty. JC thought it was sort of like Lonesome County itself. Dog Mountain was in such a remote location, word had not sprinkled very far regarding the arrest of the former congressman until JC reported it on the news.

There was a uniformed law officer sitting in the gallery with a man in a sport coat next to him. JC knew them to be the police chief and an investigator from the Dog Mountain police force. They made the arrest. JC had already interviewed them.

There was a woman in the spectator seating area. She wore a business suit. JC wondered if she was with the probation department. She might be involved later in the case.

There was another woman and two men. They wore much more expensive business suits than the probation employee. Lawyers, JC thought. One of them was seated next to him.

JC knew that television and newspaper reporters from Durango and Grand Junction were speeding in this direction. But at this moment, JC and a reporter from the Dog Mountain weekly newspaper were the only journalists in the courtroom.

The district attorney's office represented four counties: Lonesome, Moffat, Grand and Routt. There were not enough people, nor enough crime, to warrant a different district attorney in each county.

It wasn't always that way. This entire area used to be one county. But in the days of the Wild West, judges complained that there were too many murder trials to be the work of just one jurisdiction. So the big county was divided into smaller new counties.

Most of the crime in Lonesome County these days involved meth, domestic violence, drunken driving, traffic accidents, illegal hunting and fishing, fire ban violations and catching someone who was wanted by the law elsewhere and came to Lonesome County to hide.

The judge arraigning Jon Oaks read the charges and stipulations.

"Did I just hear the judge say 'suicide watch?'" JC asked the well-dressed spectator sitting next to him.

"That's correct," the man whispered.

"Alright," the judge then announced in a louder voice, filling the courtroom. "Let's allow the psychological evaluation to run its course. Then, we'll set a bail hearing. Remand the defendant to the county jail until arrangements may be made with the Colorado Mental Health Institute at Fort Logan."

The judge dropped her gavel onto the sound block, dismissing court.

The few spectators rose and headed for the exit. But one woman, sitting in the back of the courtroom, stood and walked straight for JC.

"Hello, Jean Claude."

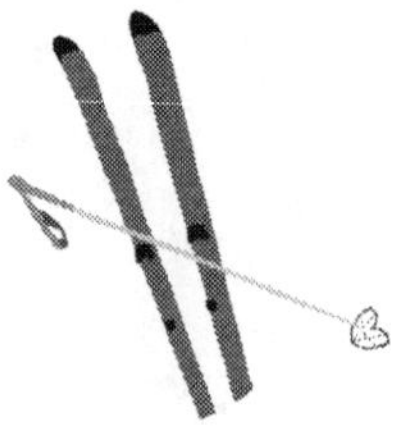

15

Robin was the only one who called him "Jean Claude." He turned toward the back of the courtroom, now in recess, and laid eyes on the exquisite redhead. His heart raced. He had no true understanding of why such a beautiful and interesting woman was drawn to him. But every time she was at his side, he was grateful that he got at least one more day in her presence.

Robin was athletic-looking, with curly red hair dropping below her shoulders. They had a standing agreement to resist public displays of affection when they were performing their jobs. He desperately wanted to feel her body pressed close to his. But there were still people in the courtroom, including Bip.

She leaned close to him though, so she could whisper in his ear.

"What country are we in?" she asked, and he laughed.

"I know," he said. "It's a bit isolated." She gave him a kiss on the cheek before she drew back.

"On my flight to Rock Springs, I saw the blackened forest from the wildfires on Cameron Pass," Robin said. "From above, it looks huge."

"It would probably still be burning," JC said. "If it hadn't snowed."

It was dark when they emerged outside. JC and Bip were committed to do a live shot from downtown Dog Mountain for the five p.m. and the ten p.m. news.

"There goes my night off," Bip remarked as they stood on the sidewalk of the cowboy town.

They found that several blocks of Main Street were closed. There were a couple of pieces of heavy equipment parked on a side street. The pavement on Main Street had been covered in snow and a few jumps had been built.

It was the start of the weekend's IcEscape carnival. The sound of music was pulling the crowd toward the bright lights.

"I tell you what," JC said. "Let's try to work a half day tomorrow. Let's get a shot of the transport vehicle taking Oaks to the psychiatric hospital. We'll get a couple of interviews and pass along any new details we know about the case. That's probably all we can hope to accomplish. Then, maybe, we can do some skiing."

"I'm hungry," Bip said to him.

"And I'll buy you dinner," JC said to sweeten the deal.

They had to work their way through a crowd, up a boarded sidewalk under a wooden awning, until they reached the hotel called the Stagecoach Stop. The restaurant appeared to be open, but everyone was outside.

The crowd lined Main Street and watched men and women on horseback pull men and women on skis who hung onto a rope. It was a sport called "skijoring."

The race course required skiers to go around slalom poles and over the jumps.

Competitors from Steamboat Springs and Leadville seemed to lead the pack. And each would try to persuade you that their hometown invented the sport.

Robin was dressed casually. She wore snug blue jeans and a blue jacket with a big white "S" on the left breast. JC had given her his letter jacket from high school.

"It's warm," she said as she pulled her hands into the leather sleeves to protect herself from the cold night air.

Inside the restaurant, they were guided by a hostess to a table in the back. The empty tables in the front were all spoken for by customers who had stepped outside to watch the skijoring.

The dining room had a Western theme. There were a few items hanging on the wall that looked like old harnesses for a team of horses, as a stagecoach would require.

"Do you think Bip is hot?" JC asked Robin as they all settled in at the table.

"Oh yeah," she said. They laughed. Bip blushed a little.

"He's got a girlfriend, you know," JC told her.

"Oh really?" Robin teased as she brushed Bip's arm. "What's her name?"

"Sunny," Bip told her, sheepishly. "Part of her Ute name is Tava," he tried to explain. "I think that means sun. So, she calls herself Sunny."

"Well," Robin teased. "I'll have to approve of her. When will you introduce us?"

"Um, breakfast?" Bip offered.

"Oooo," responded Robin. "You're moving a little fast, aren't you?"

"It's not that," Bip laughed. "You have a dirty mind. She serves us breakfast. She's our waitress."

"I must get my mind out of the gutter," Robin laughed.

"No, leave it in the gutter," JC said. "That's one of the things we like about you."

Their server at the Stagecoach approached the table and they placed their food order. They also asked for coffee.

"So, how did this whole Oaks thing blow up?" Robin asked.

JC gave her the thumbnail of the story. He told her of the affair between Oaks and Roman, the breakup, the anonymous letters, the phone calls and the hat and wig Oaks was using as a disguise when he was arrested.

"We still don't know his motive," JC added.

"You mean," Robin asked, "why would an apparently sane man do such an insane thing?"

"Yep," JC said. Robin gave it thought. They sat in silence, drinking their coffee.

"The heart wants what it wants," she suddenly said. "He still loves her."

"This is how he shows Roman that he's still in love with her?" JC asked. He had plenty of doubts about this theory.

"I don't know," Robin said. "What about the term 'madly in love?' Wasn't this a case of *madness* in love?"

"He loved her so much, he was driven to madness," JC said. "I kind of like that."

"So, does he go for an insanity defense?" Bip asked.

"He might have a case," JC said.

"*This* is insane!" Robin blurted.

Following their five-o'clock live shot, JC, Robin and Bip emerged from the satellite truck to find the skijoring competition was completed. A pair of snowplows were leveling the jumps and preparing to reopen Main Street.

The crowd had been lured in the direction of more music and bright lights belonging to the IcEscape festival, behind the school.

A foot race was being held over an ice-coated obstacle course. There were five ice sculptures plus frozen apparatus on the school's playground that competitors had to scramble over.

There were plenty of falls. And some racers seemed to have a better strategy than others.

The fastest competitors wore slick clothing, like old skiing outfits. But there was also a large man dressed as a Viking, complete with horned helmet and bare legs protruding from beneath a kilt made of fur. There were also a few women wearing bikinis.

"Talk about freezer burn!" Bip exclaimed.

"These are tough people," JC said with admiration, as they walked back to the satellite truck for one more newscast.

A crowd heading home after a night of IcEscape events stopped to watch JC's ten-o'clock live shot. The satellite truck was parked across from the Stagecoach Stop. JC explained to his audience during the broadcast that Oaks was parked outside the Stagecoach Stop when he made his last phone call to Roman Holiday.

After the live shot, they drove down 10N toward their hotel and the ski resort. Finally, their workday was done.

Robin smiled as they walked into the lobby, seeing it for the first time. She pointed out the finer points of the Western motif, the thirty-gallon wooden barrels, rifles and furs on the wall. There were mounted heads of bear, bighorn and pronghorn.

"This is really cool," she said.

"Yes, ma'am," JC said, pleased that she was pleased.

"Ma'am is your mother after she's paddled you," Robin protested. "Do I look like your mother?"

"No, ma'am," JC responded.

"Then I'm not a ma'am," she declared, tasting victory in their debate. Then, she brushed the palm of her soft hand across the side of his face and smiled. "But this is nice."

After letting Robin drop her jacket and her bag in JC's room, the three of them decided to head back downstairs and grab a nightcap in the bar. She grabbed her boyfriend's CSU hat off the bed as she exited their room.

The bar was suitably called The Saloon. They waited for their eyes to adjust to the darkness before heading for a table.

"Hey, I think that's the guy you're looking for," JC said to Robin.

At a booth in a corner, the Denver developer named Gerhard Snyder was sitting with another man.

"Do we just go up and introduce ourselves?" Robin asked. "Hi, Mr. Snyder, I'm a reporter from Denver. Would it be okay if I ask you a few questions so I can determine if you're loathsome?"

"You could try it that way," JC told her. "Or, we could just go say hi to our friend that's sitting with him."

"Hi Frank," JC said as they approached the table. The man sitting with Gerhard Snyder was Frank Green, the affable owner of the computer store.

"Hi JC, hi Bip," said Green. "I was helping Jerry resolve a problem with his computers. We decided to get a nightcap."

"You're working late," said JC. "Frank, this is Robin Smith. She works with us in Denver."

Frank Green displayed old-fashioned good manners. Robin was impressed when he stood up to greet the woman and shake her hand.

But Frank was clearly taken with Robin. So was the other man.

"JC, Bip, Robin, this is Gerhard Snyder," Frank said.

"We met, briefly," JC told Snyder. "It was at the cocktail party on Tuesday."

"Yes, of course," Snyder said. It didn't seem sincere.

JC got the impression that Snyder didn't remember him at all. But the builder was currently memorizing every line on Robin's landscape. JC chuckled to himself. *If you only knew, pal.*

The three journalists joined Green and Snyder at their booth. Bip pulled a chair to fit on the end of the table.

"You went to college at Colorado State?" Frank asked Robin.

"No," she said, pointing at JC. "It's his hat."

"You went to Colorado State?" Frank repeated, this time in JC's direction. "So did I. I met my wife there! I think I'm older than you, though. I had probably taken a job in Casper by the time you went to college."

"Great school," JC said.

"Great town," Frank added. They reminisced a bit about Fort Collins.

"And then you moved to Casper?" JC asked. "The Wonder Bar?"

"I can't believe The Wonder Bar closed," Frank said. "It was the most famous place in town."

"Legendary," JC agreed.

"So, what do you know about Jon Oaks?" Frank gasped. "I was blown away by his arrest. He wanted to sell that little girl into sex slavery?"

"I only know what we told everyone on television," JC said. Oaks' arrest, which was still only about eight hours old, was a part of every conversation in Lonesome County.

"Dog Mountain is no different than any other small town," Frank said with a smile. "We like our gossip."

The two men peppered JC with questions while the server took their drink orders. JC ordered a sour beer called Pulp Theory. It was brewed by Odell in Fort Collins. Robin joined him. Bip ordered a Storm Peak lager, brewed in Steamboat Springs.

Over their table, a classic rock album cover hung in a frame. It was from the 1970s. But it fit the décor, JC supposed, because the rock stars were dressed in cowboy outfits.

There were similar record covers on the wall. Each had an image of rock stars wearing cowboy hats and chaps and sometimes holding firearms.

JC seized the chance to change the subject away from Jon Oaks. He pointed out the album covers to Robin.

"Those are neat," she said.

"I love the artwork on old record albums," Frank said, looking at Robin.

JC was used to men staring at Robin when she was with him. But Robin pressed against JC's side in their booth. She made it obvious who she was going home with.

"Album covers are fetching a lot of money now," Robin said. "At least, if they're in mint condition."

"I've got a lot of old vinyl," Frank said. "I still like to listen to it."

"Do you take care of them?" Robin asked.

"The records? Yeah," he said.

"But how about the album covers?" Robin asked him. "Do you have Bob Dylan's *Freewheelin'?* That cover, in mint condition, can get you thirty thousand-dollars."

"I've got that album!" exclaimed Frank. "'*The Freewheelin' Bob Dylan*!'"

"Is it mint?" she asked.

"It looks like I rolled it up and tried to smoke it," he said with a laugh. "It didn't work. And it didn't taste like mint."

"How do you know so much about record albums, Robin?" The question came from Gerhard Snyder.

JC was sizing him up. He looked like he was in his forties. He was balding and had scars left on his face from acne when he was a teenager.

"I'm a reporter, Mr. Snyder," Robin said. "I recently did a story on the surprising value of some of those record covers. There are a lot of baby boomers who have those albums, up in an attic or wedged in some cardboard box in the basement. Most of the covers, though, are crumbling because of water damage or whatever. But the records still play."

"Please, call me Jerry," Snyder said. "Did you find any covers that were worth anything?"

"A few," she said. "The people who owned them were shocked. They loved me! I found that the best album covers belong to people who didn't move to a lot of different places, so they didn't drag boxes of those albums everywhere. People who live in the house they grew up in have some really nice album covers."

"So, you're a television reporter?" Snyder inquired. JC smiled a little smile to himself. He could see the hook in Snyder's mouth. Now, JC was going to watch the beautiful woman handling the rod and reel pull Snyder into the boat.

"Yes," Robin said with a smile to Snyder. "And you built the housing for the workforce here at Minnie's Gap?"

"Yes, I did," Snyder said, happy to be known for his work.

"And you have a project outside Denver," Robin said to him. "You're proposing to build over wetlands?"

The smile faded from the developer's face.

"It's perfectly legal," he said.

"I'm sure it is, Jerry. Could Bip and I come by your office here? You can explain it to us. Then, our viewers will see your explanation and the growing opposition to that project might melt away."

"Sure, I have nothing to hide," Snyder said, still smiling. But inside, he was fuming. He felt cornered, so he agreed to the appointment. He could decide later if he would cancel it.

Their drinks were done, and so was their evening.

"That was time well spent," JC said as the three journalists left the bar and headed for their rooms.

"Yes, Frank is nice," Robin said. "Don't you think he looks like a plump John Denver?"

"I thought the same thing," JC told her. "What do you know about Snyder?"

"That he cuts corners by buying cheap land or using substandard materials. His properties fall apart in ten years. But he's sold the property by then. By the time it turns to junk, he's run with the money."

"How does he get away with it?" Bip asked.

"The sharpest Realtors tell me they won't show his properties to their clients," she said. "They know what he's doing. But he's not breaking any laws. He just sells garbage with a fresh coat of paint. Most buyers don't look past the paint."

Saying goodnight to Bip, JC and Robin entered their own room. JC was ready to put his head down. It had been a long day.

"So, you think Bip is hot?" JC asked Robin as they were lying in bed.

"Well, he is," she said, her head cradled by his shoulder.

"So, how come you didn't go for him instead of me?" JC inquired.

"I ask myself that all the time," she said, laughing. She gave him a kiss. "There is a point," she added, "where being that pretty would just be a distraction. On a date, I want to be the prettiest one."

"What about when you're on a date with me?" JC asked.

"It's no contest," she smiled and gave him another kiss.

"Well, this is a lesson in humility," he grumbled.

"Wow, an old dog *can* learn new tricks," she giggled.

16

Jonathan Oaks was led out the back door of the county jail the next morning. Dog Mountain and Diamond Peak were visible in the distance.

The handcuffs and leg irons made him shuffle in canvas deck shoes without laces. He wore a blue goose-down jacket over an orange jumper. The change of clothing had been provided by his jailers.

The wind blew at Oaks' hair and his tanned face looked pale. In less than a day, the carefully manicured look of a man of prominence had been reduced to that of a captive animal.

JC and Bip had been staking out the county jail for this shot. They captured video of Oaks being loaded into the transport vehicle.

The van maneuvered through the parking lot to carry the disgraced politician away to the Colorado Mental Health Institute at Fort Logan. However, about a dozen elk chose the same moment to cross the street behind the courthouse. And, as was the custom in Dog Mountain, the transport vehicle waited for the animals to pass. Inside the truck, even Oaks and his armed escort had to smile.

The elk moved on and the transport van pulled away. JC and Bip interviewed residents near the courthouse about the arrest of Oaks.

Most of the man-on-the-street interviews expressed shock. Some said that politicians can't be trusted. One woman said that she always knew the ski resort would come to no good.

JC telephoned Oaks' home in Durango. A woman identifying herself as Oaks' wife, Brenda, told him that it was all a terrible mistake. She said that she loved her husband and hung up the phone.

Inside the courthouse, a meeting convened comprised of District Judge Victoria Rodriguez, District Attorney John Abelman and a defense attorney from Denver, Landon McNally, who would now be representing Jon Oaks.

"Gentlemen," the judge said from behind her desk inside her chambers. "I want to ask where we're going with this. John?"

"Your Honor," District Attorney John Abelman began. "I plan to prosecute Congressman Oaks no differently than if he was a guy who worked at the beer distributor. The law is the law."

"Oh, come on, John," the defense attorney from Denver reacted. "Jon Oaks is not a guy who works at the beer distributor. He's a guy who has done a hundred good things for this state. And he's harmless. He had a *consensual* affair. She wanted to break up and he didn't. That's sad, but not criminal."

"He terrorized the woman, Landon," the D.A. protested. "He threatened to sell her eleven-year-old daughter to the sex trade! If he worked for the beer distributor, he'd get one to three years in prison."

"It's a misdemeanor, John," the defense attorney rebutted. "You've got him on harassment and nothing more. This isn't the crime of the century. If you prove all your claims, he'll get six months."

"No," the district attorney insisted. "He'll be facing a charge of felony menacing. That's one to three years."

"Is that what you intend to do with the congressman?" the defense attorney blurted. "You're going to imprison a former congressman for three years because he didn't want to stop sleeping with his mistress? We've had presidents who did worse."

"John," Judge Rodriguez inserted. "The defense has a point. While the facts are salacious, does this amount to much more than bad behavior by a jilted lover?"

"Judge," the district attorney stated. "We can't allow our judgment to be altered by the fact we know Jon Oaks personally."

"Mister District Attorney," the judge sternly responded. "If you're suggesting that I am applying the law differently because of my past political relationship with the defendant, I advise you to tread cautiously."

"I am not suggesting that, Your Honor," Abelman quickly replied. Now he was on the defensive. "Forgive me if I gave you that impression. We *all* know Jon Oaks. I've even been to a party at his home in Durango.

"You asked my intentions, Judge, and I believe I have provided you with a clear answer. He terrorized that woman. I plan to prosecute this case with vigor."

The defense attorney rolled his eyes and muttered something that neither the judge nor the D.A. heard well, but certainly understood.

"Alright," Judge Rodriguez said with a sigh. "We'll proceed then. Let's see how things go with the psychiatric evaluation and we'll set a date for the bail hearing."

News Director Pat Perilla called JC and told him to edit a straight package regarding the court proceedings and send it back to the station. That meant they wouldn't be doing a live shot that evening and had the rest of the day off.

"But call me at home tomorrow, JC," Perilla said. "We have things to discuss."

Tomorrow would take care of itself, JC thought. The afternoon was free to ski.

Minnie Crouse was an accomplished woman. It was said that she built her cabin with her own hands in 1906, when she was twenty-four years old.

She borrowed books to read from a prominent Scotsman named John Jarvie, who owned the local general store and ran the post office.

Crouse's father was an influential man in Browns Park, known to close a deal with a handshake or a fistfight. He was said to have shot one man to death and was suspected of killing others.

"I like the name of this mountain," Robin said as they rode to the top of the ski area in a gondola. "Dog Mountain. Why did they call it Minnie's Gap when the actual mountain is called Dog Mountain? Who doesn't like dogs?"

"Sure," JC said, casting a sidelong glance at Bip.

"This is my favorite temperature!" JC reminded them as they walked from the gondola at the top of the mountain. It was twenty-seven degrees and sunny. They clicked into their bindings and pushed off.

They warmed up skiing cruisers named Butch and Sundance. JC snapped race turns and Bip carved gracefully on his snowboard.

They graduated to more challenging runs called Bible Back and Old Cut Rocks. They were nicknames of mountain men who trapped beaver in Browns Park nearly a century ago.

Robin was a mogul skier. They found two runs for her called Turk and Lion. The bumps made JC's surgical knees ache a bit. Robin, on the other hand, skied like she was on springs.

On the ride up a chairlift a local skier told them that Turk and Lion were the names of the oxen belonging to Snapping Annie. JC remembered that as the name of a bar in the resort village.

From the chairlift, JC saw a racing course set up for training.

"Do you guys mind if I run a few gates?" JC asked Robin and Bip.

"Come on," Bip said to Robin. "Let him flirt with another orthopedic procedure. I'll take you to some cool bumps near here."

Arranging to meet later, JC skied down to the race course. He recognized the man he met at the party.

"Does the offer stand?" JC asked. Told that he was welcome to train with the other racers, JC approached the top of the training course and pushed off.

"You're late!" JC scolded himself after a few gates, unhappy with his skiing. "Angulate!"

The reminders produced better results. His turns were precise. He began to ride the rails.

"That was impressive," the man from the party said after they took a few runs in the race course. "You should join us for the next race."

"I'd like that," JC said. He thanked the racers and headed for Bip and Robin, who waited nearby.

The three of them followed the sun for the rest of the day, riding a gondola, two six-packs and two quad chairs.

"This is my beach!" JC declared. It was one of his favorite declarations when he was skiing. Bip and Robin laughed. They'd heard it before.

There was over two thousand feet of vertical to ski, top to bottom. But JC liked to think of it as bottom to top. On top of a mountain, wearing a pair of skis, he felt like he was closer to heaven.

17

"They ate a dog!!??"

Robin sat up in bed abruptly.

Only moments ago, JC had pulled Robin into his arms, reclining in bed and looking through the window at the arrival of morning on the slopes of Minnie's Gap.

Robin had repeated her affection for the name of the mountain that the ski runs spilled down, Dog Mountain.

"Why didn't they just name the ski resort Dog Mountain? Everyone likes dogs. Think of the cute patches and stickers they could have," she said.

"It might have required a lot of explaining," JC said. "To guests."

"I don't follow," Robin said, lying comfortably on his chest.

JC proceeded to tell Robin the story about how Dog Mountain got its name.

"They ate a dog!!??"

"And that may be the tale the ski resort developers didn't want to repeat again and again," JC said. "In the defense of that exploration party, they were starving."

"I don't care!" Robin protested. "You don't eat your dog!"

"In this case," JC said, trying to mitigate the circumstances, "I think they were *very* starving."

"Good," she said. "I hope they starved to death."

"They didn't," he said, "because they ate the dog."

"Didn't they like the dog?" she asked.

"Actually," JC informed her, "I think they did. One of the explorers wrote that it tasted like mutton."

"That's disgusting," Robin said as she settled back into JC's arms. "I'm never eating meat again."

They laid in bed, nearly dozing off again. There was a light snow falling. The forecast stated that two to four inches was expected to collect.

"That was not how I expected the dog story to end," Robin said in a pout.

"I think the dog felt the same way," JC told her.

JC and Robin knocked on Bip's door and they walked downstairs to breakfast in the Rendezvous. Sunny was their waitress again. When Bip and Sunny exchanged greetings, JC had the impression that it hadn't been too long since they last saw each other.

"I've got to get this," JC said when his phone rang and he looked at the number. He rose from the table and walked out of the dining room.

"Who is calling that he doesn't want us to hear?" Bip asked as he watched JC walk away.

"I don't know what it is. But listen, you and I need to interview Gerhard Snyder," Robin said. "We're set up for after lunch."

"What did you think of Snyder?" Bip asked. "I can't think of anything he said that was offensive, but he gave me a bad vibe."

"Yeah, I got that too," Robin said.

"I just spoke with Pat," JC said as he returned to the table and pushed his phone back into his pocket.

"That's the conversation you couldn't conduct in front of us?" Bip asked. "He's our boss too. Unless you're complaining about us."

"No, nothing like that," JC said. "Sorry about leaving the table. Let's eat and I'll fill you in on what Pat told me."

Sunny brought their coffee and released them to fill up on the buffet. It was spread out over seven tables. JC and Robin headed for stainless steel chafers containing French toast and bacon.

"What was the call about?" she asked him. "Not the call from Pat. The other one."

"I'll tell you about it later," he answered. "But do you have any plans for Valentine's Day?"

"Are you asking me out on a date?" she asked.

"Yep. I have a resort in mind," he told her.

"Somewhere warm?"

"It's a constant sixty-seven degrees if you stay indoors," he responded. "Pat likes the Oaks story. He just told me he wants us to stay here at Minnie's Gap."

A new forecast was calling for more snowfall the next day. It was stoking the prospect of powder skiing at Minnie's Gap on Dog Mountain.

That would lure more skiers and snowboarders to the ski resort, where Jon Oaks was still listed on the company stationery as the managing partner.

Oaks was currently confined to a Colorado state mental hospital for evaluation. But Minnie's Gap was his baby. And his business partners were trying to evaluate if their mammoth investment was worth it, or if Oaks really was out of his mind.

18

"Call me Jerry," Gerhard Snyder said to Robin and Bip.

He had said that to her the other night when they met in the bar at the hotel. He told nearly everyone to call him Jerry. But they seldom did. Most people didn't like him very much. Thinking of him as Gerhard, rather than Jerry, might keep him at a distance.

It wasn't that he was a pariah in Lonesome County, or in Denver. He was a rich and successful developer. Who couldn't use one of those?

But that wasn't how he got started in the real estate business. And his initial dalliance into investment properties was still a significant contributor to his wealth. He was a slumlord.

In Denver, the public knew him as a builder of commercial properties and high-density residential construction. But the business that he did not publicize, that escaped the attention of casual observers, was the one that owned entire blocks of rentals for the poor. Their rent was subsidized by very reliable monthly government checks.

In Lonesome County, when he built housing for employees of the new ski resort, he deliberately proposed and built an inadequate number. That meant more housing would be needed than the ski resort could offer their workers.

So, Gerhard Snyder went about obtaining old mobile homes around the country and towing them to the Town of Dog Mountain. Renters with nowhere else to turn then paid too much money to put those roofs over their head.

Occupants of the new employee housing that he did construct, as well as occupants who lived in the trailers that Snyder owned in the town, complained about their living conditions. They said that cold air blew in through cracks around the windows. They claimed that electrical outlets didn't work. Some of the ceiling lights had water collecting in the glass shades. There was a rodent problem.

It didn't matter, really. Snyder's renters had nowhere else to go.

"Thank you for seeing me on a Sunday," Robin said, opening the interview with the developer.

"Think nothing of it," he responded. "I work every day. Sunday is no exception."

Robin asked Snyder about a shotgun that was leaning in a corner of the office. It was within his reach when he sat at the desk.

"It's a message to my renters," Snyder said. "The message is: don't threaten me and don't think you can intimidate me. Pay your rent on time and we'll get along just fine."

"Have you ever had to use it on a renter?" Robin asked.

"Once a guy, a big scary guy, came into my office telling me that he wasn't going to pay his rent," Snyder said. "And he didn't mean that he wasn't going to pay it that month. He meant that he was never intending to pay it and there was nothing I could do about it."

"That's when I leaned my chair back and reached for my shotgun," Snyder said as he smiled. "I pointed out to him that I knew exactly where he lived, which was about two hundred feet from my office and one flight up."

"Did it work?" Robin asked.

"It did!" he laughed. "And he became one of my best renters. He pays on time every month. It wasn't that he couldn't pay it. He was testing me. I guess I passed the test."

"Have you ever shot anyone with that thing?" Robin asked.

"No, no," Snyder said. "That's as close as I ever came."

Snyder wore clothing that suggested he belonged to the middle class. But Robin had done her homework. He was quite wealthy, and still only in his forties.

She supposed that he dressed below his net value when he was working, so he didn't cause resentment from the unfortunates who rented from him. They might even target him for an armed robbery if they knew how much money he carried on him.

Robin saw the cheap suit and tie that he was wearing, but also noticed the gold cufflinks and $600 shoes on his feet.

He drove a ten-year-old car to work each day. But in a magazine layout, she had seen him leaning against his British sports car. It was priced well into six figures.

She asked him about the development he had proposed in suburban Denver.

"Opponents to its approval say it is on protected wetlands," she told him.

"They're not wetlands," he told her. "They were probably misidentified when a surveyor was mapping fifty years ago. I'm working with the town to change the designation."

"Your opponents say there is an ecosystem on that property that is reflective of wetlands," she pointed out.

"There really isn't," he answered. "I've walked that property. I didn't even see a frog."

"You purchased that property for almost nothing," Robin noted. "The man who sold it to you said it was worthless because it was wetlands and couldn't be developed."

"Well, he passed up a good business opportunity," Snyder said. "But some people are hunters and some people stay back at camp and cook what the hunters bring back. This hasn't changed since we were cavemen. Hunters were honored. The cowards were merely tolerated. I'm a hunter."

She began to ask another question, but Snyder interrupted.

"Do you want to go get a drink?" he asked.

"No, thank you," Robin replied.

"How about another time?" he asked. "May I call you?"

"No," she told him. "I don't date newsmakers. It's a conflict of interest."

"Well," he said, "what if I don't do interviews with you. Then, there won't be a potential for conflict, right?"

She almost formulated her next rejection to start by saying, "I appreciate your interest but ..." That would be the polite way. But she did not appreciate his interest. She thought he was a pig.

"Mr. Snyder," she said instead, "I have a job to do. So do you. I think *my* job here is finished." She gave Bip the signal to wrap up his camera gear. The interview was over.

"I'll be waiting outside," she told Bip. "Thank you, Mr. Snyder."

"I thought you gave up meat," JC said to Robin as they ate dinner with Bip at the Peg Leg restaurant.

"Dog meat, yeah," she said.

"What did you order?" Bip asked.

"Chicken," she said. "Why?"

"It doesn't look like chicken," Bip said. "It looks like Chihuahua."

"Ha, ha," she mocked.

They were dining in the ski resort village after JC's live shot.

Their waitress wore a puffy skirt with designs of horseshoes and six-guns on it. She brought them three beers. At Bip's recommendation, they all had some of the Storm Peak, beer brewed in Steamboat Springs.

Robin's phone rang. Connecting the call, she mouthed to JC and Bip that it was their news director, Pat Perilla.

"I got a call at my home this evening," Perilla said. "It was from the developer, Gerhard Snyder. You interviewed him today?"

"Yes, I did," Robin answered.

"Well, he says he has a problem," the news director told her. "He says he rearranged his busy schedule to give you an interview. He says he knows that you are a new reporter and he wanted to give you a break."

"Okay," Robin said. She didn't like where she thought this conversation was going.

"He says that your questions were, let's see, I have it written down here," Perilla stated. "He says that your questions were naïve and unprofessional. And he says that he forbids us from airing that interview. He told me that he could ask his attorney to convey the message to me, if that was necessary."

"Oh?" It was all the response that Robin could come up with. She tried not to sound either shocked or nervous. The truth was, she was both. "What did you say?"

"He confirmed that he had agreed to the interview at his office. He also confirmed that he allowed you into his office, and he confirmed that he allowed Bip to place a lapel microphone on his jacket. And he confirmed that when Bip pointed his camera at Snyder and you asked a question, he started speaking."

"That's all true, sir," Robin said into the phone.

"I'll tell you what I told Mr. Snyder," Perilla said. "I said, 'Well Mr. Snyder, if your lawyer is worth the money you're paying him, he will tell you that there's nothing you can do.

"'It's not our fault that he gave an interview or that he said something that he now regrets. We plan to air the interview.'"

Robin felt the pit in her stomach dissipate. Perilla had defended her.

"Anything to add?" he asked.

"He hit on me," Robin said. She instantly worried that she'd pressed her luck.

"Good," the news director said. "We'll add that to the record if Snyder's attorney calls.

"Robin, you are a good reporter. You're honest and intelligent. Don't let guys like this buffalo you. And as long as I'm around, I won't let them, either."

"Thank you, Pat," she said with relief.

"When will your story be ready?" he asked.

"Tomorrow?" she said.

"Good. Write it, ask Bip to edit it and let's get it on the air tomorrow. You can go live somewhere in the town. Work it out with JC. I expect him to have a story too, so you'll have to decide on a location for our live shot that suits both of you."

Perilla ended the call. Robin thought for a moment about what had just happened and then a smile appeared on her face.

"Pat Perilla is a good guy," she said, and proceeded to tell her colleagues about the call.

Finishing their beer, the three journalists left the Peg Leg. Bip told them he was returning to his room to call it an early night.

JC and Robin stopped to sit on a bench by an outdoor fire. It was burning within a circular steel sculpture linking four images of a cowboy riding a bucking bronco.

A storm was on the way, but the sky was still cloudless and the stars above were bright.

JC told Robin that he was becoming fond of looking at the stars at night. He liked thinking that he was looking at the very same stars that humans were looking at thousands of years ago.

"It makes me feel closer to those people, and the whole human experiment," he said to her.

He said that he didn't know a lot about constellations, but he pointed out Orion's Belt.

"I read that two of the stars on the belt were the god and goddess of skiing," he told her.

"There was a god and goddess of skiing?" she asked.

"The pagans thought so. The gods were named Ullr and Skadi," he said. He laughed to himself as he thought of Hemingway.

"And you know of Ullr and Skadi how?" she asked.

"I know one of their relatives, sort of," he smiled.

19

"He was murdered by two men who robbed his store," JC told Robin.

They were standing in a small cemetery next to a Browns Park landmark, Lodore Hall. John Jarvie's grave overlooked the Green River. His final resting place was decorated by rocks and some fake flowers. The marker said he was murdered in 1909.

"He and his wife, Nell, built a hut from logs when they first arrived in Browns Park in 1880," JC told her. "He was an immigrant from Scotland. He loaned Minnie Crouse books to read."

"You've gone 'history geek' on me again, haven't you?" Robin said.

"I remember reading about how he would ice skate on the Green River when it was frozen in the winter. His white beard was so long it would almost sail behind him," JC told Robin. "People here loved him. He ran a store, the post office, a ferry.

"When he was murdered, a posse was formed, but his killers were never caught." JC looked over the landscape like he could see its history unfolding. Robin admired that in him. He could envision past events like they were unfolding before his eyes.

"It's my superpower," he'd once told her with a laugh.

Robin and JC had decided to spend the morning exploring Browns Park. Bip was editing her story, including the interview with Gerhard Snyder. It would air that night.

They had climbed out of bed early. JC wanted to watch sunrise at the Gates of Lodore, the narrow waterway that was one of the few passages into the park. There was a steep but short hike up to a vantage point.

Sunrise appeared to set a match to the rocks. The stone turned a fiery red when the morning sun first hit it.

"I've never seen anything quite like this," Robin said, still catching her breath from the climb.

They shared a cold cinnamon roll and a thermos of hot coffee as they sat on a rock and watched the sun move across the rock above the Green River.

Back in their car, they stopped at old Browns Park School, where children of all ages used to crowd into one schoolroom. Now, rabbits lived under the front stairs.

The school building was still a gathering place for local residents, having no store or tavern or post office. Not like in the day of John Jarvie.

Of course, park neighbors could now go to the town of Dog Mountain for social mingling. It was much closer than Rock Springs. They viewed that as a blessing and a curse.

Each year, Browns Park hosted "Wild Bunch Day." They celebrated the old days when the outlaws lived there. There was a flea market, a bake sale, games and crafts and music.

On every other day, Browns Park looked like it did today. Barren and beautiful.

JC and Robin stopped to examine old log cabins, places outlaws could use as hideouts.

Most of the cabins were collapsing into the soil. There were so many historic artifacts, but too few tourists to pay to preserve them.

Sometimes, the couple would just stop to scan the land. Everything they saw was untouched by man.

"Look at that butte," Robin said.

"It sure is a beaut," JC responded. They exchanged a smile.

Most of the time, theirs was the only car they could see in either direction on Colorado 318. Once in a while, a pickup truck would pull onto the highway from a dirt road. Many pulled four-wheelers on a trailer. The dirt buggies were useful utility vehicles on the loose soil, lousy roads and pasture.

Snow had begun falling. It was the beginning of the storm coming their way.

Snow in the mountains would eventually melt and provide cold clear water to the brown landscape. It would provide valuable sustenance to everyone and everything. Cattle, deer and coyote would drink the water. Cottonwoods and willows would come alive along the creeks in springtime.

Another principal product in this land of cheatgrass, greasewood, sagebrush, ravines and rocks was … silence. There was simply no sound other than the wind. That wasn't something easily found by modern man.

"This is all going to end, isn't it?" Robin asked as she surveyed the landscape. There was sadness in her voice.

"The silence?" JC asked. "The way time has bypassed this place? Will it have to change because a ski resort has opened down the road? Probably." He felt the same regret. "If it wasn't the ski area, it would be something else."

"We should probably get back," Robin said. "Thank you for bringing me here. It's magical."

They drove up Beaver Creek, turned onto Route 72 and passed below Diamond Peak. When the land opened up and got flat, they passed pumpjacks, each swinging like an ax to pull oil out of the ground. Snow was beginning to cover the road.

Robin stared out the window at a strange tree just on the other side of a knoll. The pine was without a single needle and obviously dead. It stood tall with its branches bare, almost bleached white by the sun. She thought it looked like a skeleton, a Halloween decoration.

That evening, with snow falling steadily, Robin went live from downtown Dog Mountain. She used the interview she had taped with Snyder.

JC provided a short update on the Jon Oaks arrest, saying the former congressman was expected back in court the next day for a bail hearing.

The satellite truck they were using was on loan from a TV newsroom in Grand Junction. Deals like this were not uncommon. It left the Denver TV station owing the TV station in Grand Junction a favor to be cashed in on later. Plus, Grand Junction could use and report anything that JC and Robin uncovered.

Walking away from their satellite truck, the crew from Denver grabbed a bite at the Stagecoach Stop. Dr. Hunter Anderson stopped by their table.

"I'm on my way home," he said. "I just finished eating. Why don't you come out to my house after your dinner. I'll have a bonfire going and brush the snow off of some chairs. Dress warm."

Following dinner, JC and the others stopped by their hotel to change into warmer clothing. Robin put on the old high school letter jacket that JC had given her.

"It's a tiny house," Dr. Anderson told them as he welcomed his guests inside. "That's the name that's stuck, as they become more popular. I guess that makes me a minimalist."

"It's about the same size as the little dugouts settlers used to live in around here," Robin told him. "We were looking at some today, in Browns Park."

"That's what I'm told," Anderson responded. "But they had dirt floors. I've got carpet, hardwood floors with heating coils beneath, a hot shower, electric range and a satellite TV. I'm not roughing it."

The tour of the doctor's 250-square-foot home fascinated them but did not take very long. He pointed out clever uses of every possible spot. The risers on a narrow staircase leading up to his bed could be pulled out and used as drawers. A tall cabinet concealed an ironing board. Another cabinet folded out into a desk. His cowboy hat hung on a peg.

"I have ten more on order," he said of his tiny house. "They don't have all the luxuries that this one does, but they're pretty nice."

"What are you going to do with ten more?" Robin asked.

"I have a proposal before the town board on Wednesday," he said. "The planning board already voted in my favor. I bought a five-acre lot on the other side of town. I want to place ten tiny houses on a circular road there. I plan to rent them. I think it will work. I already have an option to buy more land and I'd like to put more tiny houses on it."

"Is it a good investment?" JC asked.

"I've done the numbers," the doctor said. "It's a great investment. Those things would be the gift that keeps on giving."

"Do you expect any opposition to your plan?" JC asked. "It sounds like everybody wins. You're the only one taking a financial risk."

"There's really only one landlord in a town this size who owns a considerable number of units," Anderson explained. "He's opposing me. His name is Gerhard Snyder. He seems to be really pissed off about the whole thing."

"I've met him," Robin said with a sour expression on her face.

"I'm told that he drove here from Denver as soon as the ski resort was announced," the doctor told them. "He purchased the cheapest land on the end of town and threw old rusty mobile homes on the lot."

"He's been accused of doing the same sort of stuff in Denver," Robin told him.

"Well, it sounds like he's doing everything he can to get town hall here to vote against my project," Anderson told them. "We will see. I am not a political guy at all. I just have an idea that I think will work."

Anderson still had his arm in a sling, but he pulled it out on occasion and stretched it.

"Anybody like hot buttered rum?" the doctor asked. "It will keep the chill away. Let's go sit by the fire."

Before the arrival of his guests, Anderson had prepared the drinks in a pot and let it warm on the stones of the fire he built outside. He set out four chairs and covered them from the falling snow.

He pulled his hat off the peg and led them outside.

"I don't know when I last had hot buttered rum," Robin crooned as she settled into her seat with a hot drink. "I love this."

The others agreed and the fire pulled them into a trance as fires always seem to do.

"I have one more of these, you know," Dr. Anderson finally said, breaking the silence.

"Another tiny house?" JC asked.

"Yeah. It's up on Dog Mountain," he said. "It's a really beautiful spot. It's all by itself with a magnificent view of Diamond Peak. I go up there on the weekends, sometimes, just to be alone."

The snow stopped falling. They were sitting, staring at the flames of the fire and easing into bottles of Storm Peak beer provided by the doctor.

Cattle, belonging to a ranch that bordered Anderson's small plot, pressed against the fence and also stared at the fire.

"They want company," Robin giggled as she looked at the quiet gathering of livestock. Dr. Anderson had provided her with a blanket to wrap up in.

JC stood and approached the livestock. Bip followed him. They scratched behind the ears of the cows.

"They're Angus," JC told Bip. "The breed originated in Scotland."

Robin and Hunter Anderson were left alone at the fire. JC and Bip could be heard laughing in the background.

"You and JC seem like a solid couple," Anderson said.

"Yeah," she replied, looking over her shoulder at the two men and the cows. "He's a really good guy. What about you?"

"What about me, what?" Anderson answered.

"Are you in a relationship?" she asked.

The doctor smiled a little and poked at the fire with a stick.

"Never?" she prodded.

"Never is a long time," he said. "I was, a long time ago."

"It must have left an impression," she said. "You didn't try again?"

Anderson stood and collected two logs. He placed them on the fire and returned to his seat.

"She died," he said.

"Oh my God," Robin said quietly. "I'm so sorry. I shouldn't have pried. I'm afraid prying is becoming second nature to me. I'm not sure that I like it. It's what reporters do, though."

"It's alright," he assured her with a kind look. "I just haven't spoken about her in a long time."

"You loved her," Robin stated.

"I worshiped her," he said, reaching up to the brim of his headwear. "She gave me this cowboy hat."

"She's been gone a long time?"

"Yes," he disclosed, staring into the fire. "She died in a rock-climbing accident in the Alps."

Robin let out a small gasp.

"I'm sorry," she repeated.

"No, no," he told her. "It's alright. She was adventurous. She was a backcountry skier before it was cool. She'd explore primitive areas in Africa. She was attacked by a tiger once. She had some scars to prove it."

He smiled as he spoke.

"Up in the Arctic Circle, she was almost eaten by a polar bear," he laughed. "She flirted with death. It was her hobby."

"You were with her?" Robin asked.

"Not often enough," he answered. "We were married. But I had a busy practice as a doctor. It wasn't easy for me to take time off. And she was impulsive. She'd come up with an idea on Monday and be gone by Thursday. She was amazing."

Robin and Hunter Anderson listened as JC and Bip erupted in laughter, still petting the cows like large dogs.

"When she died, we didn't have any warning," he said softly. "We were happy and alive together, and then we weren't."

The fire popped. The two of them stared at the flames.

"It was a long time ago," the doctor repeated.

"Maybe it's time to try again," Robin said sweetly. "A romance, I mean."

"I know what you mean," he said, turning his head to smile at her. Then he shook his head. "It comes with too much risk. Too high a cost."

JC and Bip left the cattle and returned to their chairs.

"We've arranged to meet our new friends at the bar tomorrow night," JC said.

"The cows?" Robin said with doubt in her voice.

"Yeah," JC acknowledged. "They are quite attached to us. I named one after you. The pretty one."

Everyone giggled a bit and returned their attention to the fire.

"We'll have to finish this discussion at another time," Anderson said to Robin in a hushed tone.

"I'm sorry," she responded. "I shouldn't have poked my nose in your business."

"Not at all," he quickly responded. "It feels good to talk about her. It's a little like having her back for just a moment. I'll fill you in on the rest, next time. There's plenty of time for that."

"Tell Robin and Bip about your theory that we have nine lives to look forward to," JC said to the doctor.

"It's what first got me thinking about it, what we were just talking about," Anderson said to Robin. "Have you ever died?"

"I don't understand," Robin said, looking at him.

"Sorry," Anderson said. Then he turned his eyes to Bip.

"Bip?" he said. "Have you ever died?"

"You tell me," Bip laughed. "You're the doctor." Anderson and the others laughed too.

"Seriously," Dr. Anderson decided to resume. "There are some who believe you might have died three, four or even five times by this stage in your life."

He proceeded to share his theory with them, as he had with JC over lunch. He told them about the Egyptians and the Celtics and present-day folklore regarding cats.

"Think back in your life," he said as he looked at Robin and Bip, but mostly Robin. "Was there an event that made you wonder how you survived?"

"I went to a lecture once," Bip said. "I thought I was going to be bored to death." They laughed some more.

"We've all been to something like that," Anderson said patiently. "Robin, can you think of anything?"

"My mother said that she thought she was going to lose me only a few months after I was born," Robin said seriously. "She said that I had some illness that was going around. The doctor asked her who she would like to perform last rites."

"Wow," Anderson said reverently. "It must have been a relief for her when you bounced back."

"I'm sure," Robin agreed.

"Can you think of another?" Dr. Anderson asked.

"A horse accident," she said. "I fell from a horse when I was probably four years old. I don't remember it, but my parents said that I just laid there. I was out cold. They were certain that I was dead."

Dr. Anderson said nothing. He just gave her a reassuring look.

"It's weird," Robin said. "You don't think about any of this stuff. But since you asked me, these memories have come rushing back to me."

"That's how I reacted," JC said to her in a soft voice. "I don't think I had ever compiled a list. But no one had ever asked me a question like that."

"I count the avalanche as the end of my eighth life," Anderson said.

"You have already burned eight lives?" Bip exclaimed.

"Bip," Robin exclaimed. "That's not nice."

"Sorry," Bip apologized.

"No problem. I was in the military," the doctor responded. "Some combat situations. I think I used up a few lives there."

"You were in an avalanche?" Robin asked, unaware of the incident less than a month ago.

"My fault, I had so much to catch you up on," JC said. "I neglected to tell you about Hunter's experience. Frightening."

After being prodded, Hunter Anderson recalled the terror of being buried beneath an avalanche.

"So, you only have one life left?" Robin asked, somewhat alarmed.

"That's alright," Anderson said. "We're not obligated to use all nine. And one life might last, well, a lifetime."

"Couldn't this interfere with your role as a doctor?" Bip asked. "If you knew that a sick patient in your office was on his ninth life, might you just decide that their time had come?"

"I understand what you're saying," Anderson responded. "But I don't ask my patients how many lives they think they've gone through. There's no survey that my receptionist hands them when they enter my office."

They all gave it some thought, staring into the fire.

"I thought of another, you know," JC said with a grin.

"Another time your life may have ended?" the doctor asked.

"Sadly, yes," JC nodded. "I was climbing around the old quarries in Marble, probably ten years ago."

"An amazing place," the doctor said. "Near Aspen."

"Yeah. I was careless," JC said. "I jumped about eight feet down from one level to the next, and I stumbled. I was going to fall to the next level. The next level was about two hundred feet down.

"Just as my heart began to race, I saw an old rusty cable resting on the marble platform. I grabbed it and thankfully it was secured to something. I really would have died in the fall."

Robin looked at him as though she had just lived through it. There was a worried look on her face.

"You guys are clumsy," Bip snickered. "I can't think of one instance when I thought I was a goner."

"Good," JC told him with a smirk. "The next time we have to go somewhere dangerous, you're going in front of us."

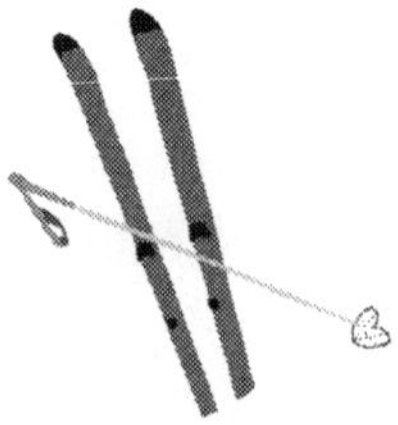

20

"He's not dead."

JC turned to Robin, not having a clue what she was telling him.

"Normally, that's good news," JC said to her. "But you don't look so happy."

She was glum. She was sitting on the bed they shared in the hotel. Bip was expecting them downstairs for breakfast.

"My father," she said, not able to look at JC. "He's not dead."

"Your father isn't dead?" JC repeated with a surprised look on his face. "But you told me he was dead. Being dead is really starting to get confusing. Do you have more than one father?"

"Only one," she said, tears brimming in her eyes. "But he didn't want to be my father anymore."

She started crying. She raised her hands to cover her eyes. She didn't like anyone to see her crying.

JC sat on the bed next to her and folded her into his arms.

He was bewildered. The conversation didn't make sense.

"I told everyone I met that my father was dead because he wouldn't talk to me," she said, and then resumed sobbing.

She held JC and cried with her head buried in his shoulder. He stroked her hair and said nothing.

"I didn't want to be one of those people who didn't talk to their family," she managed to say as she grabbed breaths between sobs. "The sister or brother who got mad and refused to talk to her own parents and siblings. It never made sense to me, and then my own father stopped talking to me."

JC knew people like that. It surprised him how many families he knew like that.

"So, I just told people that my father was dead, to avoid having a conversation about it. It was a terrible choice, but I was so hurt."

She said it without removing her face from his sweater.

"And then, I started falling in love with you," she sobbed. "And I had this lie that I had already told you."

She cried harder.

It all could have been overwhelming. JC worked to keep a calm head. She had a father who wasn't dead. And he wondered if there were more things she made up. And she just told him she was falling in love.

"I never wanted it. We had a big argument and he just stopped talking to me," she told JC as she pushed herself off of his shoulder and wiped her eyes with a tissue that he handed her. "I had just come to work for the TV station. I didn't know anyone. So, I just told people that he was dead. I just didn't want to talk about it."

She looked at him. Her eyes were red, but there came a look of recognition.

"Oh, yeah. The love thing," she said with a little laugh. "Sorry. We'll unpack all of that later."

"That's fine," he said with a gentle smile, grabbing a strand of her red hair.

"When was the last time you spoke with your father?" JC asked.

"Three years ago," she said. She was still dabbing her eyes. "Less than a year after my mom died. She wouldn't have let this happen. She was the only one who could tell him what to do. He's so stubborn."

JC handed her more tissues. He wondered what triggered the falling out between Robin and her father. But he knew that she would tell him in her own time.

"You told me that you saw his ghost," he said to her.

She began to cry again and sank her face into his chest. Her shoulders heaved and he could feel the heat of her body. He wrapped his arms around her.

"I did," she squeaked.

JC didn't say what he was thinking, that her father couldn't be a ghost if he wasn't dead.

"I guess I imagined it," she told him, not removing her face from his chest. "I guess I wanted him to tell me everything was going to be alright. It was so real."

JC was bewildered. He continued to hold her, and she continued to cry.

"Now you think I'm horrible," she said. "You think I'm a liar and wonder what else I lied about."

She began to shake, her head still not leaving his chest. He held her and they remained that way for some time. He reached into the space between them, handing her tissues.

"I didn't sleep at all last night," she told him, picking her head up off of his chest and sniffling. "All this talk about nine lives and I can't even get one right, with my father."

"Yeah, nine lives can seem like nine times the trouble, can't it?" he said to her. "It's so hard to do it right, even once."

"He called me," she told JC.

"Your father called you?" he responded. "After three years?"

She nodded.

"He called the other day," she said. "He said that he was sorry. And I said that I was sorry. He said that life is too short to let this go on any longer."

"That's fantastic," JC said. "Isn't it?"

She nodded, with a slight smile.

"I'm sorry," she said. "You must think I'm so weird. You can break up with me, if you want."

"That's not what I want," he said to her softly, taking her into his arms again. "I'm sorry that your father hurt you."

"I think we're getting a new life," she said.

So, if her father had lived, say, seven lives, did he now get one back? JC wondered that. But now was not the time to say it out loud.

21

"I was a reporter then. I went there intending to interview a woman who personally knew Butch Cassidy. She was about one hundred years old. I was stunned to learn that such a woman existed. We got there with our camera, and we were told that she had just died."

Pat Perilla, their news director, was on speakerphone. He was telling JC, Bip and Robin a story about the first time he traveled to Browns Park, as a young reporter at KJCT-TV in Grand Junction.

"That would have been in the late 1970s or early 1980s," he said on speakerphone. "I had more hair then and I wasn't fat."

"I'm sure you were a babe magnet back then," Robin told him, massaging his ego.

"Yeah," he said sarcastically. "Anyway, I have to get back to watching a Roomba clean my office. Corporate bestowed this little computerized vacuum cleaner on me. I have to admit, I find myself drawn to just watching it crawl across my carpet and bump into things. Good luck today. It sounds like you have a good story."

Perilla hung up and the news crew finished their breakfast.

"Would you like some more coffee?" JC asked his colleagues. He commenced to pour coffee in all three mugs and put the pot down. Bip and Robin were looking at him.

"What?" he asked.

"It's not just cooking, is it?" Bip asked rhetorically. JC gave him a puzzled look.

"You can't pour three cups of coffee without spilling," Bip said, waving his hand at the fresh coffee soaking into the tablecloth.

"It doesn't stop there," Robin chimed in with a grin. "He can't eat a meal without missing his mouth. He can't sit still."

"That's what it is! He can't stop moving his mouth," Bip laughed.

"Yep, that's me," JC said humbly. "I'm quite a catch." He patted Robin's thigh. "You're a lucky gal."

From their hotel, they drove to the county courthouse in Dog Mountain. Jon Oaks was back from the state mental institution. The district attorney had a fresh psychological evaluation to present to the judge. The defense wanted bail set so Oaks could go home.

Bip remained outside the courthouse with the other TV and newspaper photographers, hoping to get fresh footage of Oaks in shackles as he climbed from the transport vehicle.

The snow had resumed overnight. The parking lot of the courthouse had been plowed just before it was opened for employees to park their cars.

Inside the courtroom, there was more representation in the spectator's gallery than at Oaks' first appearance. This time, TV from Durango, Grand Junction and other Denver television stations joined JC there. There were also five newspapers represented.

JC took a quick look around the courtroom to see who was there of interest. He was curious to see if Roman Holiday would be there. She wasn't.

Oaks was escorted into the courtroom in shackles. He looked like a man who had just returned from a camping trip. He had tried his best to clean up.

His hair was combed but it looked greasy. He had been allowed to change out of the orange prison jumpsuit. Instead, he wore a suit. It looked like something had slept on it.

He had dark rings around his eyes. His face was recently shaved but he looked older.

Judge Victoria Rodriguez came into the courtroom and Oaks stood, along with everyone else. For an instant, the judge looked at Oaks and nodded her head in a gesture of respect. It was a hard habit to break.

The judge had been selected to the bench, and then won election, after winning the support of Jon Oaks when he was a powerful congressman. She served as a judge in both Lonesome County and adjacent Moffat County.

There was no debate by the opposing attorneys in the Oaks case about whether a judge who was handpicked by

Oaks could fairly rule over the trial of Oaks. When it came to district judges in the smallest of counties, there were not many to choose from.

Acknowledging that the psych evaluation had been submitted, the judge asked the attorneys if they had anything to say. The well-dressed defense attorney for Oaks stood.

"I do, Your Honor," Landon McNally said. The judge nodded her permission for the defense counsel to speak his case.

"As Your Honor can see in the report," the attorney began, "Congressman Oaks was found to be infatuated with Ms. Roman Holiday. It is something he now regrets. But this was not always an unwanted pursuit, Your Honor. My client and the source of the allegations, Roman Holiday, were recently in a consensual sexual affair. And Ms. Roman Holiday is the *only* source of the allegations, I would like to point out. There is no string of other women claiming they were also stalked by my client."

"Your Honor," the defense continued, "my client would not oppose an order to avoid contact with Ms. Holiday. He simply wants to go home to Durango to be with his wife in their house of the past twenty-five years.

"Your Honor, Congressman Oaks is no flight risk. He is well-known in this state and has deep roots in this congressional district. We would ask for no bail, but release on his own recognizance."

The defense attorney sat back down behind his table. The judge moved her eyes, and little else, toward the district attorney. It was his time to speak.

"Thank you, Your Honor," District Attorney John Ableman began. "Just to more carefully describe the findings of the hospital, the report says that Jon Oaks' infatuation with Ms. Holiday was not ebbing. It was still intensifying. His calls and letters became more frequent and inflammatory, and his threats more outrageous, right up to the moment he was stopped.

"He took on a disguise. He suggested that Ms. Holiday's little girl might be kidnapped and sold into sex trafficking. And it was all so that he could trick Ms. Holiday back into their tryst.

"He invented the specter of a dangerous kidnapper," Abelman continued. "He posed as that kidnapper and then stepped forward as the man who could apprehend or kill the kidnapper. And it was all in the hope that Ms. Holiday would fall for his ruse and again become his lover.

"Your Honor, considering the defendant's imagination and skill as a con artist, we would ask the court to carefully weigh the safety to the public if he were to be released before trial."

"Anything else?" the judge asked, surveying the two attorneys, her bailiff and court reporter.

"Your Honor?"

The judge, with a surprised look, eyed the defense attorney who had just uttered his request to speak.

"Yes?" Judge Rodriguez said.

"Your Honor," the defense attorney repeated, "my client, not fully within my advice, would like to address the court."

The judge looked at Jon Oaks and considered the request. This was not the normal juncture at which the court heard from a defendant. But the judge nodded her approval in the direction of Oaks' attorney.

With that, Jon Oaks rose from behind the defense table and straightened his posture. He was, in just a moment's time, transformed from a shackled prisoner to a congressman and an admired businessman.

"Thank you, Your Honor," Oaks began in a clear and confident voice. "This court will, in coming months, determine my suitability to walk the streets with my fellow Coloradoans. I respect your responsibilities and your judgment.

"My actions have destroyed my lifetime of public service and terminated cause for anyone to bestow upon me their admiration. In simpler words, this is not my finest hour.

"I will freely acknowledge that I temporarily suffered from some delusion, and it manifested itself into an obsession. It was admittedly a mental health problem and without any order being necessary, I plan to pursue counseling. I will not allow myself to be a burden on my community or my family.

"I only hope to return home, to the only community I have claimed as a home for my entire life, to await the outcome of this court's decision. Thank you, Your Honor."

With that, Jon Oaks returned to his seat. Everyone else in the courtroom was in stunned silence.

"That's why I voted for the guy four times," one deputy whispered to another. "He could talk a grizzly bear out of one of her cubs."

"Thank you, gentlemen," said the judge. "This will be taken into consideration."

The judge dropped her gavel with a sharp rap and court was adjourned. Jon Oaks stood as the judge departed from the chambers. The defendant was then escorted out of the courtroom and taken to a cell in the county jail.

The decision from Judge Rodriguez came only hours later. Court was not reconvened. Jon Oaks was not walked back into the courtroom. The judge's chambers merely telephoned the office of each of the attorneys to tell them a decision had been reached.

Jon Oaks would be allowed bail as the maneuverings of his prosecution played out. He would be allowed to return home to Durango. Bail was set at five hundred thousand dollars.

"Does it pass the smell test?" JC would ask the district attorney in a hallway of the courthouse. A newspaper reporter from *The Grand Junction Daily Sentinel*, taking notes, stood next to Bip's camera.

"Does it pass the smell test?" District Attorney John Abelman would repeat back to the reporter. "Let's see. The congressman who placed this particular judge on the bench asks for leniency from that judge and gets it. The victim in this crime now has to wonder every night, every time she tucks her child into bed, if he's out there, watching them. Does it pass the smell test? Sure, it stinks to high heaven."

22

"I crave something that's bad for me," Robin told him.

"I thought that's why you kept me around," JC said.

"Besides you," she smiled. "I'm thinking of chicken wings or nachos or something."

After that night's last live shot, JC and Robin walked into Snapping Annie's, next to the hotel. They were seeking bar food for dinner. Bip strolled in a different direction, telling them he was having dinner with Sunny.

JC and Robin hadn't spoken more about that morning or about her father. JC felt that Robin would say more when she had more to say.

But telling him the truth already seemed to release Robin from unseen shackles. She pressed closer to him. She truly did not know if he would accept her, after admitting her moment of untruth. But how could they proceed, she had asked herself, without taking that risk.

Snapping Annie's was teeming with the après-ski crowd. Local ski bums had windburned faces and clothing that perfectly matched the requirements of that day's weather. The locals walked the room with the comfort that comes with familiarity. They greeted each other like members of the same fraternity.

Vacationers from other areas of the country wore jackets, sweaters and bib overalls that were pulled out only for occasional ski trips. The visiting skiers and snowboarders sagged at their tables and clutched their bottles of beer, happy but exhausted. The high altitude was taking its toll.

JC spotted a familiar face, disguised behind sunglasses and under a baseball cap. She was sitting alone at a booth in a dark corner of the bar.

"Hello, Roman," JC said.

"Hi, JC," she responded with a smile.

"Is this where you come to hide?" he inquired.

"Yeah. Being next to the hotel, most of these people are out-of-towners. Even most of the ski bums are just here for the winter. They don't know me," the actress said. "I had to get out of the house. Olive is at a friend's house, studying. I got tired of hiding behind the same four walls of my home. I needed different four walls to hide behind."

"How are you holding up?" he asked.

"Eh. I don't trust anything anymore," she said. "I used to assume the sun would come up each morning. Now, I'm not so sure."

Roman was eyeing Robin who winced as she listened quietly at JC's side.

"You've been betrayed," Robin then said to the actress.

"Who is this attractive woman, JC?" Roman inquired, her eyes locked on Robin.

"Roman, this is Robin Smith," he said. "We work together in Denver. She's a fine reporter."

Robin noticed that JC didn't introduce her as his girlfriend. She decided not to read anything into it.

"Sit," Roman said with a smile, moving to make more room.

"We won't be bothering you?" JC inquired.

"No. I'm ready for some company," Roman told them. "You are beautiful," Roman said to Robin.

"Hardly," Robin replied with a laugh. "Not next to you."

A server came by and took drink orders from JC and Robin while handing them menus. Robin only wanted water. JC ordered a beer from Salida called Soulcraft.

"I've had enough," Roman said, turning down another drink and turning to JC. "When you want something stronger, ask one of the locals for the beer they make in their own basement. There is a proud tradition of brewing *strong* beer on the ranches of Browns Park. No wonder they called it firewater."

"I remember you on TV," Robin said. "I loved your show. I felt like you were my friend."

"Thank you," Roman said. She was still wearing her dark glasses. "Unfortunately, casting directors told me that was the only character I had the talent to portray: 'The nice girl.'"

"It's better than being told you're a bitch," Robin said, smiling.

"Yeah, I suppose so," Roman said grudgingly. "But there are a lot of parts for a bitch. There's not much for Little Mary Sunshine."

"Have you heard about what happened in court today?" JC asked Roman.

"I heard," Roman said. "The district attorney called me after court."

"The D.A. said outside the courtroom that he didn't like the idea Oaks was going to be free on bail," JC told her. "He didn't want Oaks bothering you again."

"He won't," Roman said. "I don't know why I say that. I didn't think he'd put on a disguise and threaten to kidnap my daughter. That's just not the man I knew, or at least, the man I *thought* I knew."

"You're probably right," JC said. "He won't bother you."

JC wasn't really certain about the truth in his words, but he didn't want to worry the woman. It had occurred to him that Roman's ranch was so far removed from another house, Oaks could be waiting in the dark when she returned home. He would be free to stare at her through a window or even sneak in an open door.

"Benny Maple helped police catch Oaks?" Robin asked.

"Benny Ray was at my house," she said. "He called police when Jon—rather, the call that turned out to be Jon came through. That must have caused Jon's blood pressure to rise when he heard that. He hates Benny Ray."

"Really, why?" JC asked her.

"Benny Ray knew about our affair," Roman told him. "He's the only one who did. And he didn't approve. He didn't trust Jon. Benny Ray said that a married man who cheated on his wife couldn't be trusted."

Oaks had been ordered by the court to stay away from Roman and Olive. He had been fitted with an ankle bracelet, so the court could be sure of his whereabouts.

"I thought I loved him, at one time," Roman said. "I thought he had everything that I wanted in a man. Intelligence, maturity, passion."

"He was married," JC reminded her. Robin kicked him under the table.

"Yes, he was married," Roman acknowledged somberly. "It was something I conveniently overlooked. Over time, I knew it could only end in disaster. That's why I ended it."

"How did he take that?" JC asked.

"Not well," she said with a small laugh. "He was furious. He confronted me with all these arguments and ideas about why I was doing something foolish. But I knew I was right. I finally had to ask him to leave."

"Did he get violent?" Robin asked. "Did he lay a hand on you?"

"No," Roman quickly said. "Jon would never do that." Then she caught herself. "Listen to me. Obviously, I didn't understand how far he would go."

She put her hands to her mouth, as though she was about to be sick.

"He killed our dog," she whimpered. Behind her sunglasses, JC knew that her eyes were filling with tears.

JC handed her some napkins. Robin rubbed Roman's other hand.

"Are you willing to do an on-camera interview tomorrow?" JC gently requested. He felt a little guilty about asking, but he hadn't lost sight of his responsibilities as a journalist.

"I'm not. I'm sorry," Roman said, putting a momentary smile on her face. She was still composing herself as JC assured her that there was nothing to apologize for.

Robin filled the silence, telling Roman how much she liked her shirt. It was a gesture to make them all more comfortable. JC admired Robin's empathy for others.

"I've got to get this," JC said as his phone rang and he looked at the number. He rose from the booth and walked outside. Robin eyed him as he exited.

Roman pointed out a few people in the bar, telling Robin an interesting story about each one.

"Do you see him?" Roman pointed across the bar.

"I do. I met him," Robin said. "Frank-something, right?"

"Yes, Frank Green," Roman said with a smile. "He grew up in Browns Park for a while. We didn't know each other very well. We weren't the same age and he moved away when I was still young. I don't remember the details."

Roman pointed out a couple. She explained that they weren't married.

"She's married to another man," Roman told her. "The two men share her. The two men know each other. She'll go on vacation with her husband and then they'll come home and she'll go live with the other man for a week. It's very unorthodox."

"It must be a scandal," Robin suggested.

"You would think so," Roman smiled. "But everyone here knows about it. It's not something anyone is trying to hide. People just let them be. Everyone tries to be friendly with everyone."

Their conversation flowed easily. They talked about relationships. Robin felt the energy of Roman's unassuming sex appeal.

When JC returned to the table, Roman informed them that she had to pick up Olive. It was time for the study group to be over.

"Dress warm, you two," she said as she stood up. "There's a cold front coming. It's going to really get cold."

She pulled on her jacket and wrapped a scarf around her neck. She adjusted her ball cap with a smirk.

"Thank you, JC, for understanding," Roman said. She leaned in and gave him a kiss on the cheek.

"I'm so glad we had a chance to meet," she said to Robin. "I hope we'll be seeing each other again. Thanks for talking. I think I needed a woman to talk to." Roman leaned in and gave Robin a hug.

When Roman left, JC and Robin ordered a glass of wine for each of them. They were told it was alright to take them next door to the hotel.

"You and Roman seemed to have hit it off," JC said as they walked outside to the entrance of The Fort, their hotel. The snow had stopped falling.

"She's really nice," Robin said. "It's horrible, what she was put through."

"It sounded like you two shared a story that I wasn't privy to," he said. "What did you talk about?"

"Lots of things. Especially something that she wouldn't have told you," Robin said with a grin. "Not even if you talked to her for a month."

"Well," JC prodded her after waiting for her disclosure. "What did she tell you?"

"Wait until we get upstairs," Robin said softly. "It's not for anyone else's ears. I'll tell you while we savor our wine in our room."

Walking through the lobby, Robin touched the rough-cut posts and ran her hands over a saddle and soft animal furs hanging on the wall. JC watched her, admiring her feminine grace.

"I like this place," she said when they were in their room. She turned switches to illuminate two matching birch-bark lamps with canvas shades. "It's fun.

They relaxed on a faux leather couch, took off their shoes and put their feet up on the coffee table, sipping their wine.

"You're punishing me, aren't you?" he said to her after waiting some minutes for the big news he thought that she had.

"It kills you that I know something you don't," she said with a smile.

"Yep," he said, after failing to find a way to plausibly deny the fact.

"Roman is in love with Benny Ray Maple," Robin said.

"She told you that?" JC blurted.

"Yes, she told me. And it's not for anyone else's ears," Robin replied. "I don't think anyone else knows.

"Not even Benny?" JC asked, still in a state of spasm.

"No. She said she hasn't told him. They're great friends and she doesn't want to jeopardize that," Robin explained. "Roman thinks that Benny will eventually come around and realize he's in love with her."

"Is that realistic?" JC asked. He had serious reservations.

"I've known a few women who pursued that tactic," Robin stated. "I don't remember it ever working."

"Wow," JC said, collapsing onto the back of the couch.

"No, you haven't heard the 'wow' yet," Robin declared.

"Really?" JC said, energized.

"Olive is Benny's child," Robin said, looking at him.

JC did not respond. He found himself speechless. A dozen different possibilities leaped into mind.

"Does Benny know?" he finally asked.

"No," Robin exclaimed. "When she found out, she told Benny that she was already pregnant when they had sex. And he's *not* going to hear it from *us*!"

JC didn't say another word. He was connecting all the dots. He looked at Robin and then looked away.

"You have superpowers," he finally said. She laughed a little at that.

"Maybe," she responded.

He thought about it some more. He was standing now.

"You could convince the Pope that he was Protestant," he turned and told her.

"I'm still working on that one," she smiled.

"You could win the Pulitzer Prize for gossip," he said.

"Funny," she said. She liked the sound of it, though.

23

"I've been wearing this thing ever since the Covid outbreak," Bip said.

"Isn't it time you washed it?" JC asked.

"I've washed it, you jackass," Bip laughed. "I just got used to wearing this neck thingy as a facemask when we had to, during the pandemic. I learned that it keeps me warm. So, I never stopped wearing it."

"Me neither," JC said.

"Me neither," said Robin. "It's toasty."

They were riding up a chairlift together. The metallic pings and rattles seemed amplified by the freezing temperatures. The cold front that Roman had warned them about had arrived.

Still, they didn't balk at a chance to ski for an hour before their workday began. JC took two more runs in the race course.

Now, he looked down from the chairlift at the skiers going by. He saw that there were all sorts of ways to accomplish the same thing.

Some skied with ankles tied together as they were taught in the 1960s. Their skis floated in beautiful unison.

Some turned using the stem-christie method. Others mimicked a slice of pie and snowplowed their way down the hill. Others leaned into their turns on snowboards.

A few ski racers went by, with their feet apart and carving precise turns.

It all looked fun. JC didn't believe that there was only one proper way to enjoy gliding across the snow. There were endless ways. And anyone who fell was allowed to laugh, get up, and try again.

The cold was another matter. Temperatures that morning fell below zero. It was the kind of cold you felt settling on your face. You felt it traveling down your windpipe and into your lungs.

Their ski jackets, built for the cold, grew stiff. And their skis would hardly glide when they left the chairlift. Friction in the freezing snow felt like glue.

"It will feel a lot better when the sun gets higher in the sky," JC reassured Robin. "At least we don't have humidity, like back East."

"Yeah, in Colorado, cold like this is life-threatening," Bip laughed. "But it's a *dry* life-threatening."

"Great," Robin complained, her voice muffled by her face mask. "I'm going to be freeze-dried to death. My nose hairs are frozen."

"Ew, you have nose hairs?" Bip teased.

Below, in the resort village and in the town of Dog Mountain, there were cars that would not start. And the smell of burning wood climbed up chimneys and hung in the air.

The three skiers explored runs that were new to them at Minnie's Gap. There was one called Dart's Danger. It was named after the great grandfather of Roman Holiday, Isom Dart.

"Are you going to race this year?"

The voice came from the fourth seat on the quad chairlift as they rode back up the hill.

"Hi, Cannonball!" JC exclaimed when he looked down to the other end of the chair. The man with the nickname Cannonball had raced against JC for years. JC didn't even know the man's real name. Skiing was full of nicknames. For many skiers and snowboarders, it helped create a persona entirely different than their less-exciting life away from the hill.

"I hope to race," JC answered. "I actually got some training in."

"There's going to be a race here," Robin said.

"I'll be racing," Cannonball added. "And I spoke with Russell Driver. He'll be here."

"I love Russell," Robin exclaimed. "I'd love to see him."

"I haven't seen you since last winter," JC said to Cannonball. "How was your summer?"

"I don't do summer, man," Cannonball responded.

They reached the top of the chairlift and Cannonball pushed off to parts unknown.

"See you at the start gate," he said as he skated away.

Flurries began to fall. They would fall for the rest of the day. They didn't accumulate to much, it just seemed like the air was turning to snow.

They reluctantly skied off the mountain after an hour, climbed aboard a free shuttle bus and rode back to their hotel.

"What time is the hearing?" Bip asked.

"The town board convenes in ninety minutes," JC said. "Dr. Anderson's proposal to rent those tiny houses is on the agenda, and Snyder has asked for time to voice his opposition. It will work nicely in Robin's follow-up to her interview with Snyder. The newsroom is expecting a live shot from you two tonight."

"And how will you be earning a living today, Mr. Snow?" Bip asked with a smirk.

"Oaks is back home in Durango trying to convince his wife that the charges against him are all a misunderstanding. So, I got nothing. Robin is the breadwinner, tonight."

"Maybe you should take up pickleball," Bip quipped. "With all this extra time that you have."

When they returned to the warmth of their hotel room, they began to thaw out. JC could feel his fingers throb as blood forced its way back into his small arteries.

"My clothing is still cold!" Robin remarked as she pulled off her outer layers of ski gear.

She turned to a dresser to undertake the search for clothes to change into. Instead, she saw flowers and slowly turned to JC.

"Happy Valentine's Day," he said with a smile. "Are you free tonight?"

The public-comment period in front of the town board drew a handful of residents who lived in Gerhard Snyder's apartments in Dog Mountain. They did not come to praise Caesar, they came to bury him.

The residents, most of them Minnie's Gap employees, complained about rodents, cracks in the walls, poor heating, and water damage on the ceilings of Snyder's rentals.

"I'm afraid the ceiling is going to cave in on me when I'm asleep," one of the tenants told the board.

They complained that Snyder didn't tend to their concerns when he received their complaints.

All of the tenants who came that night urged the town board to approve Dr. Anderson's proposal to bring tiny houses to town and rent them. The renters all wanted to escape Snyder's trailers and move into Anderson's, even though the rent would be higher.

The doctor told the board that, because the tiny houses were prefabricated, he could place them on his lot in a short time.

Gerhard Snyder sat in the audience awaiting his turn to speak. He was doing a slow burn. He stared daggers at Anderson.

The renters' testimony all sounded familiar to Robin. She had heard the same complaints from Snyder's renters in Denver. Only in Denver, it was worse.

Robin would report on television that night that Denver's police and fire departments produced statistics for her. The numbers showed they had more calls to Snyder-owned apartment buildings than others of similar rent levels.

"More fire calls, more police calls, more suicides and more crime," Robin would report that night. She quoted a renter's-rights advocate in Denver saying that Snyder was "down in a class of his own."

Snyder, when it was his turn to address the town board, said that he was providing a service that no one else offered.

"These people have nowhere else to go, without me," he said. "They'll be homeless."

One board member told Snyder, "You make a lot of money off of these people. Couldn't more of your profits go back into the upkeep of your trailers?"

"You want to paint me as the bad guy," Snyder protested. "But I'm fulfilling a service that no one else wants to offer. You know, they say that prostitution is the oldest profession. But it isn't. Visionary builders like me had to come first. We had to build the first brothel."

There were muted coughs from a couple of board members, reacting to that remark. There was grumbling in the audience.

"Let's keep this discussion civil," a board member cautioned Snyder.

"You seem to be telling us that you are doing everything that you can, Mr. Snyder," another board member answered. "That's why we're here today. Dr. Anderson wants to help ease your burden. And you are here opposing his project. Isn't there room in this small town for two landlords?"

"It would cripple me," Snyder resisted. "There is a great deal of expense that goes into what I do. If I have homes sitting empty without renters, I may just shut the whole thing down and go back to Denver. I can get a fair shake there."

But Robin would report that evening that Snyder was under a great deal of scrutiny by City Hall in Denver. He was feeling the same pressure there to perform better upkeep of his properties.

And after her reporting revealed Snyder's plan to build on wetlands in suburban Denver, that project appeared to be doing a death spiral.

At the end of the public meeting, the town board approved Dr. Anderson's plan to rent ten tiny houses on his five-acre lot. His proposal to erect more of the homes on another lot would go before the planning board soon and could also expect a warm reception.

Snyder wasn't happy. He would now have competition.

Robin's live shot that evening was posed in front of one of Snyder's trailer courts in Dog Mountain.

As she was about to go on the air, live to Denver, she stared into the camera and held the cold microphone. She waited for the news anchor to introduce her.

Gerhard Snyder, walking to his truck, passed behind Robin.

JC kept an eye on him. But Snyder never broke stride, climbing into a cream-colored pickup truck with all the amenities.

"Congratulations on your congressional bitch hunt," he yelled before he shut the door.

Following the live shot, Bip packed up his gear and they dropped him off at their hotel. Bip said that he was taking Sunny out to dinner.

JC asked Robin to remain in the car with him. He pulled away and headed back down the access road away from the resort.

But he turned onto an unmarked road that Robin wasn't familiar with. It was a mix of snow and dirt. As they rose in elevation, the dirt road was lined by pine trees and completely covered by the day's snowfall.

She asked him where he was taking her. His answer came, handing her a box in the shape of a heart.

"Oh, JC,"

"Open it up," he said.

When she pulled the box open, it was not what she expected to see. There was a toothbrush, toothpaste, soap and four small bottles of her favorite single-malt Scotch whisky.

"Don't worry, I have more," he said to her as he watched the dark road ahead of them.

"More presents?" she asked curiously.

"More Scotch whisky," he said with a smile.

A bright full moon illuminated the snow and the trees.

He slowed the car down when the lights on their 4x4 spotted a man emerging from the woods. He wore short skis and was followed by his dog.

JC pulled the car to a halt and rolled down his window.

"Why do I get nervous when I see you alone in the woods," JC asked Steven Hemingway, who currently was calling himself Ullr Skadi.

"I am not alone," Skadi, or Hemingway, responded, pointing at the dog. "I'm with him."

"Whose dog is that?" JC inquired, suspiciously.

"Mine," Skadi said. "There are a lot of things you don't know about me. In my country, we have a strong bond with dogs."

"What country is that?" JC asked.

"Norway, of course," Skadi replied.

Skadi seemed anxious to go elsewhere. He pointed his stubby skis back toward the woods.

"What are those things?" JC asked the man, pointing to Skadi's feet.

"They're Hoc skis," the man responded, stopping his trajectory into the forest. "You pronounce it like the bird, a hawk. We use them to work in deep snow, in the old country."

"The old country?" JC laughed. "Aren't you laying this Norwegian thing on a bit thick?"

"I may have overplayed my hand with the 'old country' thing," Skadi said, now sounding more like Steven Hemingway.

The skis had the appearance of cross-country skis, only shorter and wider.

"It's a lot easier when I take my dog on the trails," Skadi said. "They're pretty easy to maneuver. And there's a strip of skin on the base that gives me traction to ski uphill."

"Do you need a lift?" JC asked.

"No need," Skadi answered. "Our truck is nearby. *Ha det*!"

"And what does *ha det* mean?" JC shouted as Skadi pushed off on his poles in the other direction.

"It's how we say goodbye," Skadi shouted back.

"In Norway," JC said skeptically, just as Skadi yelled over his shoulder, "In Norway."

"He isn't from Norway?" Robin asked.

"Good God, no," JC answered her gruffly. "He's probably from California. Though it's better not to believe anything he tells you. I'm sorry I didn't introduce you. He was sort of a moving target."

Robin's phone rang.

"Hi, Dad," she answered when she picked it up. "Thank you," she cooed, when he wished her a happy Valentine's Day. She and JC exchanged a glance.

As Robin spoke with her father, JC navigated the dark snow-covered road. He hoped he was properly following the directions that he had been given.

"I love you too, Dad," she said. She closed her eyes like she was having a dream and she didn't want to wake up.

"He moved to North Carolina when Mom died," Robin told JC as she put her phone away. "I told you that my brother lives there, in Asheville. Sorry, I guess I have a lot to get you caught up on."

"I'm glad you're telling me," JC said. "You know, you're not the only person who has become estranged from a brother or a sister or a father or mother. I was lucky. Our family was always close. But I can't tell you how many people I know who are in your position."

"Despite all the drama, my dad is a great guy," she said, sniffling.

"And he's making it right," JC said. "That's something a great guy would do."

"I should warn you," she said as she smiled at him. "I have a thing for great guys."

High up Dog Mountain, JC pulled into a plowed drive and turned the car off. In front of them, there was a tiny house with the warm glow of lights shining from within. JC was relieved that he found what he was looking for.

"Oh my. This is Dr. Anderson's escape in the woods," Robin deduced as she turned to face JC. He nodded.

It was built to resemble a log cabin. There were crossed skis mounted on the wall by the door.

Temperatures were below zero. But as they climbed out of the car, they glanced up at the dark sky and just stood there.

"I've never seen so many stars," Robin gasped. There were layers of stars, the close ones, the furthest ones and all those in between. "I must be looking at a million stars."

"They say this might be the darkest sky in the lower forty-eight states," JC told her as he looked upward.

They gazed at the sky as long as they could stand the brutal cold. Then they scurried onto the small porch and into their warm retreat.

Robin surveyed the comfortable surroundings. The interior was also designed to look like a log cabin. There were a few framed vintage ski posters on the wall and another set of old skis and ski poles. There was a small kitchen and a small living room.

There was a bathroom just large enough for a shower, sink and toilet. Two walls in the corner were made of glass, to look out at the forest without fear of anyone looking in. The cabin was surrounded only by woods.

There was a narrow spiral staircase, heading up to a loft just large enough for a bed.

"You did this for me?" Robin asked JC as she slipped her arms around his neck.

"Yes, ma'am," he said with a smile.

"Don't call me ma'am," she said, smiling back. "I'm too young to be a ma'am."

"It's polite," he said.

"Is that what you intend, tonight?" she asked. "Are you going to be polite?"

"No ma'am," he said smiling and hoisting her onto the bed.

"This is wonderful, JC," she said. "Happy Valentine's Day."

24

"Why aren't you married?"

JC asked the question of Robin as though they were resuming a conversation they had started at another time.

They were lying in bed in the loft of Dr. Hunter Anderson's tiny house in the mountains.

They stared out a narrow horizontal window next to the bed. It framed the wilderness that slept on just the other side of the window. The bright full moon reflected off the snow. Trees stood like dark sentinels against a white background. Their shadows stretched across open spaces.

Robin had asked him the same question, he remembered, perhaps a year ago. But now he was asking.

"First of all," she said, "I'm younger than you. So, it doesn't make me a spinster."

"You're not that much younger," he replied defensively. "A few short years."

"Many people tell me that they thought I was your daughter," she responded with a smirk.

"Really? Not my granddaughter?" he said. "I must be aging well."

They both laughed. JC remembered that he did that a lot around Robin. He laughed a lot. They both did.

"So?" he said.

"You really want an answer?" she asked. "That's a rude thing to ask a woman."

"You're stalling," he said with a grin.

"Well, you know that I was an archaeologist," she told him. "So, my fingernails were broken, the skin on my hands was cracked, my hair was dirty and I was a little smelly. You'd be surprised at how many men are not looking for that in a woman."

"It sounds like you were hot," he said.

"I *was* hot," she said defiantly.

"But you're a television reporter now," he said. "And you're not nearly as smelly."

"Yes, now I am a television journalist," she said. "And you may have noticed that television news is full of A-type personalities and hair spray. The men wear more makeup than I do and definitely look in the mirror more than I do."

"Are you jealous?" he asked. "Because I am better at applying makeup than you are."

"I could use some pointers," she said softly. She pulled her body closer to his.

"Are you trying to compromise my interrogation?" he asked.

"Sometimes," she said with a smile. "The best action is distraction."

When they fell asleep, it was to the soft sound of the cold wind outside and the warmth of their tiny log-ish cabin.

But hours later, they awakened to the sound of car tires crushing the frozen snow. It was still dark out. JC looked at his phone. It said the time was 1:30 a.m.

JC watched the lights of a vehicle spray the nearby trees.

"Who is it?" Robin asked JC with alarm in her voice. "I thought that no one came up here."

"I'm going to look," JC said as he pulled his pants on and descended the spiral staircase.

He turned on the light and reached the window in time to see a truck back out of the driveway and proceed down the mountain road.

He opened the door of the cabin and was met by a blast of cold air. He tried to get a good look at the pickup truck. His first thought was that it was the truck belonging to Ullr Skadi, aka Steven Hemingway.

The truck was light-colored. It was big and it seemed new because the body shined in the moonlight.

To JC, it almost looked like Gerhard Snyder's truck. And he thought he smelled the faint odor of gasoline.

"Who was that?" Robin asked when JC climbed the spiral staircase back up to the loft.

"Just someone turning around in the driveway," he told her.

"That was kind of creepy," she said. "At this hour?"

"It's fine," he said. "It was nothing to worry about." He wrapped his arms around her, and they tried to fall back to sleep.

Was it fine? JC had his doubts. He remembered the faint smell of gasoline. And it sure looked like Gerhard Snyder's pickup truck.

"We're meeting Bip at nine at the Rendezvous for breakfast," JC told Robin. They were retracing their steps through the deep snow, from Anderson's tiny house to their 4x4. They saw the tracks belonging to the vehicle that pulled in the driveway overnight.

"It looks like a truck, doesn't it," observed Robin. "It's big."

"It was a truck," JC told her. "A pickup truck. Light color, I think."

"Did you recognize it?" she asked.

JC thought for a moment about how he should answer that question. On one side, he thought, he didn't want to jump to a conclusion. On the other side, Robin was a professional and had a stake in all that was happening.

"I'm not sure I recognized it," he told her. "But it sure reminded me of Snyder's truck."

"What would he be doing up here?" she asked.

"And if it was him," JC added, "why did he turn around?"

"Well, that creeps me out," she said with a worried look.

"Don't be overly concerned," JC told her. "If he wanted to find us, he did. And he turned around. He wasn't looking for us."

Listening to the radio on the way down the mountain, a news broadcast informed them that the cold snap was going to stay around a while longer. It had already taken its toll on the Western Slope.

The newscaster on the radio reported that a family of three in Craig had been found dead after using an outdoor gas heater inside their home. All three died of carbon-monoxide poisoning.

There was also an elderly resident in Rifle who had slipped on ice outside and, unable to get up, died before being found by a neighbor.

As JC and Robin entered the Rendezvous, the dining room where breakfast was served at their hotel, they saw Bip approaching.

"Did you ask Sunny to be your valentine?" Robin teased.

"She beat me to it," he snickered. "We had a fun night."

They headed toward a familiar table near the breakfast buffet but spotted Frank Green sitting at a table alone and joined him.

"What are you doing at a hotel?" JC asked. "You have a home of your own in town."

"I was working here late last night," he told them. "The company that manages the hotel for the ski area has new software they want installed on the computers in the office. Between you and me, its chief purpose is to see if anyone here is stealing from corporate. Anyway, when it got late, they offered me a free room and I accepted."

"Roman tells me that you grew up in this area," Robin said, changing the subject.

"I did," Frank said with a smile. "Browns Park. My family had a ranch. It was heaven. Riding horses every day, being around animals. It was like playing cowboy. We had to move, though, when they took our land and created the preserve and the reservoir." His face disclosed his unhappiness with the move.

"Roman told a similar story about her family," JC stated. "Did your family appeal to their members of Congress, or someone in Washington who might help?"

"Everyone in Browns Park begged Congress for help," Frank lamented. "But we didn't find a Department of Conservation. Congress is just a Department of Conversation. When there's a crisis that needs to be addressed, all they do is talk."

"I'm sorry," Robin said.

"Life," Frank told her with a grunt. "I've lived it backwards. I was born in heaven and then they made me come down to earth."

Sunny approached their table. She would be their waitress. She and Bip clutched hands for an instant. Then she poured them coffee, took their juice orders and released them to load up on the buffet.

"Wow, this is becoming serious with Sunny," Robin said to Bip as they walked together. They were both heading to the table where a chef would make them an omelet to their specifications.

"Yeah," Bip said. "What's not to like? She snowboards, she's really pretty and we have a ton of fun together."

"Right," Robin said enthusiastically. "And she lives in Utah and you live in Denver. That's a long way." It sounded like the cautionary downer that she intended it to be.

"Yeah, thanks for reminding me," he answered her with a somber expression.

"Besides," Robin said as she nudged him. "What about that woman in Upstate New York?"

"She's in Upstate New York," Bip answered, stating the obvious problem.

They gathered back at their table, drank coffee and enjoyed breakfast.

"What do you know about Gerhard Snyder?" Robin asked Frank as she worked on a mushroom omelet.

"I understand he's a little ticked off at you," Frank told her. "Don't worry, he has a bad temper but he hasn't murdered anyone, as far as I know." Frank laughed at his own joke.

"What do people think of him, around here?" JC asked.

"He doesn't have many friends, if that's what you're asking," Frank told them. "But I've done some business with him, fixed him up with the computers and the programs he needed. He's a different guy, I'll grant you that."

Frank Green proceeded to tell a story about Snyder.

"Jerry was married when I met him. I was too. So, my wife and I went to visit Jerry and his wife at his forty-acre ranch outside Denver. Really impressive place," Frank said. "The guy is loaded."

"Yeah, but he disguises it," Robin said.

"The cheap suits?" Frank asked. "Yeah, I know. Anyway, here's how Jerry's marriage ended. The four of us were having cocktails. And through the window of the living room we were sitting in, I saw an old railroad caboose in back of his house. I asked him what it was.

"At that point, Jerry's wife chimed in and proceeded to tell me that Jerry bought it and had promised to renovate it. She wanted to turn it into a cute guesthouse. But he never did, she said. He never kept his promises to her, she said. I got the feeling that Jerry had heard this complaint before. Probably more than once.

"Well, Jerry didn't say a word. He stood up and left the room. I thought he was really mad at his wife. But he returned to the room in about ten minutes and sat down again. I figured that everything was fine.

"Then, I saw a glow on the wall of the living room that we were sitting in. I looked out the window and saw that caboose engulfed in flames. He'd gone outside, doused it in gasoline and set it on fire!"

Frank, Bip and Robin were all laughing at the story. JC did too. But he was thinking about earlier in the morning, when he saw a truck that looked like Snyder's pull out of the driveway of Anderson's cabin, leaving behind a distinct odor of gasoline.

They continued to work on breakfast, chatting about the cold, Frank's thoughts about his own divorce and the Oaks investigation.

"Here's something I didn't tell you," Frank said. "The sheriff came to see me. He wanted my help."

"Really, what about?" JC asked, trying not to show his full enthusiasm when it came to learning what law officers were saying. Police would tell potential witnesses things they wouldn't tell the news media. JC hoped this would be a fine example.

"Well, they're looking into those threatening calls that were made to Roman Holiday," Frank told them. "The ones they think Jon Oaks made."

"And how did they think you could help them?" JC asked.

"They wanted my expert opinion on how the caller might have disguised the original location of the call," Frank told them proudly. "It's a kind of call-spoofing. You make a call from Omaha, let's say. But you make it seem like it came from Hawaii."

"So, the calls to Roman were call-spoofed?" Robin asked.

"Yes, they were," Frank said. "It's easy to disguise your location on the phone, if you know how to do it. That's what those robo-callers do when they show up on your phone. But it's much easier to track if it stayed in this country."

"And did you figure it out?" JC asked.

"I humbly disclose that I did," Frank said. "The calls came from here in Lonesome County, but they were rerouted through Los Angeles."

"Los Angeles," Robin said. "That's where Roman used to live."

So did Benny, JC quietly thought.

25

"Is this really you?" JC asked.

Robin and Bip listened to one end of the phone conversation as they all stood in the lobby of The Fort, the hotel where they had rooms.

Robin was looking at pieces of old bottles, and belt buckles eaten by corrosion. They were on display shelves within a tall glass case in the lobby. The artifacts were unearthed when the resort village was constructed. They appeared to be left behind by cowboys who worked in Browns Park a century ago, and maybe even before that.

"I just can't remember you ever asking me to spend time with you," JC said into the phone. "I'm flattered, honored really."

Robin gave Bip a look asking if he knew who JC was talking to. Bip just shook his head. He didn't.

"I'd like to think I'm smart," JC told the caller. "But I'm not sure that's the part of my anatomy where my best thinking is done."

JC then disconnected the call and slipped the phone into his pocket.

"What?" Robin asked.

"Robin, you're coming with me," JC said. "Bip, this makes me sound awful, but you can't come with us."

"Now I'm the third wheel?" Bip asked, not entirely joking.

"No," JC replied, feeling a little guilty. "But this guy is secretive. You'll probably meet him, but not today."

"Can I go snowboarding?" Bip asked, playing on JC's easily detected guilt.

"I don't see why not," he was told. "I'll give you a call when we're done."

Bip headed upstairs with a bounce in his step. He had to change and get his board. JC and Robin walked down a hallway to the hotel's parking garage.

"I've got someone you should meet," JC told her. "It's the guy who popped out of the forest when we were heading to Dr. Anderson's cabin. The guy is a hoot. He'll probably try to offend you, but don't take it personally."

After a short drive from the resort village, they walked down a hallway on the second floor of a building on the community college campus.

JC could hear Hemingway's voice echoing down the hall, coming from an office they were approaching. Hemingway was speaking Norwegian. JC shook his head.

"Let me go in alone," JC told Robin. "Just wait outside the door for a minute."

JC stepped into the office Hemingway occupied. The nameplate on the door read "Professor Ullr Skadi."

The office was spartan. There was a metal desk, two metal chairs in front of it and as many metal bookshelves as the room could fit, filled with as many books and loose piles of paper as the shelves would allow.

Hemingway was on a landline speaking Norwegian. He abruptly stopped talking when he saw the reporter.

"Oh, it's only you. Close the door," Hemingway said.

JC did as requested, after making eye contact with Robin, who would wait only a few feet from the other side of the door.

"I only do that when I hear students or colleagues walking down the hall," Hemingway said. "I just like them to hear me on the phone speaking to my homeland."

"Which is Norway?" JC asked in a mocking tone.

"Yes, of course," Hemingway said. A polished piece of wood facing visitors from his desk read "Dr. Skadi."

"Have you ever *been* to Norway?" JC asked.

"Technically, no," Hemingway told him. "I was in Denmark once, as a child. My mother wanted to see The Little Mermaid, the statue in Copenhagen. *And* I've been to the Norway Pavilion at Epcot in Disney World. Great water ride."

"So, what are you working on, in your role at this glorious think tank?" JC asked.

"Presently, I'm fighting for the little guy, by confusing the annoying algorithms used to track us in our computers," Hemingway said. "I've designed a computer program to search the internet for outrageous things. I'll ask if a dog with a popular name is a spy for Russia. My program will do the search thousands of times, so it becomes a thing. Then, I'll ask if some obnoxious celebrity was murdered by a Supreme Court justice. I designed a program to do it over and over again. It takes on a life of its own. My plan to disrupt the algorithms is just a theory, of course. But that's what great minds do at high-minded institutions like this."

"I thought you were a biochemist," JC told him.

"Did Thomas Edison just work on record players?" Hemingway asked. "Did he only fool around with lightbulbs? We are intellectual artists. We can't live within a fence."

"By the way," JC said, "I didn't know you ski. But you were on the mountain when you saw that avalanche."

"You never asked if I ski," Hemingway said to him. "I ski more now than I used to. I'm not bad. Repeating anything makes you better at it. That's just simple neuroscience."

"I need you to meet someone," JC said as he opened the door into the hallway. Robin stepped into the room. JC closed the door behind her.

"Well, I see you have a certain type," Hemingway said to JC, eyeing Robin's similarities with Shara.

"Actually, you may have seen her in the car with me," JC told him. "Up on Dog Mountain that night, when you were with your dog."

"Ah, yes. My dog," Hemingway answered. Then he looked at Robin. "You're not her little sister, are you? Or a twin? That would offer a world of possibilities."

"I'm afraid not," Robin said with a polite smile. She extended her hand, "I'm Robin Smith. I'm a reporter."

"Oh, fine," Hemingway remarked with his eyes on JC. "We're sharing my little secret with the world now? She is a reporter. Who on earth would she tell?"

"You can trust her," JC told him. "You'll come to understand that."

"We don't breathe a word about this odd man's charade," JC said to Robin.

"I understand," Robin replied, looking back at Hemingway.

"Robin, I'd like to introduce you to a professor in the biochemistry department here," JC proceeded. "Ullr Skadi. He's from Norway."

"It's my pleasure, Ms. Smith," Hemingway said politely with a slight Norwegian accent.

"Boy, that accent comes and goes like a mosquito on a summer evening," JC sniped. "And just as annoying."

"What sort of man makes fun of an immigrant trying to learn the language of his new country, Ms. Smith?" Hemingway asked her.

The professor picked up a book on his desk and pondered something as he looked at it.

"Would you mind dropping this off on your way back into town?" Hemingway asked JC. "I promised Benny Maple I'd get it to him."

"We'd be happy to!" Robin said and quickly snatched the book out of Hemingway's hand. "Where does he live?"

"I can give you directions," Hemingway told her. "It's not far from here."

"Is this why you asked me to come by your office?" JC asked. "You wanted me to run an errand for you?"

"Mr. Skadi," Robin interrupted, as she looked at the book she had just been handed. The book was about the early history of the area now known as Norway, Finland, Sweden and part of Russia. "Am I to understand that you are named after both the god and goddess of skiing?"

"You're much too smart to be with him," Hemingway aka Skadi said.

"I know," Robin agreed. "But he's pretty."

"If you like that type," Hemingway said dismissively while looking at JC. "And why would you know of Ullr and Skadi?"

"In 2007, an ancient shrine to Ullr was unearthed in Sweden," Robin informed Hemingway. "Archaeologists discovered sixty-five rings. Scientists believe oaths were made there, by people standing over a ring."

Hemingway studied her. He seemed to be considering how and why she knew this.

"I was an archaeologist for ten years," she said, answering the question that had not been asked. "When you stop being an archaeologist, you don't just stop being interested in archaeology."

"She is more interesting than you are, JC," Hemingway said. "But I didn't summon you here because I thought you were interesting, or even to run an errand for me. I asked you to come here because I think you have betrayed me."

"If you're referring to your secret identity," JC said, "I haven't stumbled across anyone who cares. You seem to be doing this for your own amusement."

"It's not that amusing," Hemingway replied seriously. "And yes, someone is threatening to expose me unless I enrich him."

"Someone is trying to blackmail you?" JC asked in surprise.

"Yes," Hemingway confirmed.

"Do you have any money?" JC laughed.

"That is not of your concern," the professor responded.

"Exactly my point," JC told him. "I know almost nothing about you. However, police in Montana still do not know of your very existence because I didn't tell them about you. I don't tell someone's darkest secrets unless they pose a danger to someone or something. I haven't told anyone about your alter ego, except Robin. And she hasn't left the room since learning of it."

"Well, someone knows mine," Hemingway stated.

"How serious is this?" JC asked.

"It could get very serious," Hemingway replied.

"How did you come to know this?" JC asked.

"I've received an anonymous letter and then a telephone call," Hemingway informed him. "I tracked the call. They tried to disguise its origin. It came from here and was routed through Los Angeles."

"What are you going to do?" JC asked.

"I'm going to try to catch him," Hemingway said. "Otherwise, I'm going to have to make myself scarce, disappear in the night."

"Like you did in Montana," JC said.

"Like I did in Montana," Hemingway confirmed. "Only without burning this place down."

26

"Is he for real? Or is he just handing us a best-option defense?"

The two attorneys were walking down the stone path leading from the front door of Jonathan Oaks' sprawling home in the Turtle Lake neighborhood of Durango.

All the homes in that neighborhood were properties worth over a million dollars. Many, like the Oaks house, were on wooded lots offering privacy.

"I pride myself on seeing through my clients' deceit and self-centered excuses," defense attorney Landon McNally said. "But I don't know if Oaks is faking mental illness or if he's really gone off the deep end."

McNally was accompanied by a young attorney from his practice in Denver who would be his assistant in the case.

They stepped onto the gravel driveway and stopped, looking back at the four thousand-square-foot home and three-car garage. The house was designed to look like a Mexican villa.

"We will pursue an insanity defense, won't we?" the younger attorney asked.

"Oh, it will be the Mona Lisa of insanity defenses," McNally said. "If he can keep this up, he'll repair much of his reputation by summertime. He only has to tell everyone he's nuts until a jury agrees."

Jonathan Oaks watched the attorneys from a picture window in the living room of the home he shared with his wife, Brenda.

She had only spoken publicly twice regarding the trouble her husband was in. She had picked up the phone once when JC called. Her response was all of four words.

And when a Durango newspaper reporter called, she provided the same response, "I love my husband." And then she hung up.

Oaks wore a thick sweater. He took a seat on a sofa and, without thinking, reached down to touch the ankle bracelet he was required to wear since he was released from jail.

There were conditions connected to his release on bail. He was not to have contact with Roman or Olive Holiday. And he was only to leave his three-acre property to go to see his lawyers or his doctors.

Sitting on the sofa, he ran a hand through his recently trimmed hair. He had to limit the damage to his name, he thought. He was doubtful it could be done.

His eyes examined the house he had raised a family in and launched political campaigns from. Pictures on the wall and mementos on bookshelves spoke of his success.

The home was a trophy of influence and affluence. It had rich dark wood and colorful tile. Views from the windows were among the best money could buy in Durango.

Brenda watched her husband from the kitchen, where she was preparing a meal. His elbows rested on his knees. He looked forlorn.

She walked into the living room and sat on an armrest of the sofa. She stroked his back.

"It will be alright, Jon," she said. "We'll have our old life back. You just see."

Oaks grasped his wife's hand, held it to his mouth and kissed it.

"I'm so sorry, Bren," he said. "I need help."

"I know, honey," Brenda said. "We'll get you the best doctor there is. We'll get you better."

"I'm going to meet Benjamin!"

Robin said it smiling as she clutched the book to her chest and they walked to their car.

JC thought she wasn't so much *saying* it as *singing* it.

"I'm guessing this means a lot more to you than it does to me," JC said.

"I had a crush on Benjamin Maple," she exclaimed. "I was a teenager when he was making movies. I was going to marry him."

"Do I guess correctly that your wedding plans will come as a surprise to him?" JC asked with a grin.

"Laugh if you want to," she said. "He was my first love. Well, second. Jonny Moseley was my first."

"Jonny Mosely," JC repeated. "The Olympic moguls champion?"

"He was awfully cute when I was eight years old," she said.

They drove out of the town of Dog Mountain on Route 72, heading east. In only a mile, they turned into the entrance of a cattle ranch.

There was a barn, a four-wheeler parked outside and plenty of pasture. But JC noted that he could not see a single animal that would qualify as livestock. There were dogs, though. A good many dogs.

Benny Maple appeared through the doorway of an outbuilding. He looked curiously at the 4x4 parked on the dirt courtyard.

"JC, right?" the actor said as JC and Robin stepped out of the car.

"Good memory," JC said. "Frank Green introduced us at the bar. And this is Robin Smith. She's also a reporter in Denver."

JC saw that Maple's smile did not fade as he eyed the two reporters walking his way. That wasn't always the reaction reporters received, JC thought to himself.

"We've been instructed to deliver a book to you from Professor Ullr Skadi," JC said.

Robin reached out and dropped the book into Maple's awaiting hands.

"Cool," said Maple. "Roman likes you two. Come on in for coffee. Let's get out of the cold."

Maple had wrapped his arms across his chest to protect against the wind. He turned and walked toward the door of his house. JC and Robin followed.

"Or something stronger, if you prefer," Maple said over his shoulder. "We have plenty of that too."

They walked through the door into Maple's kitchen. A pair of eighty-pound dogs followed him in. They proceeded to soft beds on either side of a fireplace as Maple placed the book on a counter.

"Do you mind taking off your shoes?" he asked. "It keeps things neat."

They pulled off their shoes and he ushered JC and Robin toward a place to sit.

They found themselves seated at an L-shaped bar with a wooden tabletop and sides that resembled varnished snow fence.

"Oh my," Robin said as she gazed at the kitchen. "This is beautiful."

She stroked a wooden post with a lantern balanced on top. All the woodwork was rough-cut. The stove and other kitchen appliances were steel and copper, reflecting the color of the wood.

"Thank you," Maple said as he pulled his long dark hair behind his head and reached for three copper coffee cups. "I designed it. I figured that I would do it right, if I was going to hide out here. I don't plan to leave and I don't plan to tell anyone that I'm here. Kind of like Butch Cassidy."

He was smiling through the whole exchange. He gave Robin a wink. When doing something as simple as pouring them coffee, JC thought that he oozed charisma doing it.

He had a child's look in his eyes, innocent and admiring the wonder of every little thing. His smile was constant, as was his laugh. And yet he surprised them with the depth of his thinking.

"What's your interest in the book, the history of Norway?" JC asked.

"Eh, my mind goes in twelve directions at once," Maple said. "I just can't leave things alone. I found some Norwegian petroleum investments in my portfolio. Someone manages my investments for me. I feel like I'm missing money somewhere and I can't figure out where."

He looked around the kitchen, as though he had lost the money on a kitchen counter or in the toaster.

"I got to thinking about Norway," he said. "Someone told me about Professor Skadi. I gave him a call."

He picked up the book from Professor Skadi and walked to the other side of the kitchen.

"You enjoy watching your investments?" JC asked.

"Oh yeah," Benny said with a grin. He placed the book down next to a laptop computer on a table near an east-facing window. "I spend every morning on this thing," he said, patting the open laptop. "I watch the sunrise, watch my investments and read about potential investments. It's a hobby. I like the research."

JC glanced at Robin. "Fixated" was the word he was searching for. She was fixated by the presence of her childhood crush.

"Where is your livestock?" JC asked Maple.

"Ha! You mean, where are the cattle belonging to this cattle rancher?" Maple laughed. "You noticed that I have quite a few dogs. Well, it didn't take me long to learn that I wasn't much of a cattleman. So, I gave up cattle and, instead, I raise a litter of Goldendoodles each year to sell.

"They have better turnaround than cattle and I have a long waiting list. I don't even have to advertise!"

"They don't shed much, do they?" Robin asked, moving her eyes to the two dogs resting by the fireplace.

"That's a fact," Maple said. "They shed a little bit, but not much. I'm kind of a neat freak. I tell them to take their shoes off too, but they just look at me like they're hoping I'm going to offer them some steak."

"You must read a lot, Benny Ray," Robin said. There was a large bookshelf extending from the floor to the ceiling. Books filled every slot.

"Well, you've certainly been hanging around Roman," Maple said. "She's the only one who calls me Benny Ray. You can call me Benny Ray or just Benny, Robin."

JC saw Robin's face flush a little when Benny actually uttered her name.

"I do read a lot," he said. "And this isn't even the library. You should see it. It's a mess."

"Do you ski?" Robin asked.

"No, I don't," he laughed. "I guess that's how I find time to read. And cook. I love to cook."

"So, this beautiful kitchen doesn't go to waste," Robin remarked.

"I should have you two and Roman over for dinner," he said.

A phone rang. It was sitting on the kitchen bar. Benny picked the phone up and made a face, before disconnecting the call.

"That was a car wash in Los Angeles," Benny said. "They told me that I had a chance to win a year's supply of free car washes, if only I'd purchase a coupon book."

"The car wash is in Los Angeles?" JC asked.

"Yeah," Benny said. "My phone number is still a Los Angeles area code. So many people have my phone number, I don't really want to change it."

"May I ask you something, Benny?" JC questioned.

"Yeah, sure."

"Why would Jonathan Oaks dislike you?" JC asked.

"Because I dislike him," Benny said with a grin. "And he knows it. He also knows that I'm Roman's friend and that I knew he was having an affair with her."

"So, he saw you as a threat," Robin asked. "For her affections?"

"Maybe," Benny answered. "I'm not that kind of threat, though. I'm Roman's friend, not her boyfriend.

"But I don't trust someone who cheats on his wife, like Oaks. If he'll betray the recipient of his wedding vows, it will be easy to betray everyone else, right?

"Trust me on this. I've slept with a lot of married women. I'm not proud of that, but that's Hollywood. And I witnessed something, that once they crossed that line, deception in general became easier."

"It's kind of like something JC likes to say," Robin told him. "The first murder is the hardest."

27

Men in armor emerged from the woods in two columns of three. They wore colorful garments beneath their chest plates, and the armor covering their legs and arms.

The two lines of men carried a large shield between them. A man was lying on it. He appeared to be lifeless. A dog was trailing behind, concerned for the man on the shield.

"You were having that dream again," Robin said. She'd awakened JC from a deep sleep in the early morning hours.

"I was. How did you know?" he asked.

"You've been huffing and puffing for about ten minutes," she said. "Maybe more, but that's when your noise woke me up."

"Sorry," he said, still groggy.

"Was it the same? Medieval knights carrying a fallen warrior out of the trees?" she asked.

"Yep," he said. "Same one. I think the dog following the men is Picabo."

"Your old dog?" she asked.

"Yep, I think it was her."

"You already know what I think," she reminded him. "I think it's some leftover DNA from your Scottish ancestors. I think it's some memory of the moments after a battle, maybe the loss of a good friend on the field."

"Or maybe it's me on the shield," he said. "It's so real."

It was still dark outside. They slipped into each other's arms.

When they awoke again, it was due to the ringing of JC's phone. The clock radio by the hotel bed said it was seven a.m. The call was from their television newsroom in Denver.

"Hi JC, I figured you'd be up by now. Idle time is wasted time." The peppy voice belonged to Rocky Bauman, the newsroom's assignment editor. He was always the first one on the day shift to arrive at work in the morning.

"Yep," JC said, having been awakened from a deep sleep for a second time in a matter of hours. "I've already washed the car and vacuumed the house this morning."

Rocky assumed he was hearing sarcasm. But discovering that he didn't really care, he proceeded with the conversation.

"When is Oaks due back in court?" the assignment editor asked.

"Not for a while," JC told him. "Right now, the case is at the stage where attorneys file motions, exchange paperwork, agree on dates. Routine stuff like that."

"Okay. Listen, JC," Rocky said. "We've talked it over and it's time to bring you home. We got some good stories out of you. The Oaks stuff has been great. So was the series on the new ski resort. And Robin had some nice stories too, about Snyder. But it's time to bring you back to Denver. Do you have anything for today?"

"I can always scrounge something up," he said, "but there's nothing breaking. I think you're probably right."

"Okay," Rocky stated. "Don't worry about giving us anything today, unless something new comes up. We'll see you back here in Denver on Monday, alright?"

"Sounds good, Rocky," JC concurred. "But listen, we probably won't come home until Sunday, so don't give up our hotel rooms. Is that okay?"

"That's fine," Rocky informed him. "We'll work it out with the hotel. See all of you on Monday."

The call was disconnected. Robin was looking at him for a report.

"We have a three-day weekend," he said with a sleepy smile.

"Let's go skiing," she said with enthusiasm unbefitting his dazed condition as he pulled himself upright in bed.

"Who wound you up?" he mumbled.

"You did," she said with a kiss. "But that was hours ago."

A light snow was falling. The below-zero temperatures had now extended into a third day.

And the wind had picked up. Some of the snow was falling down while some of it was blowing sideways.

As they rode a chairlift with Bip, Robin crouched behind JC on the leeward side of the wind.

"Do you notice how quiet it gets when it's so cold?" Robin said.

"Everyone's hiding," Bip laughed. "The birds are hiding, the elk are hiding, the squirrels are even hiding. Humans are the only fools who go out into a snowstorm when it's five degrees below zero."

They had been told that there was magnificent powder piling up below a peak on a run called Charley's Cheater. The run was named after Minnie Crouse's father. Some residents of Browns Park accused him of cheating at horse racing.

Bip, JC and Robin shielded their faces from the wind, using their masks, the ones they started wearing during Covid. Their hands were kept warmer by disposable heat packs stuffed into their leather mittens.

"How are your nose hairs, Robin?" Bip asked.

"They're frozen, you jerk," Robin snapped.

"Gee," Bip mocked. "I try to be a nice guy by expressing my concern for her nose hairs and she snaps at me."

"Some women just can't be pleased," JC said.

"My eyes are watering too!" she barked. "It's cold!"

"Pretty as a picture," Bip said as he laughed.

"You jerk," Robin laughed, her voice muffled by her mask and the fact she had burrowed her face into JC's jacket.

Getting off the lift, they chose to immediately slide below the ridge. There, the wind abated. It was a relief.

Two more skiers pulled up alongside them. One was Frank Green. The other was Dr. Hunter Anderson. He was wearing his cowboy hat and the same long wool coat that he wore to his office.

"I see you found the warm side of the mountain!" Anderson said with a grin.

"I see you're dressed in business-casual," JC responded, noting the doctor's long coat.

"My orange ski jacket was ruined in the avalanche," Anderson responded. "I guess I haven't taken the time to buy another."

"But your arm isn't in a sling!" Robin exclaimed.

"Haven't you heard?" Anderson said. "Doctors make the worst patients. I'm taking it easy. This is my first attempt to really use my arm."

"How does it feel?" Bip asked.

"It doesn't feel too bad," the doctor told them. "But if you see my surgeon, don't breathe a word of this. I'm cheating."

"Aren't you freezing?" Robin asked, eying the bare ears under his cowboy hat and his topcoat.

He looked down at his wardrobe and shrugged. He had added a black and gray scarf. His cowboy hat had a leather string extended under his chin so the wind wouldn't blow it off.

"In medical school," the doctor answered, "they taught us a method that prevented us from feeling cold."

"Teach me!" Robin quickly responded.

"You know how you don't get cold?" Anderson asked. "Mind over matter."

"If you don't mind, it doesn't matter," JC translated.

"Seriously," Robin said to them with a disappointed look.

"I had my arm in a sling for too long," the doctor told them. "Now, it's time to suck it up. This is no place to be a baby."

"That's what he tells his patients," Green laughed. "'Don't be a baby.'"

"I really don't have to," Anderson shared. "There are no babies in Browns Park. Even the real babies are tougher than us. They're born cowboys."

"They are real cowboys around here," Green agreed. "Infants come out of the womb and they're already sitting on a saddle."

"And they don't easily get cold," the doctor said. "They ignore it."

"We'll warm up if we move," Bip said. And he hopped forward on his snowboard to slide over the shelf of the hill. The others followed.

The powder was light. While Bip carved cloned arcs, the skiers fell into a pattern floating into and out of the soft snow.

JC sought unblemished powder on the side of the run, only feet from the trees that lined the slope.

"I've got to get to work," Frank Green said after they had skied down to the chairlift. "We have a truck full of inventory arriving. And a day doesn't go by when I don't get called out to someone's house."

"That's got to get annoying," Bip said.

"Not really," Green said graciously. "A lot of the people that I used to know here are dead or gone. But I'm making new friends all the time. If they have a computer, we're bound to meet."

"I'm afraid recess is over for me too," Anderson said. "I've got to get to the office. But you all ought to come over for dinner tonight."

"Would it be alright if I brought someone?" Bip asked.

"I understand you have met Sunny. By all means, bring her," the doctor said.

"It's a small town," Green explained to Bip. "Everybody knows what everyone else is doing, including you and Sunny."

"So, here's the deal," Robin said to Anderson. "We'll come over, but you have to let me cook. It was so nice of you to let us stay at your cabin. I'll cook tonight, and I won't take no for an answer."

"You win," the doctor responded.

"I hope you cook something that's hot," Bip said, shivering while they stood near the chairlift line.

"Do you have handwarmers, Robin?" Green asked.

"I do. But I could use two in each mitten!" she said.

"That's a good idea," Green said. He pulled his gloves off, pulled out his own disposable handwarmers and gave them to her. "I'm done for the day. I washed my hands just before I pulled my gloves on, promise."

"Thank you," Robin said as she pulled off her mittens and added his additional warmers. "You're such a gentleman."

They all agreed on a time for dinner that night and Green skied away with Dr. Anderson.

"Don't fall on your shoulder!" Robin yelled after Dr. Anderson.

After a day of skiing on their sudden day off, the three journalists cleaned up and headed for Hunter Anderson's tiny house. Sunny met them in the lobby of the hotel.

Climbing into their car, a check-engine light came on. They ignored it. The temperature was now fifteen degrees below zero.

"Warning lights don't like the cold either," JC said. "If it starts, you drive it."

It was a short trip to Doctor Anderson's 250-square-foot house.

"Are we all going to fit?" Robin said with a smile as she entered the doctor's tiny home.

"It's going to be tight," the doctor said, amused. "Make sure you serve small portions."

JC, Bip and Sunny squeezed in next, carrying bags containing the ingredients for dinner that Robin had selected at the little grocery store in town.

"How does your arm feel after skiing with it?" Robin asked Anderson.

"It's not bad," he told her. "I have the expected stiffness, after going without exercise for so long. But I'd call today a success."

Frank Green was already at the kitchen stove. He had arrived ahead of the others to prepare an hors d'oeuvre.

"You cheated," Robin protested. "I said that *I'm* cooking dinner."

"And this isn't dinner," Green smiled. "It's an hors d'oeuvre."

"Cheater," Robin pouted. "Anyway, that's a really cute grocery. It's like an old general store."

"They're going to build a supermarket in the resort village," Green said. "I'm planning their computer layout already."

"People are going to love that. But a lot of the ranchers grow their own food," Anderson said. "And they sell to the community too."

"By the way, Sunny, I'm Hunter Anderson. We haven't been formally introduced."

"I'm surprised that you even know my name," Sunny said.

"Oh, this town loves gossip. You and Bip are a celebrity couple," Green said and laughed. "You're the biggest news in town since the new indoor pickleball courts opened. Bip is the exotic news photographer from Denver. You're the local Utah girl. People are buzzing about you."

Bip and Sunny laughed and looked at each other.

"Well, what about these two?" Bip said, jerking his thumb toward JC and Robin.

"Oh," Green said as his eyes widened. "They're royalty. If we had a magazine in Dog Mountain, they'd be on the cover. Everyone has a story about these two." He laughed again.

"It takes the pressure off Benny and Roman for a while, as the resident celebrities," Anderson said with a smile.

The doctor had set up a long narrow table, with Frank Green's help. Six people would just fit.

"How did you find a table that would fit in here?" Robin asked.

"I made the table," Anderson said. "I literally have to unscrew the legs of the table to get it out of the house. Then, it goes into my shed. That's the key to living in one of these homes. Everything has a clever design. My clothes are in drawers hidden in the stairs, for example. And I hang my suits in that closet that is a foot wide."

They drank wine and sat at the table as Robin cooked, two feet away. Sunny and Frank Green helped her. Green demonstrated that he was a good cook.

Robin cooked a dish of chicken, cheese, peppers and rice. It was something she thought up while looking at available ingredients at the grocery store.

"She is a free skier in the kitchen," JC said. "I think she gets it from mogul skiing. Just make a plan and attack."

"How are plans going for building your park full of tiny houses, Hunter?" Robin asked.

"I've lined up a contractor to build a road when the weather warms up," Anderson said. "I found a guy who builds them, over in Craig. He has taken my order and is getting to work on them. The first ones should be available for rental by next fall. It is beautiful around here in the fall. You should come back."

A phone rang. Dr. Anderson recognized the ring. It was his. And it was on the other side of the little house six people had squeezed into.

"That is one of the few shortcomings of having this many guests," he said. "Would you be so kind, Sunny?"

Sunny, on the far end of the table from Anderson, picked up the phone and answered it.

"Dr. Anderson's office," she said with a smile, looking at the doctor. "Hold for a moment."

"That sounded like an audition," Green said. "Do you need a receptionist, Hunter?" Everyone laughed.

Sunny then passed the phone to Bip. Bip passed the phone to Green. Green passed the phone to the doctor.

"This is Doctor Anderson," he said into the phone and listened. "Yes, Edgar."

The doctor's dinner guests watched him listen to someone on the other end.

"Oh boy," he said in a deflated voice. "I'm sorry to hear that. No, I'd be happy to help," he answered. "Do you want to give me any instructions?" he asked. "Just a moment, Edgar," he said.

"Sunny, could you reach into the drawer under the bottom stair and get me a pen and paper?" he asked.

Sunny pulled out the riser beneath the bottom stair, found a drawer with a pen and paper and handed them to Bip. Bip passed the pen and paper to Green. Green passed them to the doctor.

"You're welcome, Edgar. This is a shame," Anderson said into the phone as he was writing. "I should be able to get there in a half hour. No, no trouble at all."

Anderson hung up the phone and looked at his guests. After a moment of thought, he delivered the news.

"You are all welcome to stay and enjoy your meal and each other's company," he began, as he pulled on his coat and plucked his hat off a peg. "That was the county coroner, Edgar Ringling. Someone has died. Edgar was calling from a meeting in Grand Junction. He wouldn't be able to get back for three or four hours, so he asked me to fill in for him. He just wants me to be his eyes and ears and of any help that I can be for the sheriff."

"Who died, Hunter?" Frank asked.

"I'm afraid," the doctor said, "it's Benny Maple."

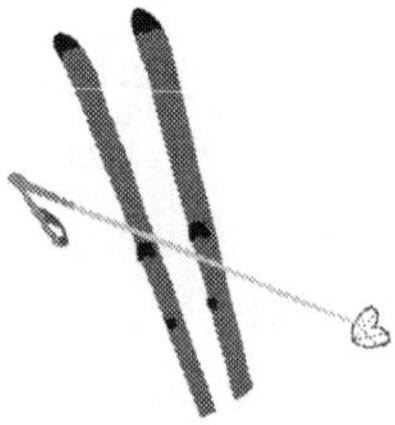

28

"Benjamin Maple, the actor, was found dead at his home in the town of Dog Mountain," JC wrote on the website of his television station. The short article was placed under a banner saying, "Breaking News."

Upon being informed of Benny Maple's death, JC, Bip and Robin rose from Hunter Anderson's dinner table. Despite being told by their host that they could continue the dinner party in his absence, the journalists knew they now had work to do.

It began with a call to their TV station from the car. Then, JC wrote that short article for the TV station's website.

"So much for our vacation from murder," Bip said as he drove up the access road to the resort village.

The news team stopped at their hotel long enough to pick up Bip's camera and batteries. They also put on warmer clothing. It might be a long night and it was still fifteen below zero.

Sunny stayed behind at the hotel with the key to Bip's room.

Upon arriving at Benny Maple's ranch off Route 72, Bip pulled the car up the driveway and parked behind a sheriff's patrol car. He worked fast. He knew what was coming.

It was dark and cold. But porch lamps and a few lights set up by the law enforcement team illuminated the building.

"Should I bring my microphone?" Bip asked. "Are we going to talk to Chief Newell?" Bip asked.

"We're just outside of town," JC informed him. "We'll be dealing with Lonesome County Sheriff Henry Nidever."

Bip shot footage of the exterior of the ranch house and of sheriff's deputies coming in and out of Benny's home.

But no more than a minute had elapsed when Sheriff Henry Nidever emerged from the house and walked straight for Bip.

"That's enough," the law officer said in a commanding voice. "I'll need you to get in your car and back it up to the road." Then the sheriff looked at JC. "Don't even think of arguing. This isn't debate club."

"Can you tell me the cause of death, Sheriff?" JC asked. "Do you know what happened? Do you have a suspect in custody?"

JC blurted every relevant question he could think of that would fit inside thirty seconds. He knew he was living on borrowed time.

"What did I say?" the sheriff barked. "Out! Or I will have you taken into custody."

Time was up.

"Well, he seems to like us," Bip laughed as they climbed into the news car.

They drove, not to the road as advised, but down the long driveway a bit. JC picked out a place where they could still keep an eye on things unfolding outside Benny's house.

"It's going to be a long night," Bip said, slipping into a more comfortable posture in his seat. "I hope the sheriff visits again. I like him."

"Nice work getting some video before he shut us down," JC said to him.

"Shoot first, ask for permission later," Bip said with a smile.

An hour passed, with the continuous sight of deputies walking in and out of the house. They could tell that lights had been set up inside the kitchen. They saw multiple camera flashes. JC noticed that all the activity was in the kitchen.

Bip discreetly slipped out of the car, grabbed his camera from the back, and shot more video. His lens could zero-in closer to the kitchen windows.

"That was a great dinner that you cooked," JC said to Robin, staying inside the warm car.

"It was fun while it lasted," she said. "I wonder if Hunter will talk to us when he comes out."

JC had been on the phone with the TV station again. They were asked to do a live shot for the ten o'clock news. The satellite truck had been dispatched to meet them on the side of the road at the entrance to Benny's ranch.

JC would also do a live shot for the TV station in Grand Junction, which was loaning them the satellite truck and the engineer who drove it.

Bip was done shooting and climbed back into the car to warm up. They saw a vehicle moving down the dirt driveway toward the road.

"That's Hunter's car," Robin said. She and JC got out of their vehicle and made themselves visible.

"Hi," Dr. Anderson said in a somber tone when he stopped and rolled down the window of his car.

"What can you tell us?" JC asked.

"I can't tell you much or the sheriff will have my head," Anderson said. "It *is* Benny," he said sadly. "He bled a lot. Roman is still in there. I'm worried about her, and how she's going to handle this. I'm going to get some medication to give her, then I'm coming back."

"Roman is in there?" JC considered the multiple possibilities. "What's she doing in there?"

"She says she found him," the doctor told them. "I don't think she's a suspect. She's pretty upset, as you might imagine."

"She's not a suspect?" JC said. "So, Benny was murdered?"

"Oh boy," Anderson said. "I'm new to this. I've probably already said too much. Yes, the sheriff believes he was murdered. I've got to go. I'm sorry."

Anderson's car pulled away.

"I don't think we're going back to Denver any time soon," JC said, looking at Robin.

Ten o'clock came quickly. Bip edited the video he had taken. And JC reported the facts as they knew them, that

Benny Maple was dead and a source close to the investigation had told them it was believed to be a murder.

Sheriff Henry Nidever emerged from Benny's home as soon as the live shot was over. He walked over to JC and a local newspaper reporter who had since arrived.

"I can give you a little bit," the sheriff said. "Not much."

The sheriff was a stern-looking man. His hairstyle was a gray brush cut. He looked like he had been a Marine until yesterday. But his face was weathered, showing he had been out in the sun and the wind of Browns Park for decades.

The sheriff waited for Bip to set up his tripod and get his camera rolling. The sheriff had learned that it was good policy to cooperate with the news media. But that only applied to things that didn't matter to his investigation.

"At approximately six o'clock this evening," Sheriff Nidever commenced, "our 9-1-1 dispatcher was called by a person saying that there was an unresponsive male at this ranch. Our units responded and found one Benjamin Raymond Maple prone on the floor of his kitchen. Deputies were unsuccessful in their efforts to revive him.

"No one is in custody, as of now," the sheriff continued. "We are classifying this as a suspicious death. If there is anyone who encountered Mr. Maple today or knows anything that might help explain the sequence of events leading to the discovery of the deceased, we ask you to call the Lonesome County Sheriff's Office."

"How was he killed, Sheriff?" JC asked.

"It appears that he was stabbed," the sheriff responded. "We have recovered what we believe to be the murder weapon."

"So, it's more than a suspicious death, then?" JC asked. "You called it a murder weapon?"

"I guess I did," the sheriff answered. "That would be accurate. We are investigating this as a murder."

Before answering any other questions, the sheriff uttered, "Thank you," and turned his back and walked away. He returned to the house of the late Benny Maple.

JC turned to Bip and asked him to tell the satellite truck engineer to delay his departure for the night. JC wanted to send that interview back to Denver.

"I have a feeling we're going to have an early start to our morning," JC said. Denver is going to want us to do live shots for the morning news."

While Bip was editing inside the satellite truck, Dr. Hunter Anderson returned. He drove past JC and Robin with a wave.

Ten minutes later, Anderson emerged from Benny's house.

"Roman is with him," Robin said. "Poor thing."

The doctor and Roman climbed into Anderson's car and headed out the driveway for the road. JC and Robin gave them room to pass.

But the car stopped. Anderson emerged from the driver's side and walked in front of his car to approach JC and Robin. Roman stayed in the car, only a few feet away.

"I'm a little concerned about Roman," Anderson said in a low voice. "Her daughter is at home, waiting for her. But I'd like an adult to be there tonight, just to make certain everything is alright. I've given Roman a mild sedative. Benny's death has come as a shock to her."

"I can imagine," Robin said.

"I asked her who I could call, to stay with her tonight," the doctor continued. "She said that Benny was the one she would always call. So, she asked for you."

Anderson was looking at Robin.

Robin looked at JC, who nodded his support for the arrangement.

"Yes, of course," Robin stammered.

"I can bring you your things," JC said.

"Thank you," she said, as did the doctor.

Robin climbed into Anderson's backseat. JC could see her lean forward to comfort Roman, who was wearing sunglasses and was seated in front of her. JC saw Roman reach back and clutch Robin's extended hand.

"They got it," Bip said as he emerged from the satellite truck. "They want a live shot from us in the morning."

"It's official, then," JC responded.

"Where's Robin?" Bip asked as they climbed into the car. JC explained her absence.

When the two men arrived at the hotel, JC told Bip to get some rest and they made arrangements to meet at five in the morning. JC said that he had to gather some of Robin's overnight things and drive them out to Roman's ranch.

JC climbed the stairs to their room. He gathered something for Robin to sleep in, her toothbrush and toothpaste and hairbrush. He grabbed a bag of something that was sitting on her side of the sink, zipped it up and tossed it in with some clean clothing.

He had somber thoughts as he drove to Roman's ranch. He thought of an old friend, Al Pine, who was also a murder victim.

JC called Robin and said that she could come outside and get her overnight bag, if Roman didn't want to be disturbed.

When JC pulled up in the news car, he saw two horses watching him from the nearest corral. They each had a blanket strapped to their back, to help combat the cold. Light poured out of an open door they could walk through, into the barn.

Robin opened the door of the house and Roman told JC to come inside. He did what he was told.

He gave Roman a hug. She held it for longer than expected.

"Someone killed Benny Ray," she said.

"You don't have to talk about it, Roman," JC said. "I didn't come here as a reporter. I just wanted to drop off some things for Robin."

"There was a lot of blood," Roman said. "He was stabbed with his own kitchen knife. In the neck. The only good thing was that they told me he died almost instantly. He didn't suffer."

She sounded exhausted. Or was it the sedative? JC knew that he couldn't, or didn't want to, report Roman's words to a television news audience until the sheriff corroborated them. Or at least until Roman repeated them when she was off medication and in a better state of mind.

"Why would someone do this?" Roman asked. There wasn't anger in her voice. It was fatigue. It was just one word stepping in front of the next.

"You don't have any idea?" JC asked. Roman shook her head.

"His two big dogs were with Benny Ray when I got there," she said. "They were laying down next to him. One of them had his head laying on Benny Ray's side. They looked so worried."

"Get some rest," JC said. "I'll check on you two in the morning."

29

A sheriff's patrol car was parked across the entrance to Benny Maple's property, preventing unwarranted entry. Frost covered the windshield. The deputy inside was asleep when JC and Bip arrived.

They brought an extra coffee for the deputy. Getting there before sunrise, JC and Bip had coffee and donuts for the satellite engineer. He was a stout man in his thirties with a beard. His name was Abel White.

A short time later, a reporter and photographer for the Grand Junction newspaper, *The Daily Sentinel*, arrived. They parked their car alongside the road and joined JC and Bip. They gratefully accepted the offer of donuts.

"We're like Meals on Wheels," Bip quipped.

The cold snap was over. The temperature at dawn was already in the teens and forecast to rise into the high twenties.

"This is ludicrous," Bip told JC. "It's fifteen degrees and it feels warm."

"Yeah," JC agreed. "Compared to the last three days."

Sunrise was spectacular. The men stood outside the truck, sipped their coffee and watched.

This was a land of extremes, JC thought. There were good men and bad men. The country was both beautiful and barren. It was so old, and yet, man couldn't resist trying to turn it into something new.

Man is so arrogant, JC thought. Human beings are almost the newest thing on the planet. And yet they behave like they invented the place.

The silence of the country morning was broken by two patrol cars as they crested a hill and approached the driveway of Benny Maple's home.

The deputy guarding the entrance backed up his car like a gate was opening. The two patrol cars, one carrying the sheriff, pulled into the driveway and proceeded to the kitchen door. The patrol car guarding the road pulled forward, sealing off entry by anyone else.

"Let's review. What have we got?" Sheriff Nidever asked two of his investigators. They stood in the kitchen and filled cups with coffee that came out of a spout protruding from a box.

"It was a knife from the victim's own kitchen," one investigator said. The investigator's name was Sid Brown. He was one of two Black deputies in a county that was over ninety-eight percent not Black. He was born and raised in Lonesome County.

"The knife hit the carotid artery," the other investigator said. Her name was Kathy Garcia. She left an unhappy life somewhere else and came here. It wasn't an uncommon story in Lonesome County.

"He had a deep cut on his chin," Garcia continued. "He may have hit it on some furniture on the way to the floor. The coroner says that death was probably quick."

"Do we know why he was found where he was found?" the sheriff asked. "If he died quickly, then he was probably standing in the area where we found him on the floor."

"We think he knew his attacker," Brown said. "At least, he was comfortable enough to turn his back on the killer. He was stabbed in the back of the neck."

"No sign of break-in," Investigator Garcia continued. "No sign of robbery. His laptop wasn't stolen. His wallet was upstairs in a bedroom drawer. There were four $100 bills in it."

"What was he doing when he was killed?" the sheriff asked.

"He may have been on his laptop," Investigator Brown answered. "His body was found in that general area. And we found scraps of paper next to the laptop that seem to contain passwords."

"Convenient for us," Sheriff Nidever said. "Let's go through all the sites we can connect those passwords to. Maybe we'll find something."

"There was also a book next to the laptop, Sheriff," Garcia added. "A history of Norway. Pagan gods and the works."

"Does that mean anything to you?" the sheriff asked.

"Not offhand," Brown said. Garcia was looking at him in agreement.

"Well, keep it in mind," Nidever told them. "Roman Holiday, the actress, found the body? Were they a couple?"

"She says they were not," Garcia responded. "Very good friends, she said."

"Do you believe her? Anything to contradict that?" the sheriff inquired. Both investigators shook their heads. "Well, keep her in mind."

Sheriff Nidever walked out the kitchen door and climbed into a patrol car. A deputy drove him to the end of the driveway where the sheriff held a brief news conference. He confirmed all that Roman and Dr. Anderson had told JC the night before. There was nothing new.

Henry Nidever climbed back into the patrol car and the deputy drove him back to the door of Benny's kitchen. The sheriff got out of the car and walked back inside the crime scene.

"How about Jon Oaks?" JC asked Bip and Robin over breakfast at the Rendezvous. "Roman and even Benny told us that Oaks hated Benny. That puts him on the short list."

Robin had joined her colleagues after spending the night at Roman's ranch. She said that Roman slept through the night, with the help of sedatives.

The actress assured Robin that she would be alright for the day. Roman's daughter, Olive, would be home with her.

"We should check in on her later," Robin said.

"We can find time to do that," JC said.

"I might spend the night there again," Robin told him. JC nodded his agreement.

"Can we think of anyone else who would want to kill Benny, besides Oaks? Benny was probably the most popular, likable guy in the county," JC said.

"His drug dealer," Bip said after drinking his coffee and giving it some thought. Sunny was their waitress, so coffee refills were frequent.

"His drug dealer?" repeated JC. "That's a really good one. He was open about his drug use. Who was his drug dealer?"

"Do you think the sheriff knows Benny was an addict?" Robin asked. "Do you think Roman told them? I get the feeling that Roman didn't tell them anything that might damage Benny's reputation."

"The medical examiner will tell him," JC suggested. "But let's go ask."

Riding in the car to Benny Maple's ranch, JC's phone rang.

"I've been expecting your call," he said.

"Yep," he said into the phone after a pause.

"Yep," he repeated.

"Can we keep Robin?" he asked.

"Yep," he repeated.

JC hung up the phone and turned to make eye contact with the two others.

"That was Rocky, our fearless assignment editor," he told them as he pocketed his phone.

"What did he say?" Robin asked.

"He asked if we could stay here in Lonesome County for a little while longer. He asked if there would be anything to report. I asked if we could keep you with us, Robin. He asked if that would make me happy."

Sheriff Henry Nidever walked out of the house when Bip drove the news car up to the door of Benny's ranch. Two investigators followed behind the sheriff.

"I thought I was pretty clear about where you could park," the sheriff snapped.

"I might have something you'll be interested to hear," JC said. "You might want to speak with us."

"Twice in one day," the sheriff grumbled. "I guess I'm just lucky."

"Is Jon Oaks a suspect?" JC asked.

Bip was at his side, his camera rolling.

"We're not presently at liberty to discuss suspects," the sheriff growled. "Besides, I thought you said you had something important to tell me."

"Oaks hated Benny," JC said.

"Would you mind turning that camera off a moment," the sheriff asked after considering the question. It sounded more like a command. "Let's talk. Then we'll see what we want to say on camera."

JC and Bip looked at each other and agreed to power down the camera.

"Who told you that?" the sheriff asked.

"Benny told us," JC said. "So did Roman."

The sheriff looked over his shoulder at his investigators, sending them a message to check that information out.

"And do you know who his drug dealer was?" JC asked.

The sheriff stared at the reporter. JC could see that Nidever was considering his next response.

"How do you know he was a drug user?" the sheriff asked.

"Again, Benny told us," JC responded. "He was kind of an open book."

Now, it was JC's turn to assess the man standing in front of him.

"You didn't know he was an addict, did you?" JC asked. It was really a statement. "The autopsy results aren't back."

"So, who is the dealer?" the sheriff asked.

"That, Benny did not tell us," the reporter replied.

"What do you want?" the sheriff asked brusquely.

"I want you to know that I'm not as stupid as I look," JC answered. "I'll share with you what I learn. I want the killer caught too."

It went without saying that JC expected some cooperation in return. But, he thought, why insult the law officer by telling him something that he already knew.

"Anything else?" the sheriff asked JC.

"I understand that you said Benny's death was pretty quick, after he was stabbed," JC stated.

"I don't remember telling you that," the sheriff said with a stern face.

"No, you didn't," JC said.

Without a word, the sheriff turned and led his deputies back into the home of Benny Maple.

JC watched the law officers disappear behind closed doors. He thought about Benny's Los Angeles phone number. The threatening calls to Roman were routed through Los Angeles. Was it a coincidence? He wondered what he was supposed to make of that.

"It's pretty nice out," Bip said, breaking the trance. He pulled off his heavy jacket.

The sky was a bright blue and temperatures had climbed to thirty. Birds were chirping again. JC, Bip and Robin leaned against their car and absorbed the sun's rays.

30

Roman heard a vehicle rumble over the cattle guard and two minutes later, there was a knock at her door. She had showered and changed back into her pajamas after feeding the horses that morning.

She grabbed a robe to pull around her. On the way to the door, she stopped at the thermostat on the wall of her living room and turned up the heat to sixty-eight.

"Do you know where my husband is?" the woman asked when Roman opened the door.

"Um, hello," Roman said, startled by the question. "Who is your husband?"

"Nat Sanchez," the stranger said. "I can't count the number of times he told me how pretty you were. I thought maybe he was here."

"Thank you, but what would he be doing here?" Roman asked with a furrowed brow. "I don't think that I even know him."

"He sells you office supplies," the pudgy woman said. "Nat Sanchez."

Roman gave this some thought. The door was only open halfway. Roman was blocking the stranger's path into her house.

Roman did remember a man coming to her ranch to set up her office when she started her horse-rescue nonprofit. But since then, she bought her office paper and an occasional ink refill for her printer from Frank Green's store.

"Nat?" Roman repeated the name. "Is he the office supply man from Casper?"

"Yes," the woman said. "He told me that he knows you. And he is right. You're quite beautiful. I thought maybe he had taken up with you. I feel a bit foolish now. I think you're out of his league."

"Thank you?" Roman said awkwardly. "He seemed like a nice man. But I think he was only here once."

"I'm sorry," the woman said as she dropped her eyes to the ground. "I should be ashamed of myself."

The woman was plump, had dark hair and wore glasses. Roman thought she wore a bit too much makeup.

"And you are?" Roman asked.

"I'm Nancy Sanchez," the woman said, lifting her eyes to meet Roman's. There were tears in the woman's eyes now. "I'm Nat's wife."

The visitor's chin began to tremble. She was trying hard not to cry. Roman stepped back from the door to allow Nancy Sanchez into her home.

"Come in," the actress said. "It's cold out there."

"Oh, no," the woman said as she entered the house. "The sun is out. It's not that cold."

Spoken like a true woman of the Rocky Mountains, Roman thought. A little cold wasn't going to bother her. But the woman walked in.

"Why would your husband be here?" Roman asked, shutting the outside door behind them. "Oh, that's right. You thought he might have taken up with me."

"I am so foolish," Nancy Sanchez said. "You're the actress, aren't you?"

"I used to be," Roman said with a smile.

"I guess Nat has left me," Mrs. Sanchez said, her chin trembling again.

"I'm so sorry," Roman said honestly.

"I just don't know what to do," the woman said. That started her crying. Roman embraced the stranger and the woman sobbed into Roman's shoulder.

"Am I just supposed to move on?" the woman wept. "I waited for him to come home. Now, I'm worried that something has happened to him."

"Why would you think he left you?" Roman asked gently.

Nancy Sanchez pulled her head away from Roman's shoulder and reached into the pocket of her heavy winter coat. She pulled out a piece of stationery.

"He left me this," the woman said, sniffling her nose and wiping it with a tissue. "It says that he is unhappy and he needs to start his life over. He says that he loves me but that he needs a new life. Without me."

Nancy Sanchez began crying again and Roman pulled her back into her embrace.

"I haven't told anyone," the woman sobbed into Roman's shoulder. "You're the first. I just kept it all inside. I made excuses when people called for Nat."

"And now you've come looking for him," Roman said softly.

"Yes," the woman choked, her head still burrowed into Roman's shoulder. "You smell nice."

That made Roman laugh quietly. She offered the woman coffee.

"Let's go into the kitchen," Roman said. She thought that a normal setting might bring the woman back from the verge of hysteria.

"This is beautiful," Nancy said, scanning the kitchen. Roman led her to a table by a window that looked out the back. They could see the horses from there.

"Thank you," Roman said, eyeing the kitchen herself. "So, you haven't heard from him since finding that letter?"

"No," Nancy said. Roman placed a cup of coffee in front of Mrs. Sanchez and joined her at the table.

"Excuse me for being insensitive," Roman said. "But did you see this coming? Had your husband expressed his unhappiness to you before disappearing?"

"No!" Mrs. Sanchez replied. "We were happy. At least, I thought we were." Her chin began to tremble again. But she fought off tears.

"And you haven't told anyone he's missing?" Roman asked. "You haven't called the police? They might be able to help you find him."

"I haven't," Nancy said, wiping her nose with the tissue.

"And why would he be here?" Roman asked. "I don't mean my house. Why would he be in Dog Mountain?"

"He always talks about this place," she said. "It's his favorite stop in his region. He knows lots of people. We spoke about moving here."

"Well, maybe he is here in Dog Mountain," Roman said. "Honestly, I'd be the last to know. But if he had a lot of customers here, maybe one of them knows where he is."

"Maybe," Mrs. Sanchez said. She now seemed emotionally drained. The tears had stopped coming. She looked in her lap a lot, not drinking her coffee.

"Are there other customers here who he talked about?"

"He talked about all of them," the woman said with a slight smile, like it brought back pleasant memories. She named names. Roman knew some of them.

The woman rose. She said that she had other stops in town. She held a list of customers who did business with her husband. She wanted to talk to them.

Roman gave Mrs. Sanchez directions to the stores and offices she was looking for.

"I'm sorry for bothering you," Mrs. Sanchez said. "You have a very nice home. You've been kind to me."

With that, the woman walked out the front door and climbed back into her car.

"Poor woman," Roman said to herself. She returned to her own affairs, including writing some remarks for Benny Ray's funeral.

It was a difficult task. It would require saying a final goodbye to a man she loved with all of her heart. He was the father of her daughter, though he would now never know.

The time would come when Roman would have to tell Olive who her father was. Was this the time? Roman had always thought the time would be when Benny Ray came to his senses and recognized that she was the love of his life.

She thought of Nancy Sanchez.

"Men," she said to herself. "Fucked if you love them and fucked if you don't."

She heard another knock at her door. She wondered if Nancy Sanchez had forgotten something. But upon opening the front door, she saw a sheriff's investigator standing there.

"I'm sorry to show up without calling," the man said. She recognized him. It was Sid Brown, one of the investigators who questioned her after she found Benny Ray's body.

"Please let me get dressed," Roman said, somewhat distressed. "Would you just give me a moment?"

She closed the door, leaving the investigator standing outside. He was always suspicious of that kind of behavior. It was typical of drug users who would close the door and quickly hide their stash.

"I'm sorry," Roman said when she opened the door again. "I should have invited you in. It's been a rather hectic morning."

She had pulled on a pair of blue jeans and a plain green sweatshirt that matched her eyes.

She gave him a smile and invited him to come inside. He returned a non-committal smile and entered. He immediately surveyed the home, looking for evidence she might have forgotten on the coffee table or an end table.

He inhaled through his nose a number of times.

"Are you sniffing for pot?" Roman asked, laughing.

The investigator didn't appreciate being laughed at. She picked up on that.

"I'm sorry," she said, still laughing a bit. "I don't know what you think you interrupted, but you're off by a mile. May I offer you coffee?"

"Sorry, ma'am," he said, having not detected the scent of marijuana. "It's my job."

Roman walked him into the kitchen and seated him at the table in the same chair where Nancy Sanchez had been seated. Placing a cup of coffee in front of him, she caught the law officer gazing out the window at the horses.

"It's a nice thing you do," he said. "For the horses."

"Thank you," she smiled, having collected her own fresh cup of coffee and joining him at the table. "Now, what may I do for you?"

"You weren't far off," he smiled a little. "I'm here to talk to you about drugs."

"Are you buying or selling?" she grinned. That made him feel awkward.

"You say that you were close to Mr. Maple?" he asked.

"Yes, very," she said. Her smile disappeared and she looked down at the steam rising from her cup of coffee.

"Then," the investigator said. "You were aware that he used a high quantity of heroin?"

"He was a heroin addict," she said. "Yes."

"Can you give me the name of his supplier?" Brown asked.

"I would if I could," she said. "Benny Ray never shared it with me. He was very discreet. He didn't discuss things like that with me."

"I thought you said you were close?" the law officer said to her.

"Yes," Roman answered. "Close enough to tell him that he was killing himself with that stuff. He grew tired of hearing me say it. Eventually, he just avoided the subject. He knew that I knew that he was using, but he never discussed it again."

She sensed that the investigator was suspicious of her. She locked her eyes onto his and pushed up the two sleeves of her sweatshirt. She exposed her arms, showing him that there were no tracks marked by a hypodermic needle.

Investigator Brown knew that there were other ways to inject or ingest heroin, aside from shooting it into your arm. But she was convincing. And he noted that the actress' bare arms were exquisite.

"Thank you. You've made your point," he said seriously. "He never gave you a name?"

"No, he didn't," she said. "I'm sorry."

"Did you ever see him in the company of someone who might be his supplier? Anyone you thought was suspicious?"

"No. Everyone knew Benny Ray," she said. "And if he didn't know them, they behaved as though he knew them and would walk right up and start a conversation. Benny Ray was always nice about it. He'd treat total strangers like they were old friends."

"Did he ever shoot up in your presence?" the investigator asked.

"Never," she said. "Not a single time."

"Then how, might I ask, did you know he was a user?"

"He told me," she said with a grin. "That was Benny Ray. I don't think he was capable of keeping a secret."

"But he kept the name of his supplier a secret from you," Investigator Brown pointed out.

"I never asked," Roman told him.

The investigator asked some more questions that Roman thought sounded routine.

"You still have no idea who killed Benny Ray?" she interrupted.

"Someone who he trusted," Investigator Brown told her.

At that instant, it occurred to the investigator that Benny Maple trusted *her*. The thought also occurred to Roman.

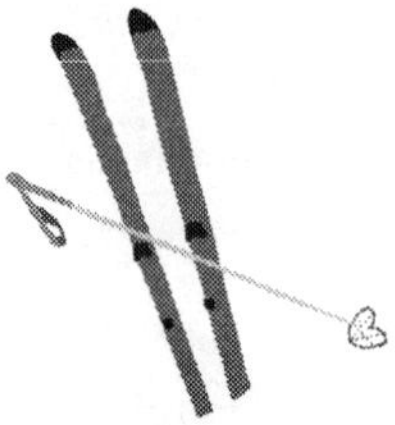

31

"Closed for the day."

Signs like that hung on the door or window of every store in the tiny town of Dog Mountain. Everyone would be attending the funeral service of Benjamin Maple.

When the sheriff released his remains, Benny would be cremated and interred in a mausoleum in Dog Mountain's new cemetery. It was Lonesome County's only cemetery currently accepting new clients.

Older burial places included the small Browns Park cemetery next to Lodore Hall, or family plots on a ranch, or graves long forgotten in a meadow or atop a hill. Indigenous people had no doubt died there, but they were good at hiding their graves.

An old diary spoke of a man who was shot for cheating at cards. An old letter discussed a rancher who was gored by a bull. Where they were buried, and others like them, was anybody's guess.

There were some Hollywood types at Benny's funeral. His agent was there. A former producer and a former co-star were there.

And there were a few women who looked like old girlfriends from the movie business. They were gawked at by the locals like balloons in Macy's Thanksgiving Day Parade.

Roman hosted a gathering at her ranch, following the funeral. Everyone was invited. Roman had been named as executor of Benny's estate.

The sheriff had not released the murder scene at Benny's ranch. It remained sealed and blocked off by yellow tape that read, "Crime Scene Do Not Cross."

JC and Bip were on the clock during the service. Bip was shooting footage outside the church. They would go live that night on the evening news.

JC interviewed Sheriff Henry Nidever before the funeral.

"We checked on the whereabouts of Jonathan Oaks at the estimated time of Mr. Maple's death," the sheriff told JC. "Mr. Oaks was confirmed by multiple witnesses to have been in Durango, some seven hours away. That finding was also backed by data from his court-ordered ankle bracelet."

"Do you have a suspect then?" JC asked.

"We are not at liberty to discuss suspects or persons of interest at this time," the sheriff said.

If the sheriff *had* been at liberty to discuss suspects or persons of interest at that time, JC had the feeling that the answer would be, "No."

Investigators continued to try, to no avail, to unearth the person or persons who provided Benny with his drugs.

"We found some notes next to Mr. Maple's laptop," the sheriff said after the interview was over. "We're looking into those. They might be passwords. We think he was on his computer when his assailant approached him from behind."

JC thought about this. While sitting in Benny's kitchen with Robin, Benny stood by his computer and said that he thought he was losing money, somehow. He borrowed that book from Hemingway, hoping to learn more about Norway, where he had investments.

But JC also considered Benny's phone number with a Los Angeles area code. Hemingway had received a threatening call that appeared to come from Los Angeles. So had Roman, for that matter.

What, JC wondered, was Benny doing on that computer? And who might have caught him doing it?

The shadows were growing long as JC and Bip drove from Roman's ranch. They had spent a brief time at the gathering after the funeral, but they had work to do.

JC watched the landscape roll by. He saw fallen logs topped by sun-glazed snow. Tall grass, darkened by death, was poking through the snow in some places. It reminded JC of black and white photographs taken by Ansel Adams.

They passed three backcountry skiers arriving at their car at the end of their adventurous day. One carried a splitboard, a snowboard that could be split in two and used as skis when climbing up the mountain.

As the hour of their live shot approached, it was time for Bip to edit his video at the satellite truck. Abel White had parked the truck across from the chapel, the site of Benny's funeral service.

On a utility pole in front of the church, the town was advertising another festival coming up in a week. It was called "The Mountain Man Rendezvous." The poster promised dogsled races and riding inner tubes down the steepest hill on Main Street. There would be archery, hatchet throwing and other contests befitting a man who could live in the mountains with only his weapons and his wits.

"You should have gotten that anchor job," the voice told JC over the phone. "You're a really good anchor, and much better than the guy who got the job."

"Thanks, Clint," JC said. "I appreciate that."

The prior summer, JC had been considered for an anchor slot at his television station. It would have meant more money, among other things. JC was never sure that he wanted the job. It was flattering to be considered, and there was nothing wrong with being paid more money. But he preferred reporting from the field to sitting at the anchor desk.

He had stepped out of the satellite truck and into the cold air to take the phone call. He wanted privacy.

"You're a reporter at heart, aren't you?" Clint asked.

"Yep," JC told him. "I knew that all along. I don't even think about that anchor job."

Clint worked for the national television network that JC's TV station was affiliated with. This was Clint's third call informing JC that he was wanted for the national news. They wanted him to move to New York or perhaps Los Angeles.

"Come report for us," Clint said over the phone. "More money, more fame, more stories that will take you across the globe."

"It's tempting," JC said. "I'm giving it serious thought. You said that I had a little time to think it over, right?"

"Yes, I did," Clint agreed. "I just want to make sure you're giving it serious thought. You've got a great gig in Denver. I know that. But think of the stories that you could sink your teeth into, up here with us. You'd spend a year or two working here in New York or in Los Angeles, and then you'd leapfrog over the more senior reporters and you'd have your choice of assignments. You're that good, JC."

"Thanks, Clint," JC said. "Listen, I've got to go. I have to get ready for a live shot for the only employer I've got, presently. I'll let you know."

"I'm not trying to put additional pressure on you, JC," Clint said. "But they generally don't ask twice."

"Gotcha," JC said before hanging up. "No pressure at all."

"He seems pretty special," Roman said.

"He is," Robin told her. "I did something really stupid. And he seems to forgive me. I don't know why. When you finally meet a good man who is really fun to be with, you almost hold your breath hoping that nothing goes wrong."

The two women were alone in Roman's kitchen. They were washing dishes and cleaning up following the funeral dinner.

"Thanks for staying," Roman told her. "It's nice to have company."

Roman had been treated at the funeral, and at the gathering at her house, like the widow. Maybe, Robin thought, Roman's secret longing for Benny wasn't as well-kept a secret as she believed.

"Do you want to spend the night?" Roman asked. "I'm fine, I'm just saying that you don't have to leave."

"Thanks," Robin told her. "But I'll get JC to come get me. I miss him."

"You're a lucky woman," Roman told her again.

Roman left the kitchen to join her daughter on the couch.

"How are you doing, sweetie," she asked her eleven-year-old.

"I'm fine," Olive said. "I'm going to miss Benny though."

"So am I," Roman said, exhaling and collapsing onto the back of the couch.

"You were in love with him, weren't you?" Olive asked.

"He was an important part of our lives, honey," Roman said.

"Was he your best friend?" the young girl asked.

"I suppose that he was," her mother told her.

"Why?"

Roman brushed her daughter's hair out of her eyes and considered that question. There was a conversation they needed to have. Roman had always hoped that the talk would come at a happier time.

But maybe, she thought, now was the best time left to her. The entire town would be mourning Benny. It might help Olive to process the information and mourn a man she never knew was her father.

"Honey, I want to tell you something that you have a right to know," Roman began. "It's complicated, but I think you're adult enough to understand. I hope I'm right."

Roman proceeded to tell Olive that Benny was her father. Roman anticipated the questions that followed.

"Why didn't you tell me until now?" Olive asked. "Then we could have been a real family."

"He didn't even know," Roman told her. "Benny Ray never knew that you were his daughter. He wasn't ready for us to be a family."

"Didn't he love us?" Olive asked. Her eyes were moist, but she didn't cry.

"He did love us, honey. And he loved *you*," Roman said.

"Then why didn't you ever tell him?"

"That's the complicated part," Roman told her. "He needed more time, I think."

"You don't really know that, if you didn't tell him," the eleven-year-old said.

That was a good point, Roman thought. If she had given Benny Ray a chance, she wondered, would he have wanted to join their family? Would he have wanted to be Olive's father and Roman's husband?

Would he have wanted to kick his heroin habit? Or would he have, however reluctantly, dragged his wife and daughter down the black hole that all drug addicts pulled their loved ones down.

When would she tell her daughter the entire story, Roman asked herself. When would Olive understand that her father loved her, but might have loved heroin more?

Roman wondered if she was wrong to refuse to risk everything on a junkie?

32

Hunter Anderson squinted up from under the brim of his cowboy hat. He saw bluebird skies. He parked at a pull-off in a cedar break on Route 72, well west of town. He had passed a number of oil and gas exploration sites as he drove to the spot.

The wind had blown most of the snow from the pull-off, exposing dirt and gravel beneath his car tires. He opened the hatch of his SUV and waxed his cross-country skis.

It hadn't snowed in a few days, so he had decided on some blue hard wax. It went on like crayon. Then he rubbed it in with a cork.

Friends of his were buying cross-country skis with fish-scale bottoms or mohair bases, for the convenience. They were tired of waxing. They said it was messy and time-consuming.

Most conversations got around to complaining about waxing with klister. It was like applying honey with your fingers. He couldn't argue with them, he just stayed away from klister.

But Anderson liked it old-school. Waxed bases provided a more efficient grip on the snow when he needed something to climb. The extra time it took to wax was worth his while. Besides, he liked gauging the temperature, snow condition and potential changes in the weather. It was part of the experience of matching wits with the elements.

He pushed off and kicked out of the cedar break and up a knoll. It would be covered in grass in the summer. There were some rock ledges to his right. To his left, the terrain flowed downhill to the road and Talamantes Creek.

He was wearing the same topcoat that he wore when he was alpine skiing. He needed to get to the store and buy something more appropriate, he thought.

Still, as the exercise warmed his core temperature, he only had to unbutton the wool coat to catch a breeze on his chest.

His skis followed another set of tracks. They were left by an animal and heading toward a large meadow covered in sun-baked snow. Anderson stopped and looked at the wildlife prints. They were no longer sharp, probably a few days old.

He guessed they belonged to a lone elk, the animal might have been moving toward the meadows in Browns Park, where winters were less severe. It would be easier for elk to find grass to graze there.

Anderson pushed on for a time. From the frozen sagebrush slopes of Diamond Peak, he could look north in the direction of Wyoming.

This was a stern test for his arm, he was thinking. He even thought that he might have overdone it.

After some miles, he skied toward a large rock. It would be a good place to rest and eat a lunch he had packed in a bag. There were crackers, peanut butter and a banana.

He gazed at an odd tree as he skied by. It was a dead pine. Without a single needle on its branches, he thought it looked like a tall skeleton, alone on the slope.

The snow on one side of the big red rock wasn't very deep. He kicked off his skis and climbed onto the stony seat to sit in the sun.

He was loving his day. His arm was tired but he was getting exercise. He was in nature and at peace with the world.

Chewing his lunch, he took in his surroundings. He believed that this was a summer pasture for cattle. They would have been moved down lower for the winter.

He thought about a new wolfpack spotted in nearby Jackson County. They had first been discovered on game cameras. The wolves' motion triggered the cameras at night.

Then ranchers began to see them. A few of the animals were legally shot by the ranchers, trying to protect their livestock.

Sitting on the rock, Anderson studied draws and gulches carved by creeks that would funnel water to the Talamantes, and eventually the Green River.

There were low cedars and piñon. He thought that if he went up near the peak, he would see the Gates of Lodore.

He looked at a pebble resting next to him on his stone seat. It was curious.

Picking it up to more closely examine the item, he saw that it wasn't a pebble at all. It was a human molar.

He turned it in his fingers. He was disappointed when he determined that it wasn't an ancient artifact left by indigenous people who used to live here. The tooth showed signs of modern dentistry.

Anderson placed the tooth in a pocket of his long black coat. Lunch being over, he slid off the big rock and retrieved his skis.

Bending over to fasten his bindings, he saw something he was surprised he hadn't noticed before. It was etched into the rock. It said *1838*, along with some letters. It looked like other letters had faded away. A remembrance left from someone gone for a long time.

He was ready to turn around and head back home. He had invited JC, Robin and Bip to dinner at his tiny house. There were six rainbow trout thawing on the counter of his small kitchen. He caught the fish last summer at Flaming Gorge Reservoir.

Returning to his little house, he jumped into the shower, dressed and prepared for company.

By the time his guests arrived, his arm was plenty sore. Pulling the fish off an outdoor grill, he winced.

The doctor greeted his friends and paraded the food inside. A salad and some buttered potatoes were already waiting.

They sat around the table he had made. There was just enough room for the five of them, with the addition of

Sunny. There was just enough room for their plates and a bottle of wine.

Bip and JC had spent the day preparing a story about Jon Oaks. He had a hearing coming up. Oaks would be returning to Lonesome County from Durango. JC had gone live via satellite outside the courthouse for the evening news.

Hunter Anderson informed them that he didn't have office hours that day, and told them about his day on skis. He said he didn't regret making the trip, despite his current discomfort. His arm would feel better tomorrow.

"Here's something interesting that I found." The doctor stood and rummaged through a pocket of the coat that hung from a peg.

"It's a tooth," he said as he revealed the day's find. He held it up between his forefinger and thumb. "Technically, it is a multi-rooted tooth of a human."

"It looks like a molar," Robin told him.

"That's exactly what it is," Anderson said, pointing at her as though she'd won a contest.

"It was sitting on a rock, right next to me as I ate lunch and admired the view," the doctor said. "In fact, it turned out to be an interesting rock. On one side, angled and protecting its surface against the weather, someone had carved the numerals 1-8-3-8. I presume it to be a date."

"How did a human tooth end up sitting alone on a boulder?" JC asked.

"That is a good question," Anderson said after giving the tooth a moment of thought. "Maybe I'll pass it along to the sheriff. Maybe someone reported they lost a tooth."

That got a laugh from his guests.

"Maybe the tooth fairy has posted a reward," Bip giggled.

Anderson deposited the molar back into the coat's pocket.

They drank more wine and had finished off the fish when the doctor's phone rang.

"Didn't this happen last time we ate dinner here?" Robin said with a smile. "I guess that's what happens when you're the only doctor in town."

Anderson returned an apologetic smile to his guests and picked up his phone.

"Yes," he said to the caller. "This is Doctor Anderson."

His eyes grew large and he stood from the table. He pushed back the curtains and looked out his window into the night.

"Yes," he said to his phone. "I'll be right there."

He hung up and gave his friends an astonished look.

"My cabin is burning," he said. "They think someone set it on fire."

33

Smoke hung in the air. It clung to the canopy of pine trees. All that remained of Dr. Hunter Anderson's tiny cabin was the masonry foundation it once sat on. The walls were gone. There was some blackened metal that was once a refrigerator, a stove, the spiral staircase.

Bip was shooting footage of the glowing ruins. Anderson and his cowboy hat were silhouetted as he spoke with an investigator from the sheriff's office. The investigator also wore a cowboy hat.

The news photographer, along with JC and Robin, was kept back from the smoking remains. Investigators didn't want them to step on evidence or provide even more tracks to the confusing collection already in the snow.

"JC, Robin?" Anderson called to them. His gesture instructed them to duck under the yellow crime tape and join him with Investigator Kathy Garcia. Sunny remained on the other side of the tape.

"I told the investigator that you two stayed in the cabin last week."

"Do you smoke?" the investigator asked.

"No," they both said.

"Did you use the wood-burning stove?" Garcia asked.

"We used the stove," JC responded. "You'd freeze to death if you didn't." Anderson laughed in agreement.

"We don't smoke," Robin added. "And we didn't light candles or anything."

"I just wanted to check," Investigator Garcia told them. "This wasn't caused by a spark from a stove that hadn't been used in a week. There's a burn pattern on the floor. Someone used an accelerant."

"So, this was arson?" JC asked.

"Shit," Garcia said. "You're a member of the news media, aren't you? Well, we would have said it in a press release in the morning anyway. Yes, this was definitely arson."

"Investigator?" a deputy called out from the other side of the cleared lot.

"Excuse me," Investigator Garcia said. "I'm being summoned."

She walked across the fire scene to the deputy. JC was about to tell her about the truck he saw on the night spent in the cabin with Robin. He decided to stay until he could pull her aside again.

"Hi doctor," a voice said. The sheriff was approaching from the line of parked cars. "I'm sorry to have to see you under these circumstances."

The sheriff recognized JC and Robin and inspected them without saying a word. JC thought the sheriff was wondering why two members of the news media had been allowed past the yellow tape. The sheriff was certain to ask his investigator. And if there wasn't a good reason, he'd have the two journalists escorted to the other side of the line.

"You have a minute, Sheriff?" JC asked. The sheriff thought for a moment before saying that he had.

JC told Sheriff Nidever about the night he spent with Robin in the cabin. He told him about the truck that pulled into the driveway, only to pull out again. And the distinct odor of gasoline.

"I'm not saying it was Gerhard Snyder's truck," JC said. "But it sure looked like the truck we saw him get into at the county building."

"Okay," is all the sheriff said, after eyeing JC for a moment. Then the law officer walked off in the direction of Investigator Garcia.

"You're welcome," Robin said so only the three of them could hear it.

"Gerhard Snyder?" Anderson repeated with surprise in his tone. JC realized that he hadn't shared the story with Anderson.

"It slipped my mind," JC told him. "I really didn't think about it a lot, until now. I half figured that it was my imagination. I'm sorry if saying something could have prevented this."

"No need to apologize," the doctor said. "I probably wouldn't have given it much thought if it happened to me.

I've had cars and trucks turn around in my driveway before. It's not that uncommon. The road ends just a bit ahead. You're not sure it was even his truck?"

"No, I'm really not," JC said. "I just thought it was worth mentioning, considering the current circumstances."

The sheriff walked past the three of them again, apparently heading back to his patrol car.

He stopped and looked at JC.

"You're sure about this?" the sheriff asked.

"I said that I'm not sure it was Snyder's truck," JC told him. "I am sure that a truck of that description pulled into Hunter's driveway and turned around."

"Okay," the sheriff said before turning and walking to his patrol car and driving off.

"You're welcome," Robin repeated, so only the three of them could hear it. They all laughed a little.

"Crud," Anderson said as his hand shuffled through his coat pocket. "I didn't show him the tooth. Oh well, I'll stop by his office tomorrow and give it to him."

Bip joined them, saying that he'd shot the fire scene from every angle. JC said that he wasn't going to wake up the satellite engineer to send the video of a small cabin fire in the middle of the night.

He'd call the newsroom in the morning and let them know what they had. It wasn't worthy of a banner across the TV screen screaming "Breaking News." But it would fit into the show, somewhere.

They left Dr. Hunter Anderson, expressing their sorrow about the loss of his cabin, and thanked him for dinner.

"You're not going to invite us to dinner again," Bip said. "We seem to bring you bad luck."

"Not at all," Anderson smiled.

It was past midnight when JC and Robin climbed into bed.

"Can I ask you something?" Robin said. They were lying in the dark, waiting to fall asleep.

"Sure," JC said.

"Who's calling you?" she said. "Bip said you got another call and you got out of the satellite truck to talk in private. That's the third time."

JC considered her question. He knew it was time to have the conversation. But it wasn't a conversation he wanted to have, at least not yet.

"Network wants me to come work for them," he said.

"That's wonderful," she said. It was dark. He could not see the expression on her face. He wondered what the expression would look like. She knew what the job offer meant.

"It would mean moving to Los Angeles or New York," he said.

"I know," she said after a pause. "We'd be fine, JC. I'd be fine."

He reached out an arm to touch her face.

"I don't know if I'm going to take it," he said.

"Why wouldn't you?" she asked. "They need you. You'd be wonderful. You'd be their best reporter."

"I'm not sure anyone is *that* needed," he said. "If they don't hire me, they'll hire someone else. They'd be fine and I'd be fine. It's not a higher calling, like God needs me. It's just a good job."

He wasn't of a mind to ask her if she'd come to New York or Los Angeles with him. He wasn't eager to become tangled in that contest, exploring whose opportunity was more important than the other person's. Robin was excelling as a reporter in Denver. But she was still new at it, still building a track record. How could he ask her to walk away from that?

"You'd be living a reporter's dream," she said. "You'd have some of the best story assignments in the country. And you'd be making fabulous money. Why wouldn't you take it?"

"Because I'm happy," he said.

Dr. Anderson was tired when he got to his office in the morning. He'd only had a few hours' sleep, but he knew that he had appointments up until lunch.

It didn't help that his receptionist called in sick that morning. But the appointment calendar was in the middle of her desk. He opened it to today's date and got to work.

He squeezed in an older man who said he had been throwing up all night. The doctor checked him out and they discussed what the gentleman had for dinner the night before. He said he baked a turkey and made a salad.

"How long did you bake the turkey?" the doctor asked.

"I don't know," the patient said. "Until it looked done."

"Did you wash the salad?" Doctor Anderson inquired.

"You've got to wash it?" the patient asked.

The patient's wife had died last summer. Her widower was learning to cook for himself for the first time.

"I know it's not easy," Dr. Anderson said. "I think you have food poisoning. The good news is, you'll probably feel better by this time tomorrow. Drink a lot of water. You're dehydrated. And think about taking a cooking class at the community college."

A five-year-old was brought in by his mother for a measles, mumps and rubella vaccination. The child took the shot without a whimper. "These kids are tough," the doctor thought to himself.

A ranch employee had an appointment to get his knee looked at after being thrown off a horse.

"I'm going to give you the names of some orthopedic specialists in Rock Springs," Dr. Anderson said. "Pick one and go see them. I suspect that you may have torn your ACL. If that's the case, it's not going to heal by itself."

The doctor grabbed his hat and accompanied the man to his pickup truck. He wanted to see how his patient was walking. It also gave Anderson a chance to get outside.

It had turned into a sunny day. There was water running off the curb into the street from snow that had been shoveled into piles.

A dark sedan drove by. Anderson wondered if his eyes were deceiving him.

"That looked like Jon Oaks," he muttered to himself.

His attention was diverted, though, when he saw a woman walking down the sidewalk. The doctor recognized her. She was coming to her follow-up appointment to see about a rash showing up on both her hands, first one and then the other.

Hunter Anderson stepped back inside with his patient and sat her on an exam table in a room down a hall behind the receptionist's desk.

After taking a look at her hands and discussing the possibilities of allergies, he gave her a tube of medicated cream.

"Rub that on the rash, once in the morning and once at night. It should clear up before you run out of cream," he said. "If it doesn't, come back and we'll set you up with a dermatologist or an allergist in Rock Springs. They'll get to the bottom of it, if we don't."

The next man to walk through the door wasn't expected. Anderson glanced at his appointment calendar and saw that the time slot was blank.

"What a surprise," Anderson said with a smile. "My receptionist called in sick. Did we forget to write your appointment in?"

"Do I need one?" the man asked.

"Not really," the doctor said as he waved his hand at the empty waiting room.

"You a dentist now?" the man asked, pointing to the molar Anderson had found on Diamond Peak. He'd set the tooth on the receptionist's desk.

"No, I found that," Anderson said. He proceeded to tell the man about his ski trip and finding the molar on a rock he was sitting on.

"I'm going to take it to the sheriff," Anderson stated. "Maybe there's a reward," he joked.

"It's probably just a tooth that belonged to an old Shoshone who died a thousand years ago," the man said.

"Only if we've overlooked the Shoshone's role in modern dentistry," the doctor said with a grin. "This is a lower molar, and it has a filling made from composite resin. He probably got it in the 1990s or so."

"Are you sure it looks human?" the man asked.

"Oh, it's human," Anderson continued to smile.

"And you can identify somebody with that?" the man asked.

"That tooth has some of the best DNA in the human body," Anderson said. "It's fascinating. The DNA is under the tooth's enamel. Enamel is as hard an armor as we have. A one hundred thousand-year-old tooth was found in Siberia about a decade ago. And do you know they were able to extract some DNA?"

Anderson turned his back on the man, to put away the file on the woman with the rash.

The back of his head exploded in blood, accompanied by the sound of bone being crushed.

Anderson fell. On the way down, his forehead slammed into the edge of the file cabinet. His cowboy hat, resting on the cabinet, followed him to the floor.

Stunned, his head gushing blood from two spots, he tried to push himself up.

He turned his head to face his attacker. Blood dripped on the cowboy hat next to him.

"That's nine," the doctor mumbled before dropping back to the floor.

The assailant picked up the molar and examined it. He put it in his pocket and looked at Dr. Anderson on the floor.

One more blow was delivered with the heavy antique Reichert microscope. It crushed the base of his unmoving skull. It was the last blow that was necessary.

34

The body of Dr. Anderson was discovered by his receptionist. She had phoned the office a number of times to say she was feeling better and would work a half-day. When no one answered the phone, she decided to just come in.

Upon discovering the body, she called the police.

"What the hell is going on," Bob Newell said, mostly to himself. The police chief of Dog Mountain was kneeling over the corpse of the only doctor in town.

His officers knew that the police chief would be leading the investigation personally. As a former Denver police detective, he had seen more dead souls than all of his officers put together.

"Wiped clean," Investigator Joe Walker told him of the antique microscope. The brass and metal instrument suspected of being the murder weapon was now enclosed in a clear plastic evidence bag.

"Let's send it to the CBI lab," the chief said. "Maybe they can get a partial print."

Chief Newell continued to kneel next to the victim and study the surroundings.

"He's got a gash to the forehead and, I'd guess, two to the back of his head," the chief said to his investigator. "You see this filing cabinet? I'd guess he got hit from behind in the head and then hit the front of his head on the filing cabinet on his way to the ground."

"What about the second gash?" Walker asked.

Still on his knees, the chief leaned over the victim's head. He pulled out his phone and triggered an app that featured a spotlight. He took a good look at the gashes. The blood in the victim's white hair was hardening. The chief then leaned back, glancing at the cowboy hat lying on the floor.

"Both blows look like they'd have dropped him," the chief said. "I suspect the first one sent him to the ground. The second one was to make sure the killer finished the job."

The chief looked around and gripped the back of a chair to rise to his feet.

"No one saw anything?" he asked.

"No, sir," Walker answered. "The receptionist had called in sick for the morning. She found him when she felt better and came into work."

"Send some officers to every store downtown," the chief ordered. "I want them to ask if anyone saw anything or anyone suspicious. Let's do it now before any work shifts change."

"Yes, sir," the investigator said. He left to dispatch uniformed officers to carry out the order.

"Anything missing?" the chief asked when Walker returned. "Any drugs, money?"

"The receptionist doesn't think so," the investigator reported. "There wasn't much money in the drawer. They didn't have office hours yesterday, so the cash had been deposited at the close of business Monday.

"And the cabinets holding the drugs are all still locked. The receptionist keeps the inventory. She thinks everything is where it should be."

"Well, that tells us something," the chief said. "Dr. Anderson was the target. Not drugs, not money. What the hell is going on?"

Bip was outside, videotaping exteriors of the scene where Dr. Hunter Anderson was murdered. Bip and JC had been at the courthouse when they learned of his death. At the time, they were awaiting the arrival of Jonathan Oaks for a hearing regarding his case.

Robin met Bip outside the doctor's office and JC returned to the courthouse. Oaks' hearing was routine, regarding the admission of evidence. The congressman's defense attorney, understandably, wanted records regarding Oaks' phone ruled inadmissible. The judge said she would make a ruling later in the week.

Oaks was in the courtroom for the hearing, even though his presence wasn't really required. The court clerk told JC that she was surprised he made the long trip from Durango for courtroom minutiae.

"Sometimes they just do it for the change of scenery," the clerk told JC. "They get bored, even when they're allowed to wait for trial at home instead of in jail. This was an acceptable excuse to get in his car and go for a drive."

Robin stood watch outside the doctor's office. She wanted to cry but was intent on doing her job. If the police chief walked out the door, she was to ask him for an interview and summon Bip.

She was cold, just standing there, even though the sun was shining. The wind blew her hair onto her face. She'd swipe her hair aside but the wind would just blow it back.

She watched a police officer carry evidence out of Dr. Anderson's office. His flattened cowboy hat was inside a clear plastic bag.

"We didn't have a chance to finish our conversation," Robin said to herself, as she thought of Anderson's lost love.

Robin wondered if she really wanted to share an orbit with clear plastic evidence bags. She questioned if this was the way she wanted to live her life. Since entering the news industry, really since she started working with JC, she seemed to meet a lot of people who were dead.

She didn't know any other reporters with JC's *murder-per-story* rate. But she was JC's disciple and JC seemed to attract a rough crowd. She thought about that.

She admired his way of knowing when trouble was stirring. But instead of backing off, he plowed ahead. Rather than be afraid, he was curious.

She'd seen him when a bear approached their campsite, last summer. JC didn't back up. He wanted the bear to come closer. He saw it as a chance to learn something, rather than a chance of being eaten.

She pondered the national TV news' offer to JC. They coveted his superpower, a nose for trouble. It made remarkable news. He would thrive. But she wondered if that was really the life *she* wanted.

Her thoughts were interrupted when Police Chief Robert Newell walked out the front door of Hunter Anderson's office. Robin notified Bip. She asked the chief to grant them an interview and he agreed. He looked at her, unable to miss the red rims around her eyes.

She didn't hear a word as the interview progressed. It was a blur. People she liked were dead.

What if she only had one life to live? Was this the life she wanted?

Chief Newell wasn't paying much more attention to the words coming out of his own mouth than Robin was. He answered in clichés and police jargon.

His attention was focused on who could have committed the murder. There was still evidence to gather and tests to run. But he couldn't help thinking that Anderson was a material witness in the case against Jon Oaks. Without Anderson to provide credible testimony and withstand cross-examination, the witness-account of seeing Oaks in the car on the phone wearing a disguise could be diminished by an effective defense attorney.

Following the interview, Robin and Bip climbed into their news car to hide from the wind. JC knocked on the window. He'd arrived with sandwiches and coffee for the three of them. They'd keep an eye on police activity at

Anderson's office in the comfort of their car. And they discussed how they were going to handle reporting the news.

"We've got to divide it up," JC said upon his return. "Robin, does it make sense for you to report on Dr. Anderson's murder while I report on Oaks' court hearing? Of course, there could be a connection between the two, if Oaks came to town to kill the doctor and used a routine court appearance as an alibi."

"I'd rather take the Oaks story," she said. "But you're right. I should report on Hunter's murder. That's where I've spent the day while you were in court."

The next hour, then, was spent in the car. Bip would keep an eye on the police activity. Robin listened to audio from her interview with the police chief and JC began writing his story on Jonathan Oaks' court hearing.

"Look at this," Bip said, calling their attention to the crime scene across the street.

They watched as Sheriff Henry Nidever parked out front of the doctor's office and walked in. JC took a special interest.

When the sheriff walked back out of the office, perhaps twenty minutes had passed. JC scrambled out of the news car and walked across the street.

"Sheriff," JC called out to stop him from climbing into his patrol car. The sheriff said nothing, but he stopped and waited for the reporter.

"A lot more people were alive before you got to town," the sheriff said with a frown. JC dismissed the remark.

"Sheriff, you're here because his cabin burned down last night?" It was a question, in form. But JC was really making a statement.

"If you say so," the sheriff said.

"Do you have reason to believe they're connected?" JC asked.

"Wouldn't you suggest that was an obvious question to pursue?" the law officer smirked.

"Anyone in custody for the fire?" the reporter inquired.

"No," the sheriff said.

JC thought about Gerhard Snyder. But he didn't want to advocate for someone's arrest. That wasn't his job.

"What did you make of that tooth that Dr. Anderson gave you?" the reporter asked.

"What tooth?" the sheriff responded.

"The tooth that Hunter found while he was cross-country skiing," JC said. "He told me that he wanted you to look at it."

The sheriff looked up and down the street at nothing in particular. JC had a feeling that it was something the sheriff did when he was buying time to think.

"What tooth are you talking about?" the sheriff asked.

JC proceeded to tell the sheriff what he knew. And he suggested that if Anderson hadn't turned over the human tooth, that it must still be in his possession.

Sheriff Nidever considered this and walked back into the doctor's office. In about a half hour, he emerged with an impatient expression on his face.

"You sure about this?" he asked JC as the reporter approached.

"I am, Sheriff," JC responded.

"We'll check his home then," the sheriff said. And he climbed into his patrol car, backed onto the street and drove away.

The sun was going down. Able White drove up in the noisy satellite truck and pulled to a stop. Air brakes hissed and there was metallic clatter. The engineer was stopped in the middle of the road and asked JC where he should park. JC pointed at a spot directly across the street from the office of the only doctor Dog Mountain had.

35

"I had a strange visitor over the weekend," Roman said to Robin. They were having coffee in downtown Dog Mountain at the Stagecoach Stop.

Another sunny day was unfolding. The bright light poured through a large window in the dining room.

Robin was glad Roman called. They both needed a distraction following thc discovery of Hunter Anderson's body the day before. Robin had not slept well.

"A woman came to my door," Roman said. "She suggested that I was having an affair with her husband. Offhand, I didn't even know who the man was."

"That's a little scary," Robin commiserated.

"Yes," Roman answered and took a sip of her coffee. "She wasn't scary, though. She was sad. I invited her in for some coffee. She was actually quite nice."

Robin laughed. Roman, she thought, was a kind soul.

"She said that her husband had disappeared, and she thought he might have come here," Roman elaborated. "I guess he had spoken about me, maybe exaggerated about how well he knew me. And this woman decided that he had run off with me."

"Do you even know who he is?" Robin asked.

"I think he's the guy who set up my office when I started my horse rescue," Roman said. "I bought a computer and printer and everything I needed for an office, and he came to set it up for me. He's from Casper."

"So, who *did* he run off with?" Robin inquired.

"I don't think she really knows what happened to him," Roman said. "Other than he didn't come home one day. Oh, and he left a note saying he was leaving her. He was unhappy, he said in the note. He spent a lot of time doing business here in Dog Mountain and at the ski resort."

"That's it?" Robin pursued. "She just decided that you weren't having an affair with her husband, after all, and she left?"

"I gave her directions to the offices of other people she believed were his customers," Roman answered. "She was hoping that one of them knew something."

"Like who?" said Robin.

"The administrative office for the ski resort," Roman answered, "Dr. Anderson's office …"

Roman stopped without finishing her list. They both felt awkward at the mention of Anderson, their friend, as though they'd see him later that day. Instinctively, they both reached across the table and grasped the other's hand.

JC thought of the mythical Hydra, a snake with many heads. Jon Oaks was awaiting trial for stalking and threatening Roman Holiday. Oaks despised Benny Maple. Hunter Anderson was murdered just days after his mountain cabin was set ablaze. Gerhard Snyder was furious with the doctor. How could there not be a connection, he wondered. And had he even seen all of the Hydra's heads?

The Hydra had nine heads, he thought to himself. Like a cat has nine lives.

JC placed a call to Sheriff Nidever.

"Did you find the tooth at Dr. Anderson's home?" JC asked.

"No," the sheriff said. "Are you sure about this?"

"He showed it to us," JC told him. "And he told me that he was bringing it to you."

"Well, we'll keep looking for it," the sheriff said on the other end of the phone. "Not sure what it means, though."

The phone call ended and JC walked alongside Robin and Bip.

"Who is Nancy Sanchez, again?" JC asked. He was confused by the story Robin was telling them.

"She thought her husband was having an affair with Roman," Robin repeated.

"Who wouldn't have an affair with her?" Bip quipped.

Bip, Robin and JC were hiking up a knoll toward a tall dead pine tree. It looked like a skeleton. Hunter Anderson had mentioned the pine when he told them about finding the tooth off Route 72.

Robin thought she might have seen that same tree on her trip back from Browns Park with JC.

"It sounds like the same place," she told them. "Hunter had said, 'I was just over that knoll. I couldn't see the road from where I was. But if you find that rock with *1838* scratched into it, you know that you're in the right place.'"

At the crest of the knoll, they would also see that three days of sun had melted a lot of snow on the windswept meadow.

They walked down the other side toward the tree and began looking for a big red rock.

"Just follow JC," Bip told Robin. "He was a Duck Hawk."

"I know," Robin answered. "He's very proud of that. He can tie knots."

"You mock me," JC said. "But the Duck Hawks trained me for this moment."

"And he can make his own bed," Bip grinned, sharing a moment with Robin.

"Fine, if I see a wolf, I'm not even going to tell you," JC replied.

"Is this where they've started seeing wolves?" Bip asked.

"A bit east of here," JC replied. "But you know they'll spread out. You can track them by following the complaints from ranchers after the wolves go after their livestock."

"Wouldn't that make them deadstock?" Bip quipped. He walked off in a different direction to get a fresh perspective of the land and shoot some video of JC and Robin walking.

JC and Robin walked together through the brush. She picked up a small stick and picked at it, her head down.

"I heard what the sheriff said to you yesterday," Robin told him. "It was strange but interesting."

"He said something like, I show up and people start dying," JC stated. "Is that what you're referring to?"

"Yes," she acknowledged. "I was in the car, but I overheard you two."

"I don't think the mere sight of me triggers people to commit homicide," JC objected.

"No. But I've been giving this some thought," she said. "I think it's like not being afraid of fire. Most people, when a fire breaks out, run in the other direction. It's part of our survival instinct.

"But you, JC. You run *toward* the fire. You want to understand it. You're not afraid of it. You might even want it to burn you a little."

They spotted the rock and began walking toward it.

"She has a point," Bip shouted from afar. He had been listening. "You're a bit of a psycho. But I like that in a reporter. It gives me something to take pictures of."

"I'm thinking of taking some time off when we get back to Denver," Robin told JC. "I'm thinking of going down to North Carolina, to see my father."

"That sounds like a good thing to do," JC told her.

"I'm not sure how many lives we get," she said. "But I want to make sure I get this one straightened out."

As they approached the big red rock, they crossed some narrow tracks in the snow. They were laid down like a railroad.

"Those are probably Anderson's cross-country ski tracks," JC said. All three of them peered in the direction the tracks had come from.

Large portions of the tracks had disappeared as the snow melted. Instead, there were patches of dead grass. Then the tracks would continue where there was snow.

"It's kind of eerie," Bip said. "Thinking he made these tracks."

Then he kneeled, focused his camera on the tracks and hit the record button.

"I was thinking about Anderson's theory," Bip said as he rose from the ground. "The whole nine lives thing." He was holding his camera by the handle like a suitcase.

"I was cliff diving up at Horsetooth Reservoir, outside Fort Collins," he continued. "I remember diving into the water. And as I approached the water, I could see the rocky bottom underwater. I realized that the water at that spot was too shallow."

"What happened?" Robin asked.

"That's the thing," Bip stated. "Nothing happened. I really thought that I might break my neck and die. But when I hit the water and came up, I never touched bottom. Maybe Anderson would say that I died. That's kind of spooky. So, Hunter would say that I've died like three times now?"

"I remembered a motorcycle crash I had," JC said. "I was riding outside Loveland. I banked a turn, slipped on some gravel and went over the handlebars just when a car was coming. I hit the ground. I was bleeding through the sleeve on my jacket when I got up. My bike was all busted up. But there was no car. I wondered where the car went."

"Wait a minute," Bip said. "You were already up to six, weren't you?"

"I think so," JC said.

"Be careful, my friend," Bip said, smiling. "That's seven."

Reaching the large red rock, they saw numerals scratched into the side. *1838*. There were also three letters. Other letters may have faded away.

That side of the stone was protected from the weather, or else *all* the scratched figures would have been gone.

"So, some guy scratched these numbers in the rock in 1838?" Bip asked in wonder. "That's a long time ago. Kind of cool, when you think about it."

They searched the ground around the rock. There was not another tooth to be found. Not there.

They began a search of the nearby landscape. Their eyes were focused on the ground, walking in circles of a growing radius. Much of the snow had melted, exposing dead grass and natural debris.

"Most humans have thirty-two teeth," JC said to no one in particular. "As many as thirty-one are lying somewhere around here."

"You're assuming he had all of them," Bip pronounced.

"That's a good point," JC said. He glanced at Robin, who had her head aimed at the ground and said nothing.

"How did Hunter know about this spot?" JC asked as he looked across the landscape.

His companions didn't answer. Anderson hadn't told any of them why he skied in this direction.

"We should check on Frank Green," Robin said. "He and Hunter were pretty good friends, I think."

The three journalists slowly walked in three different directions. Once in a while, one of them would look toward the rock, getting their bearings.

"Oh, God," Robin quietly said to herself. But she twisted in the other direction, placed her hands on her knees and vomited.

JC saw what was happening from a distance. He whispered in Bip's direction and they made their way toward Robin.

Reaching her and stroking her back, JC looked on the ground and saw a partial set of human ribs.

"I'm sorry, honey," JC said. "You're having a rough couple of days."

He walked her a few yards away from the find and left her to breathe some fresh air.

Walking back toward the ribs, he pulled out his phone and took pictures.

Bip and JC walked beyond the ribs about fifty feet and found a jawbone. One of the teeth, another molar, was loose on the ground.

JC pulled a plastic bag from his jacket. He always carried a few bags.

"What is it with you carrying bags around?" Bip asked.

"It became a habit, quite a while ago," JC told him. "It comes in handy on occasions like this, or when I'm walking a dog."

"You don't have a dog," Bip reminded him.

"No," JC agreed. "But I'd like to have a dog again. I'm just keeping my hand in the game."

"How did the Duck Hawks let you get away?" Bip remarked.

JC used the plastic as a glove and slipped the single tooth into the bag before zipping it locked.

An hour later, he entered the sheriff's office. JC placed the bag with a tooth on the desk in front of the sheriff.

"And you might want to speak with a Nancy Sanchez," he added.

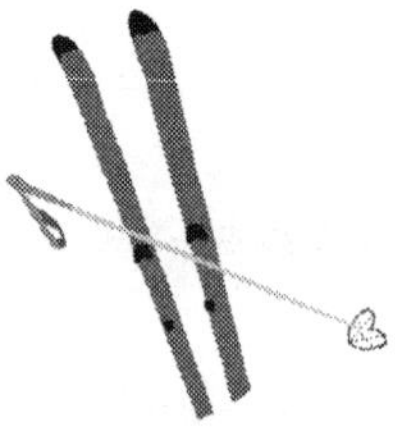

36

"This place comes with a strange story," Deputy Robinson said.

"Which one?" Deputy May Byers asked.

"Which place?" Robinson asked.

"No, which strange story?" Byers asked.

"True," said Jack Robinson. "There are a lot of them."

The two deputies were standing guard over scattered human remains discovered on Diamond Peak. And they weren't wrong about the unusual tales.

One of the stories involved the Great Diamond Hoax of 1872. A pair of prospectors salted the mountainside of Diamond Peak with real diamonds obtained elsewhere. The prospectors sold the fraudulent diamond deposit to a group of prominent investors. The belief that there really were diamonds lying on the ground on Diamond Peak briefly triggered a diamond rush to the area. It was like the gold and silver rushes in Colorado. Only the gold and silver frenzy really did produce nuggets of gold and silver.

In 1872, a lot of money was lost in the Diamond Peak hoax. The two prospectors fled East and were never prosecuted. One later became a banker and was killed in a shootout with another banker.

The pair of uniformed Lonesome County deputies looked around them, as though something might jump out from behind a rock. Things had jumped out from behind a rock before.

They wore heavy, dark blue, waist-length jackets with the county emblem on one sleeve and the American flag on the other. They wore a badge over their left breast. Their dark blue winter-weight slacks hung over black winter tactical boots. They had no-slip soles with deep grooves.

Both deputies wore Glock 23c handguns, holstered at their side.

"You ever heard that called a Halloween tree?" Byers asked Robinson.

They were looking at the solitary dead pine tree a few hundred feet away. It was the only tree of significance nearby. The weathered branches looked like bones.

"No," Robinson said.

"My mom used to call them Halloween trees," Byers said. "I heard them called that, once in a while, back where I came from."

"Did you see those numbers carved in the rock?" Deputy Robinson asked.

"I did. 1838?" she said. "Does that mean anything to you?"

"There was an old French-Canadian fur trapper in these parts named Denis Julien," Robinson told her. "He seemed to want people to know that he was here. He carved his name and the year in a lot of rocks."

From the deputies' vantage point, a portion of a rib cage could be recognized. There was also a pelvis, a femur and a tibia. A short walk away, there was more of the rib cage and another femur.

"The serving size was five hundred," joked Deputy Robinson as he surveyed the picked-over remains.

"They don't let much go to waste," Deputy Byers said, referring to the wildlife that had been scavenging at the spot. "There's not much meat left."

"Any guess?" Robinson asked her. "Man or woman?" Byers surveyed the remains and gave it thought.

"Judging from the size of the ribs," she said, "I'm going to say a man."

"Good observation," Robinson said. "I'd guess that you're right."

The skeletal pieces were found in Lonesome County, just outside the border of Moffat County.

"We're going to take our time on this," said Sheriff Nidever as he approached the deputies. There were other deputies searching the nearby sagebrush flats, gully washes, cedar breaks, and knolls.

"There won't be any passersby who stumble across us," the sheriff said. The privacy of the investigation was virtually assured. "We can take our time."

There would be no witnesses of the human variety. But maybe some birds, wolves, voles, or a coyote would come back to see if anything was left to nibble on.

The problem was: the victim was probably placed there or killed there before many subsequent snowfalls. And evidence might have washed away or been carried away by wildlife.

"Anybody missing who fits this description?" the county coroner asked Nidever.

"What description would that be?" the sheriff asked. "Someone who had bones?"

The county coroner, Edgar Ringling, got a chuckle out of that.

"Actually, there is," the sheriff said. "A woman who thought her husband ran off on her."

"How was he found?" the coroner asked the sheriff.

"A tip," the sheriff said. He wasn't in the mood to say that a television reporter led him to this spot.

"I don't see any clothing," the coroner observed. "Did you find any clothing?"

"No," the sheriff said. That got the sheriff's interest. "Can we identify him with his DNA?"

"Yes," the coroner answered. "We can if we have something to compare it with. It would be good fortune if he was in the National DNA Database or if someone has reported him missing."

"We'll get something from the woman who thinks her husband ran off," the sheriff said.

"A hairbrush would do the trick," the coroner suggested.

"And maybe we'll see if there are any missing ranch hands," the sheriff added.

"Ranch hands who weren't wearing any clothes at the time," the coroner said with a grin.

"It looks like someone tried to dig a grave," the sheriff said as he looked at a depression in the dirt. "But he realized it would be too much hard work, and just placed the deceased in the unfinished hole and pushed the dirt over him."

"So, you're looking for a weakling, Henry?" the coroner asked, amused.

"It's winter, Edgar," Sheriff Nidever said with a serious face. "The ground is hard."

The coroner considered that. It made sense.

"Where is my undersheriff?" Nidever grumbled.

"I think he's with the team searching for evidence, Sheriff," said Deputy Byers. "By the Halloween tree."

"The what?" the sheriff asked, scrutinizing Deputy Byers.

"The Halloween tree, sir," she repeated. "The dead pine."

"I've never heard that called a Halloween tree," the sheriff said dismissively as he took another look at the tree.

"It's a thing, sir," she replied. "A thing from back home."

"We don't have *things* in Lonesome County, deputy," he barked as he walked in the direction of the Halloween tree.

37

Nancy Sanchez answered the doorbell at her home in Casper, Wyoming. She had been cleaning the hardwood floors of her house. They weren't that dirty to begin with. She was trying to keep her mind off things.

When she opened the door, a Casper police officer was standing on her porch.

She thought that he looked Indigenous. He had a round kind face with short dark hair under his regulation knit cap with a patch in the shape of a shield. It said Casper Police.

"Ma'am," he said in a gentle voice. "Are you Nancy Elizabeth Sanchez?"

Her stomach was suddenly queasy. Her legs tingled. She knew that the officer had arrived to bring her closer to an outcome. She gripped the door to maintain her balance and invited him into her home.

"Ma'am, do you have a hairbrush belonging to your husband?" the officer asked.

"I believe so," she responded automatically. "Yes, of course I do."

"Would you mind going to get it, ma'am?"

It took more effort to walk up the stairs of her home than it usually did. For the first time, it occurred to her that Nat Sanchez had left behind his hairbrush and his toothbrush. And she couldn't think of any clothing of her husband's that she couldn't account for, other than those he wore when he left home on the last morning she saw him.

She asked herself, how had this not occurred to her until now? But she already knew the answer. She hadn't wanted to think it.

He hadn't taken those things with him, she now acknowledged, because he thought he would be coming home that night, just as he said he would.

She opened the medicine cabinet in their bathroom and grabbed Nat's hairbrush by the handle and returned downstairs.

"Thank you, ma'am," the officer said gently as he dropped it into a clear plastic bag. "I am going to forward this to the sheriff in Lonesome County. They'll be in touch with you."

"Wait," she said. "Don't go yet."

She walked to the kitchen and opened a drawer that held miscellaneous things like pens and pencils, paper clips, a tape measure.

She walked back toward the door and handed the police officer a piece of paper.

"What's this, ma'am?" he asked.

"It's a note my husband left for me. It says he's leaving me." Her chin trembled. She fought back tears. "I don't understand it. Take it. Maybe the sheriff will understand it better than I do. He didn't leave me, did he?"

She closed the door as the police officer left and put her hand to her mouth. She began to cry. Her husband was really gone.

Once the Colorado Bureau of Investigation lab had the hairbrush belonging to Nat Sanchez, he was quickly identified by DNA as the man whose remains were found in the meadow by the Halloween tree.

No one had seen him in a month. He had been out of contact with customers, and he was late delivering expected office supplies to stores and businesses on his route.

"It was the note," Sheriff Nidever told Investigator Brown as they sat in the sheriff's office. "His wife thought he had left her. She stayed quiet. She didn't tell friends and she didn't call the police, hoping against all reason that he'd change his mind and come home."

"The killer left the note inside her own house?" Brown asked. "Clever. It also means that he got inside her house."

"The police officer in Casper did the right thing, placing the note in an evidence bag," the sheriff said. "Let's see if we can get any fingerprints off of it."

"Yes, sir," the investigator said.

"And let's get a tech unit over to Casper to go over her house for more evidence," the sheriff ordered. "Maybe our killer left some fingerprints there when he dropped off the note. Let Casper police know that we're coming."

"Sheriff?" The voice accompanied a knock on the sheriff's office door. It was Investigator Kathy Garcia. "I just got off the phone with Mrs. Sanchez. She told me that she and her husband never locked their back door. She said that they live in a safe neighborhood in a safe town."

"So, the killer forged that note and walked right in the back door," the sheriff surmised. "He left it for her to find. Clever. Cruel."

"What was the cause of death?" JC asked over the phone. The medical examiner who performed the autopsy on Nat Sanchez was on the other end of the line.

The medical examiner was named Marvin Getz. He was a doctor with offices in Craig. He performed autopsies for both Lonesome and Moffat Counties.

"A severe blow to the base of his skull," the medical examiner answered.

"Similar to the fatal blow to Dr. Anderson?" JC asked over the phone.

"That's a good observation," the medical examiner said. "I'd have to say that it was."

"Is a strike to that area commonly fatal?" the reporter inquired.

"If it hits the right spot. It's almost one hundred-percent fatal if it hits the part of the brain that controls breathing," the medical examiner replied. "The victim dies of hypoxia. Massive bleeding can also deliver the same outcome. Blood carries your oxygen. A loss of probably forty percent of your blood will end in the same result. Your body is starved of oxygen."

When JC ended the call with Dr. Getz, the reporter briefed Robin and Bip. They were seated in Bip's room, amidst his portable editing bay, camera and extra batteries and chargers.

"I think we're looking for one guy," JC told them. "In all three murders, the victim was attacked from behind. They were probably unaware that they were about to be attacked. That means they were comfortable turning their back on the killer. They probably knew the man or woman who killed them."

"But why?" Robin asked. "What links these three victims?"

Robin and Bip had just returned from Casper. They had interviewed Nancy Sanchez.

"Mrs. Sanchez said that her husband didn't have an enemy in the world," Robin told JC.

"Gambling debts? Drugs?" JC asked. "Another woman?"

"Well, she'd already explored the 'Other Woman' path," Robin reminded him. "She seems terribly embarrassed about that. And she said she'd been spending her time going through his papers and things in his office. She said she didn't find anything that would indicate gambling. She just laughed at the suggestion of drugs. She said that he liked his beer with a splash of Fireball."

"That's disgusting," JC said.

"Is it?" Bip objected with a smile. "It's like beer candy."

"There was something else interesting that Mrs. Sanchez told us," Robin said to JC. "It probably doesn't have anything to do with all this, but do you know what happened when Frank Green's family moved away from Browns Park?"

"No," JC told her. "He seems happy to be back, though."

"Mrs. Sanchez is friends with Frank's ex-wife," Robin informed him. "She says that the federal government took a lot of the Green family's ranch, for the reservoir and wildlife sanctuary and everything. She says they left soon after that, gave up the ranch. But Frank's mom was heartbroken and passed away before too long. And then Frank's father killed himself!"

"That's pretty awful," JC said.

"Horrible," Robin said quietly. "Frank was still a child."

More death, Robin thought. She had forced herself to be resilient since Hunter Anderson's murder. She knew what her job required. But she could not alter her feelings about the murder of a friend, or the growing scent of death in Dog Mountain.

She and JC would both be part of the live broadcast that night, telling their Denver audience what they learned that day.

Robin's phone rang and she looked at the number.

"I've got to get this," she said with an apologetic look. She left the room and walked out into the hallway.

"Oh," Bip sneered. "Now *she's* getting phone calls I can't listen to?"

JC looked at the door she had just walked through, puzzled.

He pulled out his own phone.

"Have you spoken with Gerhard Snyder yet?" JC asked the sheriff when he picked up.

"We arranged to have Mr. Snyder come to our offices to chat," the sheriff disclosed. "He was accompanied by an attorney. We had a discussion, and he was allowed to leave.

He denied setting the fire or having anything to do with the death of Dr. Anderson. Without evidence to the contrary, there's not much we can do."

"He's back home, safe and sound," Police Chief Bob Newell said. JC had called him to see if they were certain of the whereabouts of Jonathan Oaks. JC pointed out that Oaks had a court appearance in Dog Mountain on the day of Anderson's death.

"If we kept a closer eye on him, we'd be tucking him into bed each night," the chief said, "He was here in Dog Mountain for his court appearance and then he returned to Durango."

"Is he a suspect in the death of Dr. Anderson, or Benny Maple?" JC asked. "Or Nat Sanchez?"

"Until we have an arrest," the chief said, "everyone is a person of interest."

"Could he have slipped into the doctor's office and still arrived at his court appearance on time?" JC asked.

"It is possible," the chief replied. "We're looking at that."

"The two locations are only a few blocks from each other," JC said.

"We are aware of that," the chief told him. "By the way, that was nice work, you going back to the meadow and finding that jawbone. It had also occurred to *me* that the melted snow might have uncovered something. But that's not my jurisdiction. It's not my investigation."

JC sensed some jurisdictional rivalry. Chief Newell was the more experienced crime investigator, but whoever the county sheriff was at the time, *he* was going to be a bigger deal than the town's police chief.

"He was probably my best friend since I moved here," Frank Green said. "He was great company."

JC and Bip had stopped by Green's computer store. Robin had suggested they check in on him to see how he was coping with Anderson's death.

She was worried about him.

"Don't tell him that we know about his family, his dad killing himself and everything," she advised. "It's not really our business."

JC agreed. He was just hoping they might get a usable soundbite about Anderson for the news that evening.

The reporter asked Green about the animosity between Anderson and Gerhard Snyder. Green spent time with both men.

"Jerry is a hothead," Green said off-camera. "But I've never seen him harm anyone. I think he's hot on the outside and cool on the inside. A lot of his so-called anger is calculated. He thinks he can intimidate people who oppose his business ventures. But it's a big bluff. I told Hunter exactly that."

It had been a long day. After their live shot, JC, Bip, Sunny and Robin had a dinner consisting of bar food and beer.

They sat at a booth inside Snapping Annie's in the ski resort village. There were empty plates in front of them with the remains of chicken wings, onion rings, barbeque ribs, and beer from Ska Brewing in Durango. And a salad. Robin and Sunny insisted that they all have some salad.

"Seriously?" Bip asked. "You're racing tomorrow?"

"Yep," said JC. "Blame him."

JC was pointing at a man approaching the table. It was Russell Driver, a ski racer JC had competed with for a decade. Russell had his son with him, Andre, who had just turned twenty-one years old.

"Hi Andre," JC said. "Are you racing tomorrow?"

"I am," Andre responded. "My dad needs to learn some humility. I am the hammer of justice."

They all laughed. Robin popped out of her seat and gave Russell a hug.

"I used to be the only Black man in the race," Russell explained to Bip. "But now my son, Andre, makes two of us. And there is probably a third racer out there who looks like us, who we haven't even met yet. And then we'll sweep the podium."

"Russell," JC laughed. "I look forward to that day. But since you will be finishing behind me, as usual, the best you can hope for is second, third and fourth."

"I'm going to come watch the race tomorrow," Robin said. "This should be fun."

"Well, then I'll have to tell you the truth," JC told her. "With Andre here, Russell and I will be fighting for second place."

"We'll see," Andre said, looking away with humility.

"And your far better half?" JC asked, referring to Russell's wife.

"She'll be at the race," Russell said. "She will be prepared to wrap my old bones in a jacket at the finish line."

His wife, Loni Driver, rarely missed a race. And at every finish line, she had a coat waiting for Russell. He was the envy of every ski racer on a cold day.

Russell was much older than the other fast racers. But he was once a candidate for the U.S. Ski Team.

"So, you have chosen to spend tomorrow chipping away at more cartilage in your knees," Bip said to JC. "Are the rest of us getting a day off? It's Sunday."

"Yep," JC told him. "It came straight from the top. The news director called and said he didn't want to pay you to work Sunday."

"Then I will see you all on Monday. But first, I propose a toast," Bip said.

"What are we toasting?" Robin asked.

"We get a day off?" Bip shrugged and summoned the server. "May we have six small beers, each with a shot of Fireball?"

38

"What's your co-pay?"

Andre Driver just grinned when the man in the ski racing suit asked that of him. It was a greeting being shared lately by ski racers.

"That's rude!" Robin exclaimed after JC explained the remark.

"It's health insurance humor," JC told her. "We'd better have insurance. Ski racers all need it, at some point or another."

"Because you go too fast," Robin suggested.

"I don't go too fast," he told her, exhibiting patience. "I just don't always remember when to turn. Sometimes, I forget to turn at all. That gets me into trouble, not going fast."

That brought a laugh from a few fellow racers sitting near them.

JC and Robin had carved out a space on a table in the basement of the ski lodge at Minnie's Gap. It was an auxiliary cafeteria without heat. Today, it was set aside for the racers to sign up for the event and get dressed.

Behind the sign-up table, there were trophies or medals awaiting the winners in each age group.

"He doesn't lack courage, he lacks brains," Russell Driver said to Robin from the next table. Russell's son, Andre, was also there.

JC was pulling on his skin-tight polyester racing suit. The fabric sometimes caught on pads or two knee braces that he was wearing underneath. Robin helped stretch the material over the obstacles.

"Hey, Cannonball," JC said as he greeted the racer they had seen on a chairlift.

"Do I even want to know why you call him that?" Robin asked. "Does he explode on impact?"

"Oh, that's better than the real reason," the racer nicknamed Cannonball said with a smile. "But look at my helmet. It's an old Jofa 2400. It's round like a cannonball."

"It's cute," Robin told him.

"I like your explanation of my nickname better," Cannonball told her. "That's what I'm going to tell people from now on."

"Hi, Crash," another racer greeted JC as he passed by the table.

"Why does he call you Crash?" Robin asked suspiciously.

"I think he's honoring my body of work," JC told her.

"So, you crash a lot?" she asked. "I've heard that."

"I'm trying to win," he said.

"But you can't win if you crash, can you?" she asked.

"She's got you there!" Russell heckled as he strapped on his own knee brace.

"There are a few flaws I'm still working out in my plan," JC laughed.

The race was a two-run giant slalom down a slope called Break Number One.

"It's named after my first surgery!" one racer declared while in line for his start. It was actually named after a creek that cascades alongside the slope during the summer.

The race itself turned out to be a testament to youth.

Andre Driver won comfortably. Two more men under the age of twenty-nine also landed on the podium. JC was fourth. Andre's father, Russell, finished fifth.

"Age is the fountain of wisdom," Russell said. "But youth is the fountain of good knees and first-place finishes."

"Perhaps I'm carrying the wrong man's coat," Loni Driver said to her husband. "We seem to have a new champion in the family."

Russell looked at his son with pride.

JC and Robin enjoyed an early dinner with Russell, Loni and Andre after the race.

"What have you done to this nice little town, my friend?" Russell asked JC as he worked on an Italian entree. "It was loving and peaceful until you showed up. Now, people are dying."

"Why does everyone keep saying that?" JC asked.

When word got out about the discovery of a body on Diamond Peak, the name of Jon Oaks was on many of the lips in Lonesome County. Ever since people had learned that Oaks was leading a secret double life, they wondered what else he might be capable of.

"Honey, you are going to have to get used to the fact that I'm going to go to prison for a little while," Oaks told his wife.

They were sitting on the couch in their expensive Durango home enjoying a particularly expensive Scotch.

Oaks knew that his wife was having trouble dealing with their new reality. She was quiet most of the time, except when she would bring up something cheerful and random and having nothing to do with the criminal prosecution he faced. And she never spoke of his admission in court to having a love affair with Roman Holiday.

Brenda Oaks blamed it all on "that tramp." Oaks didn't object. He had told his wife that Roman had pursued him for quite some time and he finally capitulated. He blamed himself for being weak.

His moral collapse occurred even while, in every other aspect of his life, he was excelling. He was publicly admired. His performance in whatever he chose to do was brilliant. The success of Minnie's Gap Ski Resort would just be his latest triumph. He was going to be Colorado's next governor.

Until this.

Brenda spent most of her days now searching for a story of his that she could live with. How, she wondered, would they live together from this point on?

But at least he was here with her at home in Durango. In part, she blamed his troubles on spending so much time away from home.

"Tomorrow is going to be a long day," he said to her as he kissed her cheek. "I'd better go to bed early and get some sleep."

Driving back to their hotel after the race, JC spotted some lights on in a building at the community college.

"Do you mind if we make a stop?" he asked Robin.

"No problem," she said. "This is my day off."

"Sort of," JC said to her.

As they walked down the hall on the second floor of the building, they heard a man speaking Norwegian on the telephone.

"Relax," JC's voice echoed down the hall. "It's just us."

They walked into the cramped office of Professor Ullr Skadi.

"I think I need your help," JC said.

"That is a common theme spoken by those who walk through that door," Skadi/Hemingway said. "Close the door behind you."

"What do you know about computers?" JC asked.

Hemingway gave him a look that suggested it was a ridiculous question.

"Everything you'll ever need to know and then some," the professor answered.

"Have you figured out who is trying to blackmail you?" JC asked.

Upon hearing the question, Hemingway dropped his eyes to his desk and looked for something to do. He shuffled some papers, opened a drawer and looked into it without pulling anything out.

"Am I to take that as a no?" JC laughed. "Mister Know-it-all can't break a simple call-spoof code?"

"It's not that simple," Hemingway protested. "But yes, I can and I will. I just haven't yet. Why are you so concerned about my welfare? Should I be flattered?"

"Nope," JC said. "But I think your blackmail is connected to the three murders. I'm not sure how, but that's what I think."

"Well, I've reached out to someone, under false pretenses," Hemingway disclosed.

"That must have been very humbling," JC grinned.

"It's what we academics do," Hemingway responded in the slight Norwegian accent of Professor Skadi. "I called Frank Green. He installed the computer system on campus. He must know how to track things in the system."

"But you didn't tell him why?" JC asked.

"No, I covered my tracks," Hemingway said.

"And you still haven't told the police that you're being blackmailed?" Robin asked.

"No, I don't want the police involved in this," Hemingway stated.

"Are you able to protect yourself?" JC asked.

"Why, are you about to attack me?" Hemingway smirked.

"Not me," JC said. "But people around here do seem to be coming under attack."

"I'm prepared, should that occasion arise," the professor answered.

"Why does that not surprise me?" JC answered.

39

"Sir, you should smell this," a deputy called out to his captain.

The captain advanced to the crumpled car and the deputy gestured toward the open door, on the driver's side.

The deputy had just pried the door open. He had been trained to know that for a short period of time, the trapped aroma of the driver's final breaths would be present.

The captain crouched so he could stick his head into the driver's compartment.

"Ah yes," the captain agreed. "The sweet nectar of negligence."

The captain stepped back so a patrol sergeant could repeat the practice.

"Yes, sir," the sergeant said. "He's been drinking."

That made three witnesses to the aroma of alcohol, should the question arise in court or at an inquest. In short time, they would be certain there would be an inquest.

The dead man was lying on the floor of the sedan. His feet were on the driver's side but the torso of his body had slipped across the center console and his head and shoulders were on the passenger side of the car.

"He wasn't wearing a seatbelt?" the captain asked.

"No, sir," the deputy responded. "There's no indication the seatbelt was being worn."

"Why wouldn't he wear a seatbelt?" the captain murmured, almost to himself. He leaned in to take another look on the driver's side of the car. "He could have survived this if he had been wearing a seatbelt."

There was blood on the victim's head and face. There was blood on the steering wheel and some on the dash.

The sergeant gently pressed his hand against the right breast of the deceased and then against the left. He found what he was looking for, a billfold, in the left inside pocket of the man's blazer.

He opened the wallet and pulled out what presumably was the man's driver's license.

The sergeant called it to the captain's attention and passed the card over the roof of the car to his superior.

"Oh, boy," the captain said after examining the document.

He pulled a cell phone from a holster on his belt and hit 1 on the keyboard. Number 2 on the keyboard was his wife.

"Sheriff," the captain said into the phone, "I think you might want to see this. The dead driver in this car is a congressman."

"A congressman?" the sheriff of Humboldt County, Nevada, asked. "Is he one of ours?"

"No, Sheriff," the captain replied. "It looks like he's from Colorado. A Jonathan Oaks."

"Well, what's he doing on Jungo Road?" the sheriff asked. "I'll be right there."

Jungo Road made the dirt roads in Browns Park look like superhighways. Jungo Road had even lost its designation as State Route 49 in Nevada.

It was a dirt path in a desert. It led from Winnemucca to a place where the town of Jungo *used* to be.

Jungo, in the Depression, had been a shipping point for the Iron King Mine. It once had a hotel, a store, a gas station and not much else. Now, there was no sign of the hotel, or the store or the gas station. There was an abandoned metal shed. Period. Jungo was officially designated a ghost town.

The road leading from Winnemucca to Jungo was unimproved. Jungo Road leading away from Jungo to who-knows-where was even worse.

There were no houses, no farms, no pump stations, no scenic overlooks, no secret missile silos. There was no reason to drive on Jungo Road.

Winnemucca, Nevada, had a population of under eight thousand. It was the only city in Humboldt County.

The pilot of a small plane called the sheriff's office. He said that he had seen the car, off the road and askew, while flying from Portland, Oregon, to Las Vegas. He dropped off his passenger and on the return flight, he saw the car again. It hadn't moved. The pilot wondered if the driver might not need assistance.

"What's your theory of what happened here?" the sheriff asked his captain.

"Walk with me, Sheriff," the captain said. "I'll tell you what I think."

They began to walk up the dirt road, the path Jonathan Oaks traveled during the last few seconds of his life. Jungo Road was no longer maintained by any government jurisdiction. If a portion of the road got washed out, it stayed washed out.

"Judging by the skid marks and knowing he was drinking, probably drunk, I'd say he was traveling at about forty-five miles an hour," the captain explained. "The road was washed out up ahead and I don't think he ever saw it. He wasn't wearing a seatbelt, the car hit the washout and his head hit the steering wheel. The car crashed and he probably hit his head a second time, this time on the dashboard. I'm guessing the medical examiner will find he died from head trauma or a broken neck."

The captain looked back down the road toward the crash site. He and the sheriff had walked about one hundred yards.

"Here," the captain said. "Turn around, Sheriff, and look down the road toward the crash. You can't even see the washout. The road on this side looks like it continues unmolested to the other side. It's an illusion. The congressman never saw the washout until it was too late. And he was drinking."

"The stretch of road looks seamless," the sheriff agreed. "Alright, unless we find something else, we'll call it an accidental death."

The sheriff of Humboldt County eventually placed a call to the sheriff of La Plata County in Colorado. Durango was the county seat and Congressman Oaks' driver's license said that was where he lived.

The sheriff of La Plata County called the sheriff of Lonesome County. Everyone in Colorado knew that Oaks faced legal problems in Lonesome County.

"In where?" Sheriff Nidever asked. The sheriff of La Plata County repeated what he had learned. But he advised Sheriff Nidever to talk directly to the sheriff of Humboldt County in Nevada.

Nidever did just that. He was again told where Jonathan Oaks' body had been come upon, inside a sedan leased in his name, on Jungo Road.

"Well, what's Jungo Road near?" Nidever asked the Humboldt County sheriff over the phone.

"Nothing," Humboldt County's sheriff replied. "Even by our standards. It's near nothing that you've ever heard of. If you drive one hundred miles northeast of Reno, you'll get to one end of it. It might take half a day to drive from there on Jungo Road to get to where we found the congressman's car."

He's supposed to be under house arrest in Durango, Sheriff Nidever thought to himself. He's supposed to be wearing an ankle bracelet.

"So, would he have been driving to Reno?" Nidever asked.

"It wouldn't make any sense if he was," Humboldt's sheriff answered. "Assuming he got on Jungo Road in Winnemucca, there are faster ways to get to Reno."

"Was he wearing an ankle bracelet?" Sheriff Nidever asked.

"I can't say that I looked," the sheriff in Winnemucca said. "Hold on a minute."

While he was on hold, Sheriff Nidever called deputy May Byers into his office. She happened to be walking past his open door.

"Will you call the police chief's office and find out where Chief Newell is? Tell them I've got something he's going to want to hear," the sheriff told her.

"He was not wearing an ankle bracelet," the sheriff of Humboldt County reported when he returned to the phone. "I got that straight from the medical examiner. But he says chafe marks on the congressman's skin look like he had been wearing one."

"Was he drunk?" Police Chief Bob Newell asked. He'd driven over to the sheriff's office upon being informed of Jonathan Oaks' death.

"The medical examiner in Nevada says it would appear that he was drunk while he was driving," Sheriff Nidever said.

It was a rare occasion for the police chief to appear at the sheriff's office. When the two highest-ranking law officers in Lonesome County disappeared behind the same closed door, there was quite a stir amongst employees of the sheriff's office.

"Suicide?" the sheriff asked, alone with only the police chief in the room.

"That's one possibility," Newell responded.

"But the sheriff in Nevada is calling it an accidental death," Nidever said. "Unless he hears otherwise."

"That certainly makes it easier politically," the police chief stated.

The two men discussed a wide range of possibilities. Reporters from across Colorado were beginning to call. Some news crews were already on their way to Lonesome County.

"Is Oaks a suspect in the murders of Benny Maple?" the chief asked. "Or the Sanchez fellow on Diamond Peak?"

"Oaks didn't like Benny," the sheriff said. "But I don't have any evidence that he killed him. And we don't have any solid leads on the death of the fellow on Diamond Peak. What about Dr. Anderson's murder?"

"Oaks was in town when Anderson was murdered," the police chief said. "We were arranging with the congressman's lawyers to question him. That's when you called me with this. I thought Oaks was wearing an ankle bracelet, under home arrest."

"I'm waiting for a call from the sheriff in Durango," Nidever said after a loud exhale. He rubbed his face with his hand. "The sheriff himself is delivering the news to Oaks' widow. And he's going to gently inquire as to why he wasn't at home under court order, and how he went about that."

"You're not sending your own people there?" the chief asked.

"Of course, we are," the sheriff said. He was annoyed by what sounded like the police chief questioning his procedure. "But I asked the sheriff down there to make the initial contact. I didn't want the widow of a congressman to first learn of her husband's demise when a reporter called her on the phone, or she saw it on television. It's a long drive to Durango. I have two detectives on the road heading there."

There was an icy silence in the room, broken by the ring of the phone sitting on his desk.

"This is the sheriff," Nidever answered into the receiver. He listened to the update and stole a glance at the police chief while doing so.

The police chief didn't know why Sheriff Nidever hadn't put the discussion on speakerphone, so everyone could be in on it. Instead, Newell felt he was being treated like a junior officer waiting for instructions from his superior.

Perhaps, the chief thought, that was precisely what Nidever intended.

"He cut the bracelet off and his wife was covering for him," Sheriff Nidever said when he hung up the phone. "The probation department had called the house and Mrs. Oaks lied, saying her husband was on the toilet or something. She swore he was there and they believed her."

"What does she say he was doing on Jungo Road?" Newell asked.

"She had never heard of Jungo Road," Nidever said. "Oaks told his wife he was driving to Denver to talk to some people who could help with his case. He told her that prosecutors were watching his every move and he didn't want to tip them off about the defense he and his attorneys were planning for court."

"Do you believe that?" Chief Newell asked.

"No," the sheriff responded with a chuckle. "He was only making matters worse for himself. Once the court was informed that the bracelet had been cut, bail would be revoked."

"He'd sit in jail until his trial date," the chief added.

"My understanding is that he was planning to plead guilty to harassing Roman Holiday," the sheriff told the chief. "He was preparing an insanity defense and hoping to get the more serious charges dropped in exchange for the guilty plea. He knew he'd spend some time in prison, but he was angling for a minimum-security setup."

Television station news crews, along with newspaper reporters, began arriving in Dog Mountain to cover the strange case of former Congressman Jonathan Oaks. The sheriff and the police chief held separate news conferences to accommodate the news media.

Roman Holiday stayed inside her ranch house and stopped answering the phone.

JC and Bip ran into a news photographer named Fred Shook. He had worked with JC at his former television station in Denver.

"Has he gotten you shot at yet?" Fred asked Bip with a grin.

"No," Bip replied with a laugh. JC also found it amusing. He liked Fred.

"Well," Fred said. "You still have that to look forward to."

"He got another one of our photographers shot at," Bip said. "At the Snow Hat ski resort."

"Oh yeah. I remember hearing about that," Fred grinned. "He got me shot at in Montana."

"I heard," Bip said, smiling.

"You two should put together a photo album," JC said with mock indignation.

They surveyed the growing collection of news media.

"When did your crew get here, Fred?" JC asked.

"Let's see," Fred said, looking at his watch. "About two weeks after you broke this amazing story. Our TV station was nuts to fire you."

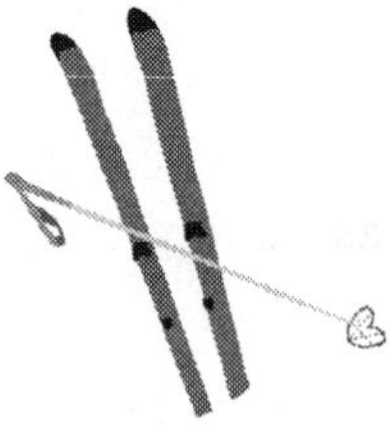

40

Television reporters were lined up shoulder to shoulder. They were clustered in the parking lot of the Stagecoach Stop Hotel in downtown Dog Mountain.

The on-air talent would stand out in almost any crowd, but especially Lonesome County. They all looked like they had just come from a hair salon, both men and women. And their faces were more attractive than those around them. Their winter coats were costly and new. Each wore a colorful scarf exposed around their neck.

The police chief was determined to prevent the town of Dog Mountain from becoming a media circus. So he sequestered every satellite news truck to the same parking lot at the Stagecoach.

The news crews could come and go freely, but if their satellite truck was parked within the town limits, it had to be parked in the lot next to the Stagecoach.

Because there was one particularly good vantage point from the parking lot, every tripod, camera, microphone, light stand and electrical cable were laid out side by side. That background provided the TV cameras with quaint Western-style buildings and fairy lights lining Main Street. It was the same spot where JC had been doing his live shots, off and on, for over two weeks.

Now JC was nearly rubbing shoulders with five other television reporters as their respective evening news programs came on the air. There were two other TV stations from Denver, two from Grand Junction and one from Rock Springs.

The death of Jonathan Oaks was the lead story on each TV channel. So they went live at the same time. The TV reporters standing in Dog Mountain were all speaking at once to their respective anchors and audiences back home. The reporters could hear each other talking. Sometimes it got a bit distracting. But their sophisticated microphones only sent their voice to their audience.

"Sources say that Jonathan Oaks was believed to be the killer in all three murders here in Lonesome County," one reporter said.

JC heard her. She was next to the reporter who was next to him.

Who told her that Oaks was the killer? It was not what he was reporting. Who was she talking to, he wondered. And was she right?

For the last newscast of the evening, all five TV reporters again went live, shoulder to shoulder, at the top of their shows. This time, a second reporter said that he was told that "Oaks' suicide solved the three murder investigations in Lonesome County."

JC and the other reporters were *not* reporting Oaks had been determined to be the killer. Nor was there any official finding, that JC was aware of, that Oaks committed suicide.

Following that final round of live shots for the evening, JC and Bip saw high-fives being exchanged among the journalists who had first reported that Oaks was the killer. They were celebrating having scooped the competition. They cast sidelong glances at JC and Bip.

JC called both the sheriff and the police chief. They weren't answering their phones.

Robin had taken the car and was positioned outside the sheriff's office, even after being told by the desk sergeant that he was not there.

She didn't believe it. Both the chief and the sheriff were clearly avoiding the news media since their individual news conferences.

"Did you hear what those two TV stations are reporting?" Robin asked JC when she called him on the phone. "The cops think Oaks committed all the murders?"

"Yep, I heard them," JC replied. "Are you getting anyone to confirm that?"

"Not even close," Robin said. "Where are those reporters getting their information?"

"I have no idea," JC told her. "If they're right, they're better at this than we are. If they're wrong, they're going to look like idiots. But I'm not going to report that Oaks was a serial killer just because they're reporting it."

Robin's response was interrupted by an incoming call.

"I've got to get this," JC told her.

"I've got a call coming in too," Robin said. "I'll talk to you soon."

"Hi, Clint," Robin said to her caller.

"Professor Skadi?" JC said to his. "Are you watching the news?"

"Why would I start doing that at this late stage in my life?" Skadi, aka Hemingway, answered.

"I think you're about my age," JC protested. "That's not the late stage of life."

"Thirty-seven was old age in my country less than two hundred years ago," Hemingway said.

"You're not from Norway," JC retorted.

"Anyway, I think I've got something for you," Hemingway said.

"Regarding the call-spoofing?" JC said. "Your blackmailer?"

"Yes," Hemingway said. "I tracked down my blackmailer. And the reason it took so long was because we were looking at it the wrong way."

"How so?" JC asked.

"I was using my time looking for someone *out* there who was getting *in*. But all along, we should have been looking for someone who was already inside."

"It was an inside job?" JC asked.

"In a manner of speaking," Hemingway answered. "The very creator of the new computer system at the community college built a door in the software that he could use to get in and out of the system without being detected. He had free access to personnel files and even our computers."

"I thought you said Frank Green installed the new computer system at the community college?" JC remarked.

There was silence on the other end of the line. Hemingway felt he had said all there was to say.

"Have you told this to the police?" JC said.

"That is something more up your alley," Hemingway said. "I don't 'do' police, remember?"

"How could I forget," JC said. "Thanks, Spook."

"Don't call me that," Hemingway replied and hung up.

JC searched the list of contacts in his phone and punched one.

It rang three times and Roman Holiday picked up.

"How much did you know about Benny's financial matters?" he asked.

"I came over each month and paid his bills for him," she said. "He didn't find paying bills very interesting. They wouldn't get paid if I didn't do it. He was intelligent, but he found things like that boring."

"And he thought someone was stealing money from him, right?" JC asked.

"Yes," she acknowledged. "He was about to go to police. He thought someone was using his passwords to get into his investment accounts. The stock market goes up and down. He told me it wasn't easy to track if money was missing from time to time."

"Did he say who he suspected?" JC asked.

"No," Roman replied. "Benny Ray told me that he wanted to talk to someone first. What's going on, JC?"

"I've got to go," he said. "I'll fill you in later."

"Oops, someone is at the door," she said. "I've got to go."

Hearing the phone disconnected, JC called Robin.

"Do you have Nancy Sanchez' phone number?" JC asked. She did and gave it to him.

"Yes," Nancy Sanchez told JC when he called. "Frank Green was a friend of ours. He was always helping us out with our computers."

"Did your husband ever suspect that money was being stolen from your accounts?" JC asked.

"I don't know," she said. "I really don't. But I've been going through more things in Nat's office."

"Have you found anything of help?" JC asked.

"Maybe," she told him. "I did find Frank's name on a calendar in Nat's office. It was for the afternoon of the day Nat disappeared. It looked like he had an appointment with Frank. It said, 'Bring a sandwich.' But Frank told me that he didn't see Nat that day."

JC was sitting inside the Stagecoach to order three coffees and get warm. Bip was still wrapping up his camera gear and helping Abel White lock down the satellite truck.

"What do you think?" JC asked Robin. He'd called her and detailed the evidence pointing to Frank Green.

"It's circumstantial, JC," she said. "He always seems like a nice guy. We can't just go accusing him on Hemingway's word."

"*And* Mrs. Sanchez saying Nat had an appointment with Frank on the last day he was ever seen," he said. "But you're right." They were both silent on the phone while they thought it over. He listened to her breathing and it made him smile.

"Maybe we can get Hemingway to look at Benny's computer," he said. "He knows how Frank does it now, some secret door. And remember how police found a batch of passwords by Benny's computer? Maybe Hemingway can find evidence Frank was getting into Benny's accounts."

"I'll call Roman and see if she can get us into Benny's house," Robin said.

"Thanks, I'll call Hemingway," JC said. "Then come pick us up. If he's willing to do it, we'll all go to Benny's."

41

"Roman's not picking up her phone," Robin said when she called JC back.

"I spoke with her fifteen minutes ago. Maybe she's got company," he replied. "She said that someone was at the door when we were hanging up."

"Someone was at her door and now she doesn't answer her phone?" Robin stated. "That doesn't make me feel any better."

"Come get us," JC said. "We'll take a ride out there."

It was a short drive to the Stagecoach Stop Hotel from the sheriff's office.

Robin collected JC and Bip and they headed for Roman's ranch, driving south on Route 10N.

Rumbling over the cattle guard, Robin drove up the driveway cautiously as they looked for a sign of Roman. Parking the car in front of the house, Robin handed JC the car keys as they got out.

"I don't have a good place to put them," she explained.

He stuffed the keys in his pocket as they heard the nicker of a horse in a nearby corral.

It was dark outside. They were under a canopy of white stars on a black sky.

There were lights on inside Roman's home, but the curtains were drawn.

JC knocked on the door. There was no answer. He pushed on the handle and found the door was locked.

"Roman?" Robin called out.

There was no answer.

"Maybe she's in the barn," Robin said. "I'll go around back and check. Try the side door into the laundry room." JC and Bip walked around to the side of the house and found the door. The handle turned and the door opened.

"Roman?" JC called as they entered the home. There was no answer. But they heard a thump coming from elsewhere in the house.

The laundry room was dark. Their path was blocked by baskets of clothing on the floor.

"Roman?" JC called out as they picked their way over the laundry baskets and a few shoeboxes.

"This is a fire hazard, Roman," Bip said in a loud voice.

Advancing, they heard the sound of weeping coming from the living room. Arriving there, they saw Roman on the floor. Olive was cradling her. There was blood on Roman's face.

"Help her! Please!" Olive begged them.

"Where's Frank Green?" JC asked the child. Olive pointed to the open back door.

JC instructed Bip to stay with Roman and Olive and call 9-1-1. JC headed for the open door leading into the backyard and the barn.

"Robin?" JC called as he emerged through the door.

There was no answer.

He saw a light on in the barn. That was where Robin said she was going to look for Roman.

He heard a horse kick his stall. He heard another one whinny.

As JC walked into the barn, a pair of horses poked their heads over the wall of their stall. Their eyes were open wide. One was pacing. The other was fidgeting.

JC thought something was making the animals nervous. He crouched near a bucket of stones and picked one up. It was about the size of a baseball.

"JC!" a voice shouted before being muzzled. It was Robin's voice.

In the shadow of the tack room, he saw Robin in the door. And then he saw Frank Green behind her.

Green had picked up a utility knife off a table and now held it against Robin's throat.

"You can't win this, Frank," JC said. "You're used to sneaking up behind your victims. But I'm looking right at you."

"Yeah, but I've got her," Green said, his arm firmly grasped across Robin's torso. He was a foot taller than she. He had to stoop to use her as a shield.

"Are you sure, Frank?" JC questioned. "It's not as easy when someone knows you're there. If she struggles, you'll probably miss the carotid artery on your first try. And in that time, I'll be on you."

"Put down that rock, JC," Frank said. "That, or I'll put your theory to the test. Whether three lives are taken or four, the prison sentence is the same."

JC looked at Robin. She was frightened, but she was alert. He thought she was ready to offer resistance.

"Frank," JC said in a calm voice. "We know what happened to your family. We know they took your land."

"They killed my family!" Frank shouted. "They killed me!"

"We understand," JC said to the enraged man. "We sympathize with you. It must be awful. But Robin had nothing to do with that."

"Everyone is trespassing!" the man with the knife shouted. "This is OUR land. It doesn't belong to skiers or bankers or people building vacation homes. These were OUR RANCHES! OURS!"

"Let her go," JC said calmly. "It's not her fault."

"You're all at fault!" Frank screamed. "It's time YOU feel what I feel. I lost EVERYTHING! I want YOU to see how that feels!"

Robin looked at JC. She didn't see fear on his face. He looked analytical. He was thinking, problem solving. He was walking into the fire.

"PUT DOWN THAT ROCK!" Frank yelled, as he pressed the knife into Robin's neck. It drew blood.

"I don't have to put down the rock, Frank," JC said with confidence. "I can hit you from here."

He could see Frank weigh his options. His eyes would dart toward possible exits from the barn.

"Let her go and you can have the keys to our car," JC negotiated. He pulled the keys from his pocket and tossed them to Frank's feet.

"Did you know that I was a pitching prospect for Major League Baseball?" JC asked him. "I had a seventy mile-per-hour fastball. I didn't make it because that's a little slow for the big leagues. But my placement was perfect. I could hit a ping-pong ball if it was sixty feet, six inches away."

Frank pulled on Robin's hair to bring her to her knees. He crouched to grab the keys. He pulled the knife away from her neck quickly, to snare the keys and then return the blade to her soft exposed tissue. It opened another cut on her neck. She grimaced.

"I don't need your keys," Green sneered. "But I've got them now."

JC was angry with himself. He felt that he'd missed a chance in the moment that knife was off her neck.

Frank forced Robin back to her feet.

"Babe, when this is over, I'm going to take you to New York City," JC said. He spoke to her, but he never took his eyes off Frank Green. "We'll go to Chinatown. I know a place where you have to order the duck twenty-four hours in advance. I love duck."

"That's because you're a Duck Hawk," she told him. Her voice was strained.

"Your girlfriend is not getting out of this, JC," Green jeered. "Unless you drop that rock and get out of my way."

JC saw alarm in Robin's face. She was on the verge of tears but trying desperately not to crack.

"Robin, just move your head to the left, away from the knife," JC instructed.

She gave him a strange look, but she moved her head away from the blade. Green responded in violence. He grabbed her red hair near the top of her head and yanked it. She screamed.

Now, with one hand clutching her hair and the other hand holding the knife, JC saw that Green really didn't have a firm grip on his captive.

"Anyway, what was I saying?" JC said calmly. "My favorite dish? Oh yeah, duck."

Robin's head was twisted away from Frank. But she looked at JC from the corner of her eye.

"What?" she said, choking.

"Duck!" JC blurted.

With all of her might, Robin lurched to the side, away from the knife. She was able to loosen Green's grasp for just a moment and ducked. It was only an instant before Frank clawed to pull her back.

But a moment was all JC was asking for.

He released the rock at a fierce velocity. The skin on Green's forehead split as the projectile landed. It made a sickening thud, something hitting a hard shell holding soft ingredients.

The man dropped backwards to the ground, the knife bouncing once on the hard dirt next to him.

JC rushed forward, prepared to punch and kick until his adversary was subdued.

But Green didn't move. He lay on his back with blood trickling from his forehead. His arms and legs were splayed like the four directions on a compass. His eyelids fluttered involuntarily.

Robin was on her hands and knees on the earthen floor of the barn. She was panting, only breaking the pattern by coughing. She spotted drops of blood falling on the dirt.

JC examined her from afar as he kicked the knife beyond Green's reach. He was satisfied that Robin's wounds were superficial. He was relieved.

"How do I get the lights on here?" JC asked, looking into the tack room.

He heard Robin grope for air. She coughed and mumbled a response.

"What did you say?" He saw her pull her hand away from a wound on her neck and stare at the blood.

"It's a flesh wound," he told her with nonchalance. "Don't worry. Where's the light switch?"

"Fuck … you … switch … on wall," she choked and growled at the same time.

He turned on the lights. And on the wall hung a dozen lassos.

"Wow," JC said. "This is better than the feed and tractor store."

He grabbed a coil of rope and rolled Green onto his stomach. He was still unconscious. JC tied the captive's hands and then tied his ankles together.

Robin was still on her hands and knees. She hadn't moved much. JC grabbed a towel in the tack room and kneeled down next to her, gently dabbing the two knife wounds on her neck.

"You make a lousy pin cushion," he told her. She didn't laugh.

But his hands were gentle. He dabbed at the blood and inspected the wounds.

"You're going to be okay," he whispered. "You were incredibly brave. I'm sorry."

She began to cry. Her shoulders shook, but she thought it might be from fatigue. She felt exhausted, like she wanted to sleep.

"They're superficial wounds," he told her with a nurturing voice as he kneeled beside her. He brushed her hair out of her face and pulled her into his embrace. "The bleeding has already stopped. You did great."

"You were a major-league pitching prospect?" she said slowly, as though learning again how to speak. He looked at her closely, searching for symptoms of shock.

"No," he responded. "I exaggerated."

"But you were a good baseball player?" she asked with a hoarse voice.

"I never played baseball," he admitted.

"You lied?" she asked innocently. It hurt her to talk.

"I lied to *him*," JC pointed out. "I wasn't talking to you."

"How," she said and then paused to catch her breath and think about it. "How did you know that you would hit him in the head with the rock instead of hitting me?"

"I never gave it much thought," he said with a grin.

A look of horror appeared on her face. His grin broadened.

"I was aiming for him," he said.

"And how do you know that … you are good at aiming a rock the size of a baseball … a game you never played?"

"That's a fair question. You're a good reporter," JC said after giving it some thought. "But I hit him, didn't I?"

"But what if you had hit me?" she asked, not realizing that her breathing was returning to normal and her heartbeat had slowed.

"But I wasn't aiming for you," he said a little defensively.

"Admit it," she demanded with a weak voice. "You could have killed me."

"Hardly," he told her. "I didn't kill *him*."

"How do you know?" she persisted as she looked at Green. "He hasn't moved."

"True," JC said as he also peered at his victim, still motionless. "He looks comfortable, to me."

She cautiously shifted her weight just enough to roll backwards and come to rest sitting on the dirt floor and leaning against a barnwood wall.

"Are you mad at me?" he asked.

"I'm not mad at you," she said with slightly less gravel in her voice. She was very tired and she closed her eyes. "I love you, more than anyone I've ever loved."

He slid his back against the barnwood wall and came down sitting next to her.

"Me too," he said. And he kissed the tangled red hair on top of her head.

She leaned against him. She placed a dirty hand on his far shoulder and laid her head on the shoulder nearer her. She seemed to be drifting off to sleep.

Bip entered the barn and walked toward them. He noticed that they were filthy but had the sense not to say it.

"I called 9-1-1," he said. "They should be here soon."

Bip looked at Robin, her eyes closed, her head resting on JC's shoulder. She looked asleep.

"Is she okay?" he asked.

"She'll be okay," JC told him. "She's tough."

"Well, *he* is tied and tagged for market," Bip said and laughed a little as he looked at Frank Green.

"How is Roman?" JC asked, tired and afraid of the answer that was coming. Robin opened her eyes and lifted her head, also awaiting the answer.

"She'll be okay," Bip told them with a smile. "He punched her in the face when he heard us coming in through the laundry room. She said that if we hadn't interrupted him, who knows what would have happened."

Bip looked over Robin and JC, still sitting against the wall. He asked again if they were alright. They assured him that they were.

"Wow," Bip said to Robin. "He must really love you. He only tries to get you killed if he really loves you."

42

"You thought you would take matters into your own hands, huh?" Sheriff Nidever said to JC. It sounded like a complaint. "I heard that about you."

Sheriff Nidever showed up at Roman's ranch after his deputies had secured the scene and took a dazed Frank Green into custody.

Deputies found Green's car parked behind a shed on Roman's ranch. He'd parked it there so it couldn't be seen from the road.

Roman said she didn't hear the car cross the cattle guard, probably because she was on the phone with JC.

JC and Robin were still sitting on the dirt floor of the barn, resting against a wall, as the sheriff loomed over them.

The two reporters were physically and emotionally spent. Robin's eyes were closed, her head rested on JC's shoulder.

"Did you tell reporters that Oaks killed someone?" JC asked Nidever.

"No, I don't know where they got that. The reporters made it up, I suppose," the sheriff said. "Oaks didn't kill anyone but himself. And that might have been an accident."

"What was he doing in Nevada?" JC inquired.

"I have no idea," the sheriff replied impatiently. "I was hoping you could tell me, since you seem to think you know everything."

The sheriff walked away without another word, as though the journalists had done a disservice by catching the real killer.

"You're welcome," Robin said softly, without opening her eyes or moving her head off JC's shoulder.

Frank Green had a long night. As there was no longer a doctor in town, and the sheriff didn't want to take him eighty miles to the closest hospital, an EMT examined the suspect for a probable concussion and his head wound was dressed. This was all done under the watch of three sheriff's deputies.

Green was taken to the county jail. He was photographed and fingerprinted. While still in the booking room, Sheriff Nidever walked in. A deputy ordered Frank to empty his pockets. He was told the things from his pockets would be placed in an envelope and he would be given a receipt.

Frank Green pulled assorted cash adding up to $152. He pulled out his wallet and two sets of car keys. One, presumably, belonged to JC Snow. The photographer who worked with Snow—the sheriff couldn't place his name, Bambi or something—assured him that they had another set of keys.

Green continued to unload his pockets. There was a three-foot USB cord. And he pulled out a tooth. It looked to the sheriff like a human molar.

"Well, looky there," the sheriff said with a grin. The sheriff looked at Green and Green looked back at him with an expression that showed he understood the severity of the find.

The sheriff placed a call to Chief Newell, informing him of the molar's discovery. Anderson was murdered within the town limits. That meant the police chief had jurisdiction over the murder investigation of Dr. Hunter Anderson.

After a short night's sleep, JC and Bip visited the chief at his office the next morning.

"The sheriff found the molar," the chief informed JC. "It was among Frank Green's belongings, in his pocket."

"If the tooth belongs to Nat Sanchez," JC asked, "will that convict Green of Hunter's murder?"

"I suspect that the tooth *does* belong to Sanchez," the chief responded. "Who generally walks around with human teeth in his pocket? And if it *is* the victim's tooth, then Dr. Anderson has been talking to us from the grave."

"How so?" JC asked.

"Dr. Anderson was a smart fellow," the chief said. "He had written a full set of notes regarding the molar. We found them in his office. The tooth was clearly in Anderson's possession before Green. The notes even said that Frank Green recommended that location for a cross-country ski trip. That was long before Sanchez was murdered. Green must have forgotten about telling the doctor and thought of the same place when he needed to dump Sanchez' body."

JC told the law officer that he specifically remembered Green telling him, at Jon Oaks' office, that he had never been to that spot with the 1838 inscription on the rock.

"Which means he lied," the chief stated as he wrote himself a note. "By then, he'd killed Sanchez and dumped his body. Now, we've got to find Mr. Sanchez' car. When we do, I suspect that we'll find Frank Green's DNA on it."

"So, If Hunter Anderson hadn't found that tooth," JC inquired. "Would you guys ever have found Nat Sanchez?"

"I'm not sure that we would," the chief said. "I understand there wasn't much left of him as it was."

"So maybe Anderson knew he only had one life left," JC muttered. "Maybe he wrote those notes in case he wasn't going to be around."

"Yeah, he told me that nine-lives theory of his," the chief said. "Funny thing is, he'd just gone to a lawyer and obtained a last will and testament. And he'd just paid off a bunch of loans. I don't know that I believe that nine-lives stuff, but Dr. Anderson was a smart fellow."

"What now, for Frank Green?" JC asked.

"Frank Green is negotiating for the best situation he can get in prison," the chief said. "He knows that we have him on at least two of the murders, plus assaulting Roman Holiday and assaulting your colleague, Ms. Smith. We're also finding victims who have had their computers hacked. In fact, many customers of Green's store have been hacked."

"There's no death penalty for murder in Colorado," JC noted.

"No," the chief acknowledged. "But Green's attorney must have told him he is sure to spend the rest of his life in prison."

"And Green admits to everything now?" JC says.

"He's talking like a parrot now. The sheriff questioned him early this morning. Green is trying to see what kind of deal he can make," the chief said. "I guess he told the sheriff that he went out to Roman's house because he was sure Benny had told her that Green was stealing from his investment accounts.

"Green lives inside the town limits. So it was our job to go to his house. We found stacks of passwords belonging to all sorts of people. As we match the passwords with a business or individual, we're telling them to check to see if their security had been breached. He was inside the Stagecoach Hotel's computers, and the community college. I'm sure we'll find more."

"Was he stealing money from everyone he hacked?" JC asked.

"The ones who had money worth taking. He was also blackmailing a couple. It's only the next morning and we have victims coming forward," the chief told them.

"And he'd kill if he thought it was necessary to cover his tracks," JC supposed.

"It's a good thing you showed up out at the ranch of Ms. Holiday. Who knows what he would have done. I'm not sure he even had a plan anymore. He was getting sloppy. He lost track of his loose ends."

As the interview ended, Bip packed up his camera gear. Newell didn't hide his happiness at being able to close the case file on the unusual occurrence of three murders in little Dog Mountain and Lonesome County.

"Honestly," the chief said as he stood behind his desk, "I thought Gerhard Snyder was going to be our man in Dr. Anderson's killing. I don't know how the sheriff's investigation is going, but I'm certain that Snyder burned down Anderson's cabin."

"Do you think that was his truck I saw at the cabin that night?" JC asked.

"This is off the record, right?" the chief declared more than inquired.

"If it has to be," JC replied. Newell nodded that it did.

"I think it was his truck you saw," Chief Newell told him. "I think he came up there that night with the intent to burn that cabin down. But he saw your car parked there and signs someone was inside the cabin and he left. He's an arsonist, I guess, not a killer."

In a few months, JC would learn that Police Chief Bob Newell had begun to circulate petitions to run in his political party's primary for county sheriff. He was going to challenge Henry Nidever for his job.

Any pretense that there wasn't a jurisdictional rivalry between the two most powerful law enforcement officers in Lonesome County would now evaporate.

Robin summoned a rideshare car to take her out to Roman's ranch. Roman was home from the hospital in Craig after being held for observation overnight.

Olive was outside. She held a new cell phone and was using the camera to take pictures of the horses.

"I got her a new phone," Roman told Robin. "We can be in better touch with each other that way. She's out there taking pictures of the horses for Missy, her dog that was killed. She says she's going to post them on social media so the dog can see them and know that we still think of her."

"My God, that's sweet," Robin said.

"We both have a lot of grieving to do," Roman said.

Roman's face was a collection of shades of bruising. She was swollen around her nose and eyes. It made her voice sound nasal.

"I'm sorry. I look awful," she said. "But the doctor says that as everything heals, my Hollywood good looks will be unchanged. Ready for my comeback."

"Are you going to do that?" Robin asked. "Make a comeback?"

"No," Roman said, smiling and dismissing the remark as a joke. "Ouch, smiling makes my face hurt."

"It's still nice to see you smile," Robin said in her nurturing way.

"Are *you* okay?" Roman asked, seeing the bandage on Robin's neck. It covered a few stitches and some bruising.

"I'm alright," Robin smiled.

"We're getting two new dogs!" Roman said with some excitement. "We're going to take the two Goldendoodles who lived in the house with Benny Ray. They're comfortable around me because I was at his house so much. I think they'll be happier here than anywhere else. And it will be good for Olive."

Roman also told Robin that she would see to it that the other dogs at Benny's ranch were adopted to good homes.

JC knew that he and Bip and Robin would be heading home to Denver soon. But they were probably obligated to two more nights of live shots from Lonesome County.

First, they would cover a court appearance by Frank Green. They would also have to provide their newsroom with images of Dr. Hunter Anderson's funeral. Bip would shoot the footage, then place the camera in the back of their car and join JC and Robin inside the church. They too would mourn the loss of their friend who hosted dinners at his tiny house.

The services for Anderson would draw nearly every adult in the county. Many of them were Anderson's patients. All of them were his friends.

Bip slowed down the car as they passed Anderson's medical office.

"Too bad he didn't have one more," JC said.

"One more life?" Bip asked.

"Yeah," JC responded as he stared at the locked door of the doctor's office. "At least one more."

"Frank Green did a lot of damage to this area," Bip said. "He killed their biggest celebrity. And now, they don't have a doctor and they don't have anyone to keep their computers running."

"He didn't go to Colorado State University," Annie Green sneered. "He learned how to fix computers in state prison. This won't be the first time he's been locked up."

Nancy Sanchez, the widow of Nat Sanchez, returned from Casper to Dog Mountain. This time, she wasn't looking for her husband. This time, she wanted to make sure Frank Green was going to rot in prison for killing Nat.

Nancy Sanchez brought Annie Green with her. She was Frank's ex-wife.

"He's a con man," Annie told JC. "He gets everyone to think he's a great guy and then he robs them blind."

"So, you're not surprised by what happened here?" JC asked.

"Nah, I could tell you stories," she said. "But I never thought he was capable of murder. Honestly, I think his life began to fall apart when his family moved away from Browns Park—his mom dying, and then his dad dying that way."

"Did he talk about it?" JC asked. She nodded her head.

"Poor Nat," Annie said and hugged Nancy Sanchez. "We were all friends. The four of us, we used to play cards together and have barbecues!"

Nancy Sanchez told JC that a police lab had found Green's fingerprints on the note left in her kitchen. The note from Nat, saying he had walked out on Nancy, was forged by Green to cover for Nat's disappearance.

"What could cause a man to be so evil?" Mrs. Sanchez asked.

"They all think they have a good reason," JC told her in a subdued tone. "But it comes back to their own rotting heart."

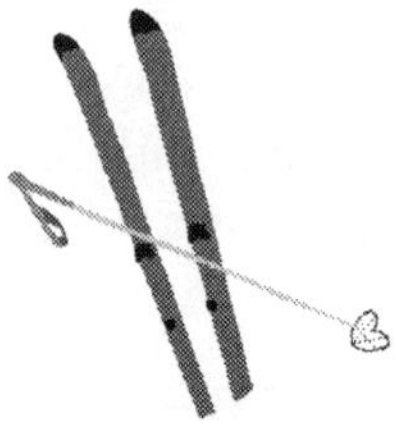

43

Some said Minnie Crouse was Butch Cassidy's girlfriend. Minnie insisted that they were just good friends. She said that she admired the way he could handle horses.

Besides, she said, he was nearly old enough to be her father. Minnie had plenty of young men her own age who fancied her. Life was fanciful for Minnie Crouse in the remote area of Colorado called Browns Park.

JC had tried to get things wrapped up so that he and Robin could head back to Denver on Saturday, after his ski race.

He had stopped by the office of Professor Ullr Skadi on Thursday to say goodbye and express thanks for leading him to Frank Green. But the office of Skadi, aka Steven Hemingway, was empty.

On the windowsill, there was a plain white envelope with JC's name on it. Opening the envelope, there was a note inside, saying:

When you are dead, you do not know that you are dead.
It is difficult only for the others.
It is the same when you are stupid.
—Unknown

"Professor Skadi informed us that a family matter required his immediate return to his home to Norway," someone in the administrative offices told JC. "We'll miss him."

The professor was already gone.

They will never see him again, JC thought. They should be grateful that nothing was set on fire.

"You should have seen Gerhard Snyder," Robin said the next morning as they dressed in their hotel room. JC would pull on his race suit, pull on some warm clothing over it, and walk to the ski lodge.

He had spent his last evening on Dog Mountain waxing his skis for the race and having dinner with Russell Driver and other racers. Robin spent the evening at a meeting of the Dog Mountain town board. Her neck was still bandaged.

"Snyder's face got so red, I thought his head would explode," Robin told JC as he sat on a chair and fastened a brace to each knee.

"The town slapped him with a reimbursement fee of $100 for each fire call and police call to the slipshod mobile homes he rented. And his property assessment was raised. His taxes are going up!"

"He might find motivation to murder someone yet," JC laughed, pulling his speed suit over his legs, but tying the sleeves around his waist.

"He was screaming bloody murder last night," Robin snickered. "I understand that the city of Denver is looking at taking similar action against him there."

"What about the fire at Anderson's mountain retreat?" JC asked.

"I spoke with the sheriff," she told him. "They know Snyder came back and set that fire. His truck tires match the tire tracks they found in the snow. The sheriff thinks they have plenty of evidence. They're talking to the district attorney now. How did he think he'd get away with it?"

"Can't fix stupid," JC told her.

The sun was rising over Minnie's Gap Ski Resort. The wind was kicking up and blowing snow across the freshly groomed surface.

Racers grimaced as they were hit by glacial gusts while locking their skis to a rack near the chairlift. Then they hustled out of the cold into the warm lodge.

JC unpacked the bag containing his ski boots and other gear. He saw the reflection in his goggles as he unsheathed them from their protective cloth sleeve. He placed them next to his helmet.

He had an egg, bacon and cheese breakfast sandwich and a paper cup of cappuccino next to him. Robin had purchased the food from the cafeteria upstairs.

With her help, he pulled his tight gold and green race suit up over his pads to protect an injured shoulder. The suit, left from his days as a college ski racer at Colorado State, had a few small tears in it. He liked the effect. He thought it looked like it had been to battle.

"Be careful today," she said.

"I can't win if I kill myself," he responded with a smirk. "Though I like Hunter Anderson's theory. I may die and lose this race. But in the next universe, I don't die and maybe I win the race!"

He smiled. She didn't.

"I was thinking. Didn't you tell me about a big car crash you had in Arizona?" she asked.

"Yep," he said as he zipped up his speed suit. "Winslow, Arizona. Oh, you think that I died? Maybe."

"That's eight," she said. "And didn't you tell me about getting lost in the hot desert there?"

"Technically," he told her with a smile. "That was the same trip. I went hiking while they were repairing my car. Yes, the desert was really hot."

"So, that could be nine," she said with a worried look. "Be careful out there."

JC gave her a smile and a racer dropped JC's racing bib in his lap.

"They told me to bring you this," the racer said.

"Thanks. Where are you from?" JC asked, not recognizing the face nor the brand on his jacket.

"We're from Berkshire East," the racer replied, looking over his shoulder at some racers in similar garb. "It's a ski area in Massachusetts. A bunch of us try to come West every few years to get some skiing and racing in."

"I've skied Berkshire East," JC said.

"If you can ski the East, you can ski anywhere," the racer said.

Conversations like this were going on at ski areas across the country. Skiers and snowboarders found common experiences to exchange, no matter where they woke up that morning.

At Mammoth Mountain in California, Crested Butte in Colorado, Gunstock in New Hampshire and Nubs Nob in Michigan, skiers and snowboarders had their own language, their own reason to be.

JC pulled the tight bib over his head and adjusted it so the number would settle across his chest. He didn't even notice his bib number. But Robin looked at it silently. Number nine.

JC wrestled his stiff ski boots onto his feet and pulled his warmer all-mountain pants and a jacket back over his race suit.

The sun was just beginning to top the trees when it came time to brave the cold.

The event would be a super-G. It would be high-speed and high-risk. One run, winner takes all.

Some racers conspired in small groups, waiting for their turn at the top of the hill. Some gathered together depending on what language they spoke.

The course was set up on a run called Minnie's Mile. With the race underway, Russell Driver posted the fastest early time for the men.

JC's name was called, meaning he would be out of the starting gate in about five minutes.

"Be careful. I'm going to watch from halfway," Robin said as she gave him a kiss and skied away.

JC could see that the wind was making some racers nervous. If he were brave, he told himself, he'd have a better chance of winning.

"Good luck," the skier from Massachusetts said.

JC gave him a conspirator's smirk. "Let's go kill the hill," he said.

He pushed into the start gate and slipped his ski poles over the start wand. Studying the course that he could see, there were five gates before he'd plunge out of sight.

The starter activated the timer. It would begin counting as soon as JC kicked through the wand.

"Five-four-three ..." the starter counted.

JC pushed off and headed past the first gate. He felt joy as the wind hit his face. His turns were clean and on edge. He felt like he was doing everything right as he plunged out of sight from the steep start.

"Angulate," he thought to himself.

As long as the wind didn't blow uphill, JC was convinced that he would have a good day.

Instead, the wind blew directly across the course, carrying a curtain of loose snow into the air. Icy crystals froze on his goggles, blinding him.

The cause of sharp pain in his right knee went unseen. He was sightless as he reached down with one hand to grab his leg.

He collapsed onto his side and was sliding off the side of the slope. He struck a tree with his chest. He hit another tree with both legs.

Slipping further into the woods, he was able to raise his skis and use his feet to catch the next tree heading his way.

He lay motionless on the side of the trail.

In his mind, he began to conduct a damage-control report. His brain asked each limb to respond. He was furious that a good race had gone bad.

Volunteers and coaches who had been lining the course rushed toward him.

"Are you alright?" the first asked JC.

"Is he alright?" another asked as he arrived. "My God, did he hit a tree?"

"Did you hit a tree?" the first man asked.

"Two," JC said with a bit of a grin and a grimace.

There was now a small crowd of coaches and volunteers standing over him.

"Don't move," he was told.

"No, I can get up," JC said. The last tree had taken his skis. They lay in the snow next to him as he rolled over and rose to his knees. "Just give me a minute."

He managed to stand in the snow and sank into it. Then, his legs collapsed beneath him.

"JC!"

He recognized Robin's voice. She had crossed the racecourse, discarded her skis and was now pushing through the loose snow toward him. He was back on the ground.

"I'm fine, hon," he said. "I just need a minute."

"You're not fine," a race official with a British accent told him. "We're getting a blood wagon for you."

"A blood wagon?" Robin repeated in horror. "My God!"

"Relax, hon," JC said to her. He was still regaining his breath. "That's just what the British call a ski patrol sled. It's a bit dramatic."

Members of the ski patrol in their bright red jackets arrived. So had a few other ski racers.

"Are you the one who caught Hunter Anderson's killer?" asked a ski patroller who was also an EMT.

"Yes," Robin asserted when she saw that JC was without words.

"We'll take good care of you," the EMT assured his new patient. "Hunter was a friend of ours. I'll stay with you to the hospital."

"Are you going to stay with him?" another ski patroller asked Robin.

"Yes," she said. "He'll be my patient when you're done with him."

"How many lives is this for you?" the EMT asked JC. He was engaging the injured skier to see if he had a concussion. He also noticed JC's bib number.

JC looked at the man with a knowing smile but said nothing.

"Hunter shared his nine-lives theory with all of us," the EMT said. "It was interesting. He was a good guy."

"Would this be nine?" JC asked, getting a bit woozy.

"Or ten," Robin said, looking at him with impatience.

"If you guys can help," a ski patrol member said to those in earshot. "We can get him on this board and carry him out of the trees. Then we can put him on a sled and get him down the hill."

And they did. Three men were on each side, carrying a fallen warrior on the board out of the woods. The sight, and the outfits of red and blue and green, froze Robin. She thought of JC's dreadful dream.

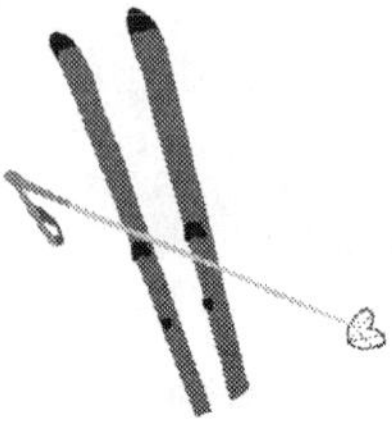

44

He was familiar with the aroma of disinfectant in hospitals. It brought back childhood memories for JC. His father was a doctor.

JC and Robin were alone in an examining room in Craig, about eighty miles from Minnie's Gap. An ambulance had taken them there. JC was laid out on a bed. Robin sat in a chair next to him.

"When I was little and there was no one else to watch me on Saturdays, I'd have to go with Dad to the hospital," JC told Robin while they waited for a doctor. He sounded drowsy but lucid.

"He'd have work to do and I'd get bored," JC told her from the steel-frame bed. "But if I didn't make a nuisance of myself, I would be rewarded with enough coins to get a candy bar out of a vending machine down the hall."

"Cute," Robin said.

Twice, a nurse brought a heated blanket to wrap around JC. He thought it was ecstasy.

The curtain providing him with privacy was pulled back and a ski racer appeared, Russell Driver.

"Are you all right, my friend?" Driver asked.

"They brought him down the mountain in a blood wagon," Robin said, now amused by the term.

"I'm fine," JC told him slowly. "Thanks."

"Good," Driver said. "Then I shall commence ridiculing you. You are metal and the ground must be a magnet. You just cannot resist its pull."

"Thank you," JC said with a smile. "How did you do in the race?"

"The younger men keep pulling away in the distance from where we stand," Russell said philosophically. "But I won my age group, and I certainly would have beaten you."

Robin laughed at that. Russell Driver departed after saying that they should arrange to have dinner over the summer.

Bip phoned, saying he had heard about JC's crash. He told Robin that he was going to pack everything in their rooms, check out of the hotel and be on the way with the car. They'd be going home to Denver from the hospital.

"Is it March yet?" JC asked Robin when he shifted his head on the pillow and his eye spotted a wall calendar. "We get good snow in March."

"It is not yet March," a doctor said as he entered the examining room. "And I hope you like watching snow fall from your window. Because your ski season is over."

The doctor introduced himself and showed JC the images that had been taken of the pipes and corridors inside his body.

"I looked at your history," the doctor said. "I suspect that you have an orthopedic surgeon in Denver that you're familiar with?"

"I've spent more time in bed with him than I have with her," JC grinned, looking at Robin. The doctor laughed.

"The good news is we didn't find any internal bleeding," the doctor explained. "But I think the ACL in your right knee is detached. You'll probably want to fix that. How much does your left thigh hurt?"

"A lot," JC said.

"You have a deep bone bruise in your left leg," the doctor informed him. "It hurts like heck, but it will heal itself."

"He hit trees at high speed," Robin informed the doctor.

"So I hear," the doctor smiled. "You ski racers seem to think we keep spare parts here at the hospital. Anyway, you also have a meniscus tear in your left knee. And you suffered multiple bruises on your torso. I'm surprised that it's not worse. But I don't see anything that won't heal, aside from that ACL. You can decide on the meniscus later."

JC refused the offer of any painkillers stronger than ibuprofen.

"Good for you," the doctor said. "Do you have someone who can look after you for a while?"

"I'll be looking after him," Robin said.

"What about North Carolina?" JC asked.

"Dad said he'll wait," Robin smiled. "He told me I was welcome any time."

The patient was then provided with a pair of crutches and told he could leave.

They moved into the lobby of the ER and waited for Bip to arrive with the car. They sat and stared out the window.

"If you do this again," Robin told him. "I'm taking you to the hospital run by the 'Dumb Friends League.'"

"Wait, isn't that a hospital for dogs and cats?" JC asked, his head still groggy.

"Usually," she responded.

They looked out the window for Bip. JC was trying not to doze off until he was situated in the car.

"What if something happens to you?" Robin asked.

"What could possibly go wrong?" JC slowly responded with a smile.

"Seriously, Jean Claude," she said. "You could be killed ski racing or doing one of the other idiotic things you do."

"It would appear that I have more than nine lives," JC told her slowly, grinning. "The devil took a look. He doesn't want me."

"I couldn't bear it," she said softly.

JC slept in the backseat during most of the drive home. He woke up when they stopped for gas in Kremmling at the Kum & Go.

When Bip was done gassing up the car, Robin emerged from the large store that accompanied the Kum & Go. She was carrying a small paper bag and wearing a smile.

In the car, she opened the bag and pulled out a small bobblehead doll replicating a Ute chief.

"Isn't that disrespectful?" Bip quipped.

"I think he looks distinguished," she said. "It has a sticky bottom on the pedestal. I'm going to put it on the dashboard of my car. He will bestow wisdom when I need directions driving."

JC fell back to sleep in the backseat. Bip drove, explaining to Robin how he and Sunny had left things. She was going to explore making a move to Denver.

"She's going to come visit me in a couple of months," he said.

"It's a lot to leave behind," Robin said. "Her family, her culture."

"She'll have your Ute chief to talk to," Bip said, grinning.

At the end of the long drive, Bip stopped the car in front of JC's apartment building in Larimer Square in Denver. A large set of glasses looked down on them, over an optometrist's store on the other side of the street.

It was a warm winter night in Denver. Music was playing from the Denim Vinyl Bar as JC slowly removed himself from the news car.

The walk up three flights of stairs to his apartment was a familiar inconvenience. He was now headed for his sixth knee surgery. He was getting used to climbing stairs on crutches.

"Beer or bed?" Robin asked after getting him situated on the couch.

"Bed," he told her. "Sorry, I don't have my wits about me. All I can do is sleep."

He woke up to the sun shining into his bedroom and bouncing off the bare brick walls.

"I can't find the spatula," Robin said. "I'm making you some eggs."

She placed a steaming cup of coffee next to him on a bedside table.

"Did you look in the drawer under the coffee machine?" he asked.

"Yes," she said. "I found tee shirts in that drawer."

"Oh, yeah," he said.

"What about the drawer below it?" he suggested.

"White athletic socks and some compression shorts," she told him.

"Right," he said and pursed his lips.

"Never mind," she said as she turned back to the kitchen. "You are the worst cook I've ever met. You don't even know what a kitchen is for. If we were on the first floor, you'd probably park your car in it!"

Shortly, she returned with two plates of fried eggs, sunny-side up, and a buttered bagel. One plate for each of them.

His body might be damaged, but he found that it was hungry. They ate in silence for a while.

"It was your dream, wasn't it?" she asked soberly as she settled onto the bed next to him.

"I think so," he said after giving it serious thought. "I've had that dream so many times."

"So, for two years," she said. "You've been dreaming of that ski crash. Of the ski racers and ski patrollers carrying you out of the woods?"

"It would appear so," he told her. "I just didn't recognize it for what it was. In my dream, I thought it was medieval knights."

"Didn't you say there was a dog following you?" she asked.

"Yeah," he said. "Maybe the ghost of my dog, Picabo. She was still looking after me."

Robin smiled at that.

"Look at this," he said to her. He slowly navigated the discomfort and pulled up his tee shirt.

"What *is* that?" she asked, looking at the marks running across his torso.

"They go down across my left thigh too," he said. "Bruises in the shape of tree bark. Kind of cool. I guess I hit those trees pretty hard."

Robin's phone rang. She looked at the number and began to get up off the bed. Then she sank back down and leaned back against a pillow.

"Hi, Clint," she said.

JC recognized the name and turned his head toward the conversation.

"Nothing has changed since I left you that message," Robin said into the phone. "Thank you so much. It means a lot to me. I'm not saying never. But I'm saying, 'not now.'"

She hung up the phone and looked at JC looking at her.

"Clint? From the network news?" he asked. She nodded.

"When you turned them down, they asked me if I wanted the job," she told him.

"And you turned it down?" he asked. "Are you crazy? You'd be great."

"Were you crazy?" she asked him.

He looked at her, hoping she wouldn't regret her decision.

"Are you sure?" he asked. She nodded.

"Because I'm happy," she said.

He kissed her and told her she made good eggs.

"Maybe I should stay here for a while," she told him.

"Here in my apartment?" he asked.

"Yes," she answered.

"But where will *I* stay?" he asked.

"You will be here too," she told him, amused.

JC thought about this. His heart began beating faster. It wasn't because he didn't want her to move in with him. It was because he suddenly realized how desperately he wanted her to.

"Do you understand what you're getting yourself into?" he asked.

"I believe so," she said, looking at him. "Do you?"

"You realize that you would see me here every day," he told her. "Day after day."

"I'm counting on that," she said with a smile, leaning in to kiss him. "Nine lives may not be enough."

Acknowledgements

COVID-19 altered the way I normally would have researched and written this book. Toward the end of 2020, I couldn't submerse myself in the actual setting of Browns Park. I had been planning to write this novel for quite a while.

I first visited this remote landscape and its spirited inhabitants decades before, as a reporter in Grand Junction, Colorado, for KJCT-Television. Happily, I was finally able to visit again, as a novelist.

My thanks to Colorado Parks and Wildlife for their guidance and advice. Thanks to the National Park Service and especially Ranger Rob Cannon for their help when I finally did get back to Browns Park.

And while awaiting my return there, I must also acknowledge the insights I gained from Diana Allen Kouris' thoroughly entertaining autobiography about growing up in Browns Park, *Riding the Edge of an Era: Growing Up Cowboy on the Outlaw Trail.*

Also, Lula Parker Betenson and Dora Flack's *Butch Cassidy, My Brother.*

John Weinstock's book, *Skis and Skiing: From the Stone Age to the Birth of the Sport,* was also quite useful.

Thanks to West Mountain in Queensbury, New York, for accommodating us in so many ways, including the lift operators who steered Chair 54 according to our desires.

Thanks to the Bromley Ski Patrol in Peru, Vermont, for patching up the wounded. Shooting cover photos can be dangerous.

Susan Wagner, the founder and president of Equine Advocates, and her fine staff provided an education in the horse-rescue movement. equineadvocates.org.

In the Department of I Couldn't Do It Without Them: Thank you to my editor, Deirdre Stoelzle and to Debbi Wraga who does the formatting and all the other things that seem impossible.

I arrived at the names of four law enforcement officers in this story by giving them the names of real mountain men who were early arrivals to Browns Park: Robert Newell, Henry Nidever, Joe Walker and Jack Robinson.

Browns Park is nearly as remote and unpopulated as it was a century ago, nearly as untouched as two hundred years ago when fur trappers first set eyes on it.

To write this story, I had to invent the town of Dog Mountain and the ski resort of Minnie's Gap. They would be the very source of population density and man-made illumination that, to date, Browns Park has avoided.

About the Author

Phil Bayly was a television and radio journalist for over four decades. He lived and worked in Denver, Fort Collins, the Eastern Plains and the Western Slope of Colorado, as well as Wyoming, Pennsylvania and New York.

He attended the University of Denver and is a graduate of Colorado State University.

He was born and raised in Evanston, Illinois, and now resides in Saratoga County, New York.

For a short while, he carved tombstones for a paycheck. He's been a ski racer and a ski bum. He's lived at least nine lives.

You can learn more about Phil and his books at murderonskis.com.

Made in the USA
Middletown, DE
02 November 2023

41828788R00224